THE WITCH THIEF

LORI DEVOTI

TORONTO NEW YORK LONDON
AMSTERDAM PARIS SYDNEY HAMBURG
STOCKHOLM ATHENS TOKYO MILAN MADRID
PRAGUE WARSAW BUDAPEST AUCKLAND

Recycling programs
for this product may
not exist in your area.

ISBN-13: 978-0-373-61883-5

THE WITCH THIEF

Copyright © 2012 by Lori Devoti

Dear Reader,

The Witch Thief is the story of dragon-shifter Joarr and the witch Amma.

A century earlier, Amma stole the dragons' most prized possession and fled. Joarr followed, but instead of catching her, got caught himself and was trapped for a hundred years in his dragon form.

Joarr is bent on revenge, and Amma on trickery, but neither can foresee the journey before them.

Joarr is the strong alpha male who thinks he cares for nothing or no one.

He is, of course, very wrong.

Amma is a lost soul who has spent her life wondering where she belongs. She thinks she has the answer now and a plan to finally be happy, but Joarr and the dragons could take it all away. And she will do anything to keep that from happening.

Or will she?

I hope you enjoy reading their tale and meeting perhaps my most unique character yet, a blood-drinking dwarf.

For more information on my other works, visit my website at www.loridevoti.com.

Lori Devoti

This book is dedicated to all the fans of the *Unbound* world who have waited patiently for this book. You rock—each and every one of you!

Books by Lori Devoti

Harlequin Nocturne

*Unbound #18
*Guardian's Keep #32
*Wild Hunt #41
Holiday with a Vampire II #54
   "The Vampire Who Stole Christmas"
*Dark Crusade #62
*The Hellhound King #82
Zombie Moon #91
The Witch Thief #136

*Unbound

LORI DEVOTI

grew up in southern Missouri and attended college at the University of Missouri-Columbia, where she earned a bachelor of journalism. However, she made it clear to anyone who asked that she was not a writer; she worked for the dark side—advertising. Now, twenty years later, she's proud to declare herself a writer and visits her dark side by writing paranormals for Harlequin Nocturne.

Lori lives in Wisconsin with her husband, daughter, son, an extremely patient shepherd mix and the world's pushiest Siberian husky. To learn more about what Lori is working on now, visit her website at www.loridevoti.com.

Resisting Joarr was like resisting a promise from the gods.

But hard as it had been, Amma *had* resisted.

And then he had shocked her by somehow shutting off her attempts to drain his magic. A skill she hadn't realized dragons had, but now that she did, she would be smarter and not let any opportunity slip by.

She had to get him to shift as frequently as possible and soak up the resulting magic like a sponge, silently and unobtrusively.

He had no idea who she was or what she was capable of. He also had no idea what was at stake for her.

She placed a hand on her abdomen. The dragon couldn't learn her secret. Couldn't learn she'd found a way to get the family she craved....

Prologue

One hundred and one years earlier...

Lips, fiery hot, trailed down Amma's neck. Her lover lapped at her skin; the fierce heat of his breath and touch sent tingles of anticipation down her spine. She pulled her hair from his path and bared her neck to his caresses. Her fingers wrapped around his biceps. His skin was cool to her touch.

Sweat beaded between her breasts; he found the tiny drops and licked them away. His eyes flickered like blue flames in the dark. She nipped at his chest, caught a bit of flesh between her teeth and pulled. His hands grabbed her around the waist and he tumbled them over until he straddled her, stared down at her. She let him, let him capture her wrists in his hands.

They'd played this game for hours, as they'd played it once before, weeks earlier right after she'd first met him and allowed him to lure her to his home. She'd been bored then, looking for something...someone... new to entertain her, and she'd found him—Joarr, her first dragon lover. Who knew the heat between them would be so intense—both literally and figuratively? But she'd soon discovered he offered her more than that. The dragon had a secret...a treasure. Of course, she'd heard tales of dragon treasure, but who really believed the stories to be true?

And since she'd left him, she'd found a buyer for one particular piece she'd seen tossed in the back of his cavern. One tiny piece she doubted her lover would even miss—a cup. Gold and engraved with a dragon's image wrapping around its side, but nothing as impressive as other pieces she'd seen and mentioned to the Collector.

One tiny, stemmed cup and the Collector would give her what she craved—her family, her past, the truth of where she came from. She was different from her sisters, always had been. Now she would know how. Now she would find where she belonged.

Joarr whispered in her ear, a language she didn't understand, but his smile said his words had been daring, challenging probably. She wiggled her fingers; power sizzled from their pink tips. He grabbed her hand and pulled her fingers down the length of his chest, let her magic sputter against his skin. He was showing off, showing that her magic wouldn't hurt him.

She smiled to herself. So he thought, but he had no idea of her real power. She'd hidden that from him, presented herself as an average witch with average powers. But she and her sisters were far from average. She had been alive perhaps as long as the dragon. She hadn't asked him his age, but she knew dragons lived for centuries, longer than hellhounds or garm. Perhaps longer than elves.

She circled his nipple with her tongue. Then, her face still pressed against his chest, stared up at him. Dragons were so crafty and secretive. How lucky was she that she'd found the one who wasn't?

The cavern was darker than Amma remembered. On her last visit the dragon must have had some light she hadn't noticed. Now she hung from the wooden ladder that led from Joarr's living room down into the cavern. The dark almost impenetrable, she could do nothing except hold on and continue her descent. One foot below the other. She felt for the firm wood under the thin sole of her slipper before shifting her weight down. Finally, instead of a thin strip of wood, she felt a cold slab of rock. She twirled, her skirt whirling around her legs as she did, and with her back pressed against the wooden ladder, she called a ball of power into her cupped hand.

The space around her flooded with light. She took a step forward, eager. The treasure…had been to the right before. And it still was. Gold and jewels winked at her. The pile was even bigger than it had been a week earlier, taller than her now.

She hurried closer and fell on her knees in front of it. Piles of gold. An insane amount of riches. Humans would kill—decimate continents—for such a hoard. Had killed. But the dragon had tossed it along with broken chairs and other worthless objects into a corner.

Left it piled there as if owning it was enough. He probably never spent the coins, never visited his riches.

She ran the pad of her finger over one shimmering jewel and sighed.

There was no way he would miss one tiny piece. She clutched the gemstone in her fist, then laid it back where it had been.

And that was all she would take. Just one piece. She had no use for money. No need to see herself clad in jewels. She only wanted the cup and the truth it would buy her.

She held up her hand and let the light play over the pile of gold and old furniture. In the back in the same place she'd seen it last, she spied the cup. She leaned forward, causing a line of coins to slide onto the rock floor. To her ears the noise rivaled the roar of an avalanche. She froze and waited for the trapdoor she'd lowered behind her to be jerked open, waited for the dragon to lower his head through the opening and roast her... or try to.

Could she defeat a dragon? Her heart hammered against her ribs as the thought twitched in her head, caused her eyes to dart back toward the ladder. The tales were all of heroes tricking a dragon, never a witch facing one in a fair fight. But who knew, perhaps her father had been one of those heroes, perhaps even a god.... Her sisters and she shared the same mother, but none knew their father. Amma's could be anyone, anything.

A thrill raced through her, but uncertainty, too. She didn't want to fight Joarr; she'd enjoyed their time together. If she hadn't been here under false pretenses she might even have convinced herself she cared for him. He was confident, masculine and reeked of magic. Just being near him made the hairs on her arms stand with awareness. Pressing against him, feeling him explode inside her...she'd never felt so alive.

She stayed frozen, waiting. Finally, after no movement came, after enough time had passed she felt safe again, she let out the breath she'd been holding.

After a last glance over her shoulder, she shook the moment of weakness off. The dragon was as she'd assessed him earlier—sloppy. And he was nothing to her. If she needed to fight him, she would. But the cup...the cup was her path to finding out who she really was, to uncovering her own secrets.

She leaned forward, her breasts brushing against gold, and grabbed the cup.

Then with it shoved under her shirt, she climbed back up the ladder and sneaked out the dragon's front door.

With the dragon still slumbering inside the small house, she found the horse she'd ridden here and turned his nose toward the portal.

At the crest of the first hill, she stopped and blew a kiss back toward the dragon's home. His cockiness had cost him; perhaps the lesson she was teaching him was worth the price of the cup.... Either way, she would remember him fondly. Her lips curling into a smile, she kneed the stallion into a canter.

Chapter 1

Present Day

"**W**here is the chalice? What did you do with it?" Joarr Enge picked up the dented metal lantern and peered through the glass. Amma, the witch whose spirit was trapped inside, refused to answer.

He shook the lantern. The needle that he'd used to pull Amma's spirit from the body she'd occupied rattled against the glass windows. The body hadn't been Amma's. A misguided princess, thinking she would gain the witch's powers, had forced Amma's spirit into her body, but she had underestimated Amma's stubbornness. Just as Joarr had. Amma would still be there, annoying her hostess, if Joarr hadn't used the needle to pull her free. But he had and now he had her where he wanted her...or where he had thought he wanted her. Things were not going exactly as he had planned.

He glowered at the lantern. He should roast it, let an explosion of fire escape from his lungs until the object was no more than a bubbly puddle of melted metal and glass.

He let his thoughts pour from his eyes.

The witch inside the lantern stayed firmly hidden.

His fingers tightened around the metal handle and he dropped it to his side, hiding his frustration from her in case she was watching without his knowledge.

She is in there, he assured himself. She just refused to come out, had refused for the past month since he'd brought her back to his home. A home he hadn't seen in over one hundred years, in great part because of this witch.

He cricked his neck from one side to the other, his mood growing darker as he remembered where he'd been, the state he'd been left in.

One hundred years stuck in his dragon form in a room that barely allowed him space to breathe much less turn around or stretch his wings. Nothing to look at but a blank stone wall. Nothing to smell but dirt and the hapless beings locked in the room he guarded. Nothing to taste…at all.

He blamed the witch for the experience. The least she could do was tell him what she'd done with the damn cup she'd taken from his cavern one hundred years earlier.

He growled and pulled back his arm. He was about to toss the lantern against the limestone fireplace when a knock sounded at his door.

Slowly, he lowered the lantern and placed it on the table. He tapped his finger against the top. "Saved for now, my witch thief, but not for long. Dragons' memories are never-ending, but their patience is short. And mine is about used up. I want my treasure returned."

With a muffled curse, he strode to the door. Whoever was waiting on the other side had already lifted the knocker again and was in the middle of pounding the hunk of iron once more against the door. Joarr yanked it open.

Rike Nyhus, his dark brows drawn together in a V, stared back at him.

Without bothering with a greeting, Joarr turned and walked back into his small home's main room, to the table and Amma. Let her hear what the representative of Ormar, the dragon army, had to say. In her current state, she wasn't going anywhere or talking to anyone—not even him. Besides, he had no loyalty to the Ormar; he wasn't obliged to keep their secrets.

He flung one leg over the worn wooden bench and waited for Rike to follow his lead. The lieutenant paused, the wind whistling behind him and snow blowing into the room around him. Finally, he stepped into the house and pulled the door closed.

Joarr folded his hands on the top of the table and waited. The Ormar had been harassing him since his return, insisting he pay the past century of taxes. Warm, fuzzy group that they were, not one had asked where he had been for the past hundred years. Not one had expressed concern, joy or even dismay at his return. He'd walked into his home and been greeted with their threats.

Not that he'd expected anything less from their cold, reptilian hearts.

Rike stopped beside the table. His dark gaze was steady. Joarr returned it with the same bored confidence he'd shown at each of their visits. But this time something was different. Rike looked tired...worried.

"It is good to see you, Chalice Keeper," the lieutenant said.

Joarr cocked a brow, instantly wary. No dragon used his official title. He'd thought...hoped...they'd forgotten it.

"Rike," he responded.

The lieutenant glanced around the room. "You have been gone awhile."

"I explained why when you were here the first five times seeking your taxes."

"Yes, the taxes." Rike looked around again. Giving Joarr the distinct feeling he was looking for something. Though tempted to glance to the side, Joarr kept his gaze away from Amma's lantern, instead staring steadily at the older dragon's face.

"Have you had a change of heart?" Joarr asked. It was an asinine question. It was hard to change a heart that didn't exist. "Have you come to remove your demands?"

Joarr expected the lieutenant to laugh. To his surprise the other dragon didn't. Instead he leaned forward. "As I said, you've been gone a long while. Has anything gone missing in your absence, like, say, the chalice?" There was a flash of fire in his eyes.

Joarr's lips formed a line. How could they know?

He laid two fingers against his brow, as if Rike's question bored him. "I know how important the chalice is. Don't you think I'd have mentioned it if it had gone missing? I am the Keeper."

"A job I know, since being orphaned, you take seriously," the lieutenant replied.

Joarr kept his expression bland. They both knew Rike's words were far from the truth.

Joarr hadn't asked to be entrusted with the dragons' damned holy artifact. Hadn't asked for anything except to be left alone. He'd inherited the job as a child when his father's death had left him orphaned.

His fingers twitched. Again he resisted glancing at the lantern. He had every intention of getting the chalice back, would have had it by now if the witch had cooperated just a little.

Rike touched one hand to his own shoulder and jerked the dragon-army badge off his tight-fitting shirt. Joarr's gaze traveled from the bare place where the patch had been back to Rike's face. This time it was harder to keep his expression blank.

"I am not here as a representative of the army," Rike said. He angled a brow. "Am I still welcome?"

Joarr flipped both hands up. "More so." He leaned back, his gaze on the lieutenant. This conversation was not going where he had expected. It at least might prove interesting.

Rike followed Joarr's example and straddled the other bench. "Will you produce the chalice now?"

Joarr didn't reply. It was obvious the lieutenant knew he'd lost the thing.

Rike let out a breath, a hiss actually. "It's true. You've lost it. How? For how long? Has it been missing the entire time you've been gone? Are you that irresponsible to leave us unguarded?" He stood up, knocking against the table, shoving it into Joarr and causing Amma's lantern to rattle.

Joarr placed his hand over the top of Amma's lantern, stilling it, then replied, his words calm and controlled. "What makes you think it is missing? What great catastrophe has befallen the dragons? I've been home a month and no one has asked about the relic, no one has come to me with tales of apocalypse. Are you saying I missed this massive disaster, or that you just forgot to mention it until now?"

Personally, Joarr didn't believe the legend that surrounded the chalice; he never had. His desire to get the thing back had nothing to do with its supposed power and everything to do with the Ormar believing in its power. If he had been able to find a fake that would have satisfied their skeptical eyes he would have tossed it where the original had been and gone on.

But an ancient artifact, with or without real power, was hard to fake, especially when dealing with dragons.

Rike placed his palms flat on the table and stared into Joarr's eyes. "Things have happened. We didn't see reason to tie them to the chalice since we believed it here, safe. We believed the Keeper would have told us, if it wasn't."

Tsk-tsk. Joarr had been a very bad Keeper indeed. He raised both brows. "I repeat—it couldn't have been that bad or—"

Rike leaned across the table, grabbed Joarr by the front of his sweater and jerked him close. "A dragon died—a young, strong dragon—for no reason. No wounds, no tales of glory-seeking heroes. He. Just. Died."

Joarr closed his lips, cutting off the rebuttal that had already started to form in his mind. Dragons didn't just die. Yes, they were killed, like his father had been, but even that was rare. Dragons were the most magical and strongest of all the beings in the nine worlds. They feared no one.

Seeing that his words were having an effect, Rike loosened his grip. "And yesterday, there was a second. Exactly the same—young and strong. No battles, no wounds." He let go of Joarr and fell back onto his bench. He turned to the side and stared at the dishes still piled in Joarr's sink from breakfast. There were shadows under the older dragon's eyes, and his hand trembled when he reached up to run it over his face.

"About five years ago, the first one, one of our youngest, went off to play—roamed the nine worlds. He was gone for a year, nothing unusual, but when he came back he was tired and stayed to himself. We left him alone, until we realized it was more than that. He had seemed normal at first, was able to shift, to fly, make fire, everything, but as time went on he grew weaker and weaker. He lost one ability after another until he was nothing but a shadow of himself. Our physicians could find nothing wrong with him, and we couldn't tie what was happening to anything he'd encountered while gone. He'd been to all the worlds, been in fights, stolen treasure, done all the things the young do before settling down. We didn't even know if it was connected to his travels. As he continued to fade, we tried all we could think of—potions, magic, even brought in witches—but in a few months, he was dead."

"Was he poisoned?" Joarr asked.

Rike turned his head to look at him. "Does it matter? Does poison kill dragons?"

The answer was obvious. No, nothing killed dragons, nothing that fit this description.

Rike growled and turned back to the side. "Six months ago, another boy left and returned. Same story, same symptoms, same outcome."

"He's dead?" Joarr asked, his blood turning cold.

Rike nodded. There was tension in his neck and his jaw was tight. "He lasted a month. Again we tried everything. This time we sent scouts to all of the worlds, but it was like searching for a fleck of gold in a mountain of earth. He'd told us some of his travels before his illness became obvious, but after that…he got so weak…there was likely more he forgot than remembered."

"Who was this dragon, Rike?" Joarr had to ask; the lieutenant's emotion wasn't normal—not for the Ormar.

Rike didn't move, just kept staring at the dishes. "My son. My only son. And he wasn't alone. His cousin was with him. Ari returned, but Brandt didn't. Ari said they separated for a while, were supposed to join back up, but Brandt never showed. When Ari realized he was getting sick, he came home alone. I suspect whatever took Ari, took Brandt, too. He just never made it back to us."

There was nothing for Joarr to say. He and Rike weren't close, barely tolerated each other actually, and even if they were, dragons did not console one another in grief. Instead he did the kindest thing; he redirected the conversation. "And you think because of two mysterious deaths, and one disappearance, I've lost the chalice?"

The dragons believed the chalice kept them safe, that the chalice was what made and kept them the most undefeatable beings in the nine worlds. Joarr thought the idea ludicrous. Even more ludicrous in his mind was that he was stuck with the job of guarding it by lineage. Tradition said only the Keeper and his heirs could control its magic, could even handle the damn thing.

"Yesterday, I got this." Rike stood and pulled an envelope from his back pocket. There was nothing ominous about the item, just a plain white envelope that could be found at any office-supply store in the human world.

Rike pulled a letter from the envelope and dropped it onto the table in front of him.

Again nothing special—white paper, black ink, printed by some type of computer printer.

I know where the chalice is. If you want it back, send one dragon to the portal. He will get more directions there.

Joarr's lips twisted to the side. It smelled like a trap. "You believe this?" he asked.

Rike cocked a brow. "Tell me I shouldn't. Tell me you have the chalice."

When Joarr didn't reply, the lieutenant shook his head. "We should have realized before. We've never been weak like this, been preyed on. No one has that ability. How could they? Not with the power of the chalice protecting us. We should have realized when the first dragon came back sick that the chalice was missing, but we were too caught up trying to cure his illness, then with my son, find his killer. When all we needed to do was retrieve the chalice." He paused. "Or you. All you need to do is retrieve the chalice."

Of course.

Chapter 2

The cavern was dark and cool. Joarr hadn't bothered to bring a working light. He could see in the dark almost as well as in the day. He tucked the folded note into his pants pocket and held up the lantern. Amma had made no sound, given no sign she was inside, not since Rike had left. He wondered what she had heard, if she was rejoicing in the pain she had caused him, could cause him still.

Before leaving, the dragon lieutenant had reminded Joarr of his taxes and added a threat. If Joarr didn't find the chalice and bring it back, the Ormar would take everything. Joarr's home would be burned, his treasure taken and the entrance to his cavern sealed. He would be exiled.

Exiled dragons became wyrms, brainless bipedal creatures unable to shift to any other form, unable to do anything besides feed the hunger that blazed inside them. Greed for food, power and treasure consumed them.

The witch and her tricks had brought Joarr to this.

He moved to the back of the first room, past his treasure, which still lay in the pile as it had when he'd discovered Amma's pilfery. The rounded grooves where her breasts had brushed over the gold were still visible. He could probably still smell her there, too, if he would allow himself to get that close. But he wouldn't. The sight and scent last time had sent him into a rage. He wouldn't fall victim to that again. No, this time he would deal with Amma and her treachery the same way she had dealt with him—with cold calculation.

In the back was a narrow passageway, barely wide enough for him in his human form. It led to a bigger room, one he rarely visited, one saved for only the things he truly treasured…didn't just feel the dragon-obsession to own. The room was empty aside from a six-foot-long table and the cloth-covered form that lay on top of it.

Amma's lantern held over his head as if the object were actually emitting light, he jerked the cloth from the table. A gasp sounded from the lantern. It began to vibrate.

Joarr smiled. Amma had seen a ghost…herself.

Her body. The new rulers of Alfheim—a hellhound and the elf princess whose body Amma had shared for a while—had sent him Amma's form. She had been separated from it not long after she had stolen his chalice. She'd gone to Alfheim, apparently in search of family, but been turned away. According to stories, she became crazed and with the help of her sisters, attacked the elves. The elves had been unable to destroy her, but they had managed to separate her spirit from her body. Her body had been kept in Alfheim while her spirit had been locked in a vessel and sent to the in-between land of Gunngar.

Gunngar…where he had been trapped, too. He and Amma both had been prisoners there for one hundred years. She locked in a gemstone, he locked in his dragon form. He'd dreamed of the day he would see her again and seek his revenge, but now that the day was here, revenge was the least of his concerns.

He needed his chalice, and while Rike had provided him with the note, he knew simply following its directions would be foolhardy. He needed more information—like what Amma had done with the cup all those years ago.

He ran the backs of his fingers over the witch's still, cool cheek and shook his head at the irony of her appearance. "You are a beauty. Deceptively innocent-looking with your golden hair and blue eyes. What color do they call that? Cornflower, I believe. Just a hint of purple if I remember correctly. And big…angelic, except in bed. Then they crackled with life…your true nature showing through. Wicked little thing that you are." His hand hovered over her face, his thumb brushing over her lips.

"According to Rike and what I've heard from others, the elves tried everything to destroy your body—every magical tool they could dig up, but did they try a dragon's fire? I know of nothing that can survive the full force of that." He pulled in a breath, then released it, a tiny puff of smoke escaping his lips as he did.

Lowering the lantern an inch, he peered through the glass. "Are you willing to talk now?"

Amma swirled around the inside of the lantern like she'd done a thousand times before, searching for a crack, a pinhole, anything that would give her an opportunity to escape. Her body! The dragon had it. How had he gotten it?

She stared at the form laid out on the table—the lantern gave her the ability to see when she chose to use it. Not a hair seemed out of place. There was no dust or grime, nothing to indicate her body had been treated with disregard, much less abuse.

Unable to form another cognizant thought, she pummeled her spirit against the glass.

Joarr jerked, then stared into the lantern. His blue gaze froze her in place. He dangled the lantern over her body's closed eyes and murmured against the glass. "Help me find the chalice and I will return you to your body."

Her spirit stilled, but her thoughts began to move as swiftly as a cat's tail when its owner had spied a fat dove. If she helped Joarr recover his property, she would in essence be saving him from whatever veiled threat the older dragon had tossed out before leaving. She hadn't understood the significance of what Rike had said, but it had been obvious Joarr had. He had paled considerably as his visitor stormed out the door.

And Amma had no desire to help Joarr. She was no fool. She knew he was angry at her for stealing his chalice and that was before the other dragon's threats.

Now? Now she could only imagine he wanted her to return to her body so he could roast it with her inside.

Still, the chance to be herself again, to truly feel and experience the world overwhelmed all else.

Her decision made, she gathered herself together and stared at Joarr. He pulled back. She didn't know what he saw when he looked into the lantern, but she could tell by the startled look in his blue eyes that now he could see her or some representation of her, and he knew she was ready to deal.

"Release me into my body and I will help you," she murmured, hoping the words flowed, that Joarr could understand her.

He smiled. "Tell me who you gave the chalice to and I will release you."

Amma pulled back into herself, hiding again. Dragons were known for their craftiness. If she gave Joarr too much information there would be no reason for him to keep his word.

"A dwarf," she said, testing him.

He sighed. "That isn't even a fraction of an answer." He picked up her lifeless hand and held it to his lips. At first Amma thought he intended to kiss it; then she saw the flicker of fire escape his lips.

"Stop," she yelled, before realizing the word had even formed. Annoyed that she had slipped and shown her concern, she immediately pulled back into herself again. She had no idea if her body could survive a dragon's fire. As he'd said, little could.

"What?" He angled his head. "I only thought a fraction of an answer deserved similar payment...a fraction of your body." He laid her pinkie flat on his palm. "One finger perhaps? Frozen, it should snap off easily."

Amma ground nonexistent teeth. She'd forgotten he had the dual powers of fire and ice. It made him an even grander adversary.

Joarr stroked the limp digit. "No? Do you have a counteroffer?"

Amma fixated on that pinkie, how it would feel to feel again. If she was in her body, the dragon wouldn't toy with her like this. She would use her magic, blow him to bits before he had a chance to so much as breathe on her…

"Half," she yelled.

"Half a body?" Joarr eyed her lifeless form with exaggerated disbelief. "That will be much messier."

"No, you lout. I tell you half of what you need to know and you release me into my body. Once I'm safely back and confident everything is working, I'll tell you the rest." Except there was no rest; she'd sold the chalice to a dwarf. There was little she could tell the dragon past that.

Joarr lowered Amma's finger and trailed his hand down the length of her body. "Yes, must make sure everything is working. That could prove entertaining."

Amma ignored him, or tried to; she couldn't keep from watching as his fingers traced the low neckline of her peasant blouse, paused at the indentation between her breasts.

Without warning, he pulled his hand back. "You tell me half, I release you. Then you come with me. Once I have the chalice, you will go free."

"I tell you what I know—that's it. I'm not responsible for whether you are or aren't capable of getting the cup back."

"You stole it. You make sure I get it back."

Amma counted to ten. Conversing with the dragon made her want to scream. He had the upper hand and he was using it, abusing it. She didn't know how long it would take him to find his chalice; it was insane to demand she stay with him until he did.

Revenge, she realized. This was part of his revenge.

She muttered a curse, thinking what she would do when he didn't have the upper hand, when she was free... She shook herself. She was letting the dragon get to her. She wasn't thinking clearly. She had nothing to lose by agreeing with him. Once she was back in her body, she'd leave. He'd only asked for her word that she wouldn't. Dragons apparently were as arrogant as the tales made them out to be.

"Agreed," she said.

Joarr held the lantern to his face; his blue eyes filled her world. Amma kept herself from reacting, from saying something that would weaken her bargain.

"Agreed," he replied.

Amma's spirit expanded inside the lantern. She didn't know if Joarr could see her joy, and she didn't care. Her bodyless state was about to come to an end.

As she was celebrating, the lantern jolted. Joarr had sat the thing down, and only feet away from Amma's body. She could see herself laid out, her golden hair in waves around her face. Her favorite skirt, patched and with a worn fringed hem, still fit perfectly. It was neither too loose nor too snug. She hadn't gained or lost an ounce, which made her wonder what had happened to her body. What state would she find it in once she returned to it? Perhaps this was all a trick; perhaps she would find herself trapped inside a body that wouldn't come back to life…

Joarr brushed by, quickly, Amma catching nothing but the flash of his white sweater, but it was enough to snap her out of her moment of panic. Her body was fine. Everything inside it was fine.

Joarr came back into view, stepping toward her.

Soon she would be herself again, and she'd teach the dragon not to make the same mistake twice, not to trust so easily.

Chapter 3

Two weeks earlier...

Dark rock music screamed from the speakers. Somewhere in the back of the bar a patron screamed, too. Walking along the plank that hung from the twelve-foot ceiling, Fafnir didn't bother to glance down. It was midnight, time for a drink. A very special drink. The dwarf had been waiting for his father, Hreidmar—known to those he did business with as the Collector—to disappear before leaving his post at the bar's entrance.

"Where you going?" Regin, Fafnir's brother, blocked his path. "You're supposed to be on the door. Some humans tried to get in without paying."

Fafnir scowled. "Too much for you? You losing your skill?" He glanced at his brother's waist where a slim blade hung.

"It's not my job—it's yours. I'm busy. Someone

broke into the vault again. Dad was not happy when he left."

Fafnir pretended surprise. "Anything missing?"

Staring down at the heads of their customers, Regin spoke without looking back at his brother. "No, nothing has disappeared since the chalice."

Fafnir shrugged. "An object Dad had no use for, anyway."

Regin turned back, his gaze assessing. "Dad has use for everything, even if we don't know its purpose." His fingers, unusually long and nimble for a dwarf, tapped the handle of his blade. "Have we had any more dragons through?"

Fafnir stiffened. "You know dragons don't wander to the human world often."

"True. But they are known thieves. And I heard one was spotted in the human world only a few weeks past."

Fafnir's heart sped, but he kept his tone bored. "Near here?" What he had said to Regin was true—dragons didn't wander into the human world too frequently, but even less so since the last had fallen.

Regin shook his head. "Not particularly."

Fafnir hesitated, not wanting to give away his interest, but if a dragon was roaming the human world, he needed to know. He needed to find him. He was also, however, concerned over his brother's interest. "Why do you ask, anyway? About dragons coming through?"

Regin's pebble-hard gaze held his. "The cup, of course. Its magic has something to do with dragons, and until its disappearance, we'd never seen one. Do you think it attracts them?"

How Fafnir wished the chalice attracted dragons.

He glanced over his brother's shoulder, to his office where his drink was waiting. He was eager to get to it, but Regin was now fully blocking his path again.

"Does Dad know what the cup does?" Fafnir asked. If Regin was going to cost him time, he might as well pay for it with information.

"If he does, he isn't saying."

Fafnir licked his lips. The pressure to get to his drink, to feel the cool, thick liquid sliding down his throat, was overwhelming. "I'm sure it's nothing, then." He pushed against Regin, forcing the slimmer dwarf to step to the side—a risky move considering his younger brother's prowess with a blade, but Fafnir's insides were crawling. He had to have that drink.

This time Regin let Fafnir pass. Fafnir scurried as quickly as his short legs would carry him over the boards, sending them swinging back and forth. When he hit the intersection of four paths, he turned to the left, putting his brother back in his view. The younger dwarf stood sure-footed, not even bothering to hold on to the hand ropes as the boards swayed.

"Do whatever you're so hurried to do, then get back to the door. I don't have time to be hauling off bodies, not tonight."

Fafnir held up one hand in agreement, then trotted the last few yards to his office. Normally, he wouldn't have taken Regin's orders so easily, but his drink…

He stepped into his office, shoved the door closed and slid the lock into place. Confident his brother wouldn't "remember" something else he needed and walk in on him, Fafnir scuttled to the safe that lay hidden behind a floor-to-ceiling mirror. The mirror was his father's, but unlike the chalice Fafnir kept locked up behind it, the mirror had been a gift.

He touched a spot on the ornate frame and the secret door swung open. Inside was a small room, lined with metal Fafnir had forged himself. He didn't have the same skill with metals his brother did, but like all dwarves, his talent was still impressive. On a shelf in the back, further obscured from accidental view by an ancient helmet, was the dragon chalice.

With both hands cupped around its rounded sides, he brought the chalice to his lips. The liquid inside was almost gone. A sip a day from the magic cup was all he was allowed. The dark elf who had sold him the tale had emphasized that. Too much and the magic would be too strong, too much for Fafnir to control. The darkest part of the dragons' power would swallow him, devour him, make him into what all dragons, all beings, feared…a wyrm.

The blood in the cup now was old and stale. His last harvest from a living dragon had been months earlier. According to the dark elf, the cup's magic only worked with fresh blood, drawn from a pumping heart, but the dragons' stronghold was on lockdown.

Fafnir had spread tales of treasure, thinking the stories would lure a few young dragons to the bar, but months had passed and nothing.

Now, though, maybe there was hope. Regin had mentioned a dragon being spotted.

Feeling more alive than he had in weeks, he pressed the gold against his parted lips. *One sip, one sip,* he chanted. It was so tempting to take more, but he had to maintain control. If he didn't, if he got sloppy, when he had fresh blood again, he would slip.

He took a breath, but didn't inhale the scent. Instead he thought of fresh blood, remembered how it warmed his mouth, how his body tingled as the magic contained in it flowed through him. He concentrated on that, and as the liquid rolled down his throat, a tiny bit of the craving subsided, but not all, not by a long shot.

He closed his eyes and stood with the cup still pressed against his lips. He breathed in and out, and recited his chant again. Then slowly he forced his arms to reach for the shelf, his hands to slide the cup back behind the helmet and his fingers to release their hold.

His hands empty and his heart bereft, he turned and left the vault. With the mirror closed over the opening, he stared at his reflection.

He looked the same. Short, bandy legs, wide shoulders and an oversize head—compared to the humans that frequented the bar that was. For a dwarf he was perfectly proportioned, attractive even. But he wasn't doing this to change his looks. He was doing this for power beyond physical strength. He was tired of being the grunt of the family, bossed around by father and brother. Nothing more than hired muscle. He needed magic—dragon magic.

When he had it, when he could shift into the mighty beast, he would have everything, would take everything. His father's treasures would be his, and his brother's blade. Anything and everything he could ever want would be his.

He rounded his lips and blew out a breath. Smoke, black and smelling of sulfur, puffed from his mouth.

He grinned. He flexed his hands, envisioned being a dragon, his body growing, a tail extending from his back… Nothing happened. His grin faded.

Three cups of fresh dragon blood he'd drained and half a cup of old. How much longer until he could shift?

He angled his head.

Who was he fooling? He would never turn into a dragon without new blood. He had to find another dragon, and soon.

Chapter 4

Present day

Joarr picked up Amma's prison. He held it for a second, contemplating his choice. He wasn't afraid of setting her free. She might be a witch, but she was no match for him. The Ormar's steadfast belief that losing the chalice weakened them was nothing but superstitious nonsense. As he'd told her, little could destroy a dragon. Dragons' weaknesses were well documented: their own greed and their opponents' craftiness.

Greed wasn't an issue—the chalice was one piece of treasure he would be happy to be rid of, if the legend that went with it disappeared, too. So, that little dragon weakness was no threat here.

And so far as outwitting him? Tales of dragons being outwitted were popular, but that popularity far outranked their reality. Dragons' adversaries tended to repeat the stories that showed themselves as the victors. But no one spoke of all the other humans, dwarves and would-be heroes who failed, who were toasted or frozen or just left walled up inside some dragon's cave.

Dragons might well be greedy, but they were not stupid—especially not this one.

So, all in all releasing Amma held little risk for him. Plus he would get the benefit of keeping her from complete freedom for a while, repaying her for at least a fraction of her crime. And if she cooperated, she could help him reach his goal—bringing the damned chalice back to those who believed in it and saving himself from becoming a wyrm.

He strode to her body and pulled out the item he had stored under the table. Amma might think he was a fool, but he wasn't.

His safeguard in place, he held up the lantern and stared inside. "Time to pay. What did you do with my treasure?"

Smoke thickened inside the thing, changing colors as it did. Amma thinking, he guessed. Trying to figure some way out of her deal most likely. He shook the lantern. "Give me a name and a world."

The fog stilled, a pink cloud trapped behind the glass. Then waves appeared and words formed inside his head. It wasn't a voice really—more like cue cards flashing in rapid succession in his brain.

"Collector. A dwarf."

The name rang no bells, and the note Rike had shown him looked as if it came from the human world, not Nidavellir, home of the dwarves. Joarr tapped on the glass. "The truth, or I won't let you out."

"It is the truth." The cue cards flashed like neon in his head, emphasizing Amma's annoyance.

"Why did he want the cup?" he asked.

"Don't know. He COLLECTS things."

She was getting testy or testier. It should have made Joarr reluctant to release the witch from her cell, but strangely it had the opposite effect. His spine tingled with anticipation. Even after one hundred years without a body, the witch still had spirit. Maybe that was the point. It was all she'd had. The idea of battling with her, playing with her, maybe celebrating her return to her body with her...reminded Joarr that he'd been a prisoner, too. Been cut off from many of the same physical pleasures Amma had.

Perhaps they could rediscover them together.

He lowered the lantern, thinking. He'd planned to get more information out of her before giving her what she wanted most, her body. But actually, once in her true form she would be easier to control and read. In his dragon shape, he could read minds. He doubted the witch realized that. It would be a handy surprise.

Decision made, he snapped the manacle around his wrist and flipped open the tab that held the lantern's lid in place.

"Fly home," he whispered.

Freedom. Amma could smell it. Not literally, not yet, but it was close.

She flew from the lantern. Outside of its magical glass walls, she lost her sight, but it didn't matter. She had developed strange talents over the past hundred years: the ability to sense life in a room, to feel the pulse inside a body—not of blood…of existence.

Joarr was close and huge. His force was so strong Amma was moving toward him automatically, drawn, fascinated. His voice stopped her.

"Are you in there?"

He was bending over her body; he had to be. She slowed herself, focused on the space beside Joarr where she knew her body had to lie. Slowed the wild need that was coursing through her and remembered what she was seeking—not any life force, not Joarr, but herself. She was searching for her body, to restore her life force.

Centered, she reached out, groped for some sign that would show her guess was correct, that Joarr was beside her body, but there was nothing, no pulse, nothing. She hesitated, her earlier fears of being trapped in a lifeless body returning. But what was her choice, this? Staying in spirit form…maybe trying to wile her way back into someone else's body? The last time had been all kinds of unpleasant.

She had no choice. She focused on the area beside Joarr and winged closer.

"Amma?" Joarr leaned over the witch, watching for some sign her spirit had returned to her body. It hadn't occurred to him before this that she might not be able to return, or that it would require anything more than opening the lantern and setting her spirit free.

Somehow, he'd thought Amma would figure the rest out herself.

But now, as the seconds ticked past, he was beginning to wonder, and worry. Left free in her spirit form, what havoc could Amma wreak? And, he realized, he felt a strange sense of responsibility. He'd threatened the witch numerous times, but at the idea that because of him she might be left floating for eternity without even the lantern to anchor her, something damn close to panic shot through him.

He turned to grab the lantern, to look inside. The manacle attached to his wrist jerked. He twirled back. Amma's body had moved. Her arm spasmed, and his arm, bound to hers by the manacles, was yanked again.

Her chest moved up and down with shallow breaths, but breaths all the same. Unable to fully lift the hand manacled to his wrist, she raised her other hand and rubbed her fingers across her eyes.

"Amma?" he prompted. "Are you in there?" Realizing his words were sharp, he took a breath and regained his normal tone. "Can you hear me?"

Her eyelids fluttered open, and there were her eyes, huge and cornflower-blue just as he'd remembered them. He stood lost for a second, unable to do anything except stare into their depths.

Her lips, full and soft, parted. "Dragon?" she murmured.

He leaned closer, until he could feel her breath puff lightly against his cheek. "Are you hungry…thirsty?" he asked. His voice was deeper than normal. He cleared his throat and tried to loosen the lump that seemed to be blocking his words.

"I…" Something flickered in her eyes, but Joarr barely took notice. He was too occupied inhaling her scent…inviting, like sun-warmed earth.

She shivered.

"Are you cold?" He reached with his free hand and felt her arm. It was cool to his touch.

She shook her head, then nodded. "A little. Will you help me?" She fluttered her fingers, telling him she needed his help to sit. Instantly, he slid his free arm behind her and propped her against his chest. Her face fell against his neck; her hair clung to his face. She was tiny, seemed fragile, in need of protection and care.

He liked her this way, almost forgot the hellion he'd hunted and lost. He bent his face to hers. She breathed against his lips. He captured the air that had just escaped her lungs and lowered his mouth to hers.

Her lips were soft. They showed no sign that her body had been without life for a hundred-plus years. He didn't know what power had kept her so perfect, but as he cuddled her against his chest, as her tongue stroked his and fire began to build in his core, he blessed that power.

He ran his fingers up the curve of her neck, into her hair, and tilted her face more completely to his. His manacled hand twitched with the need to touch her more. Her hand lifted; he followed her movements, keeping the chain connecting them loose. He sensed she didn't realize it was there. She would be angered when she did, and he didn't want that, not now, not yet.

Her fingers spread over his chest. He covered her hand with his own and intensified the kiss. The heat inside him continued to build. He let it escape through his skin, warming her and revealing his desire. It was a dragon ritual. A female dragon, if she enjoyed the act and wanted more, would return the favor, sharing a portion of her fire in exchange—not a lot—just enough for the male to feel her excitement. Female dragons were much more guarded than males when sharing their fire. They rarely released total control. If they did, it meant something—to both dragons. Joarr had yet to experience such an exchange, but he was never stingy in sharing his own flame.

And even though Amma wasn't a dragon, had no fire to share, he wanted her to feel his.

She murmured and moved closer. He tightened his arm behind her and engulfed her in warmth.

Her palm pressed flat against his chest, then she moved her free hand to his back and did the same there. He waited, inexplicably expecting her to do as he had done, share her heat… She was a witch, he reminded himself. She didn't have the ability.

He felt a tug. Power…magic being pulled from his body.

He stiffened.

He shared and she took. He had offered his fire, but as an exchange. She wasn't sharing. She wasn't caught up in a moment of passion. She, the damned manipulative witch, was stealing. Again.

He forced himself not to react, visibly at least, but he cursed himself silently for forgetting who and what she was and what she'd done to him in the past.

She was pulling power from his body. It made sense: witches didn't create power of their own; they stole it from other sources. And forandre—shape-shifters like dragons, hellhounds and garm—were magical beings. They emitted waves of energy when they shifted, but were always letting off some amount.

And no forandre was more magical than a dragon.

He could afford the magic and could understand that she would want to rebuild her reserves, but he also realized this was Amma—the witch who had tricked him once before. Innocent and feminine as she might appear, she was also deadly.

He tipped her face up to his. "I think that is just about enough." Then he snapped down his shields.

Her eyes rounded, then narrowed.

He shook his head and made a tsking sound. "Didn't know I could do that, did you? If you're going to steal from someone, you really should study their defenses better."

She shoved him away, sitting up and flinging her legs over the table's side as she did. Her eyes flared. "What defenses? You left the cup lying about like a discarded rag. You practically gave it to me." She paused; her gaze darted around the dark cavern. He could see her coming back to herself, stepping away from her annoyance and slipping into the role that had sucked him in before.

Her eyes rounded, back to innocence. But it was too late; he'd seen the truth. He'd felt it, too.

He ran his hand down his sleeve, smoothing the wrinkles that had formed. "You know I'm not referring to the cup, but to the magic you were so sweetly siphoning out of me. I realize having such power so near has to challenge your self-control, but really, if we are to make this arrangement work, you will need to learn to keep rein on yourself." He angled his head and arched one brow, playing a role of his own—cocky and condescending.

It worked. Her eyes snapped with anger again.

"Lucky for me I don't see a need to make this work. I don't see a need to be near you at all." She lifted her palm; a burnished silver ball of power was cupped inside it.

They were only a foot or so apart. At such close range the sphere winging toward him would have killed any other being, but Joarr wasn't any other being.

It really was time for Amma to realize that.

He shifted. The elfin magic inside the manacles allowed for a massive change in his size. Unfortunately in the small space he was only able to change in shape, not mass. Still, he knew the shift was impressive. In his dragon form he was more silver and dazzling than a thousand of the little toys she'd tossed at him, and he saw it on her face. He had only a second to enjoy her expression. But he had no doubt there would be more opportunities, had no doubt that Amma would challenge him again. And next time he wouldn't be limited by the walls of his cavern. He looked forward to it.

The ball inches from his head, he opened his jaws and blew…ice this time. He loved having the choice, loved how it awed his victims, left them guessing what would come next.

The sphere hit the icy shield his breath had formed and shattered it into what looked like a million diamond-sharp shards.

Amma gasped and tried to run, but chained to Joarr, she fell instead, dangled half on, half off the table. Joarr flung out his wing, shielding her from the blast. Magic shot up and back, striking the ceiling and wall of the cavern. But the caverns were strong. They had been around long before the dragons discovered them. It would take more than one magical spitball to down them.

As the magic rained down around them, he glanced at the witch. She was lying on the floor, her chest moving up and down in gasping breaths. Her gaze was fixed on her wrist and the chain that connected her to the giant silver dragon.

"Is that all you've got?" Joarr asked, transferring the question into her mind. "Because, really, I was expecting more."

She spit out a curse and spread the fingers on both hands. Energy sizzled between them, forming a powerful, dangerous web. Dangerous for most, that was, but again, not for Joarr, not in his dragon form and not while Amma's body was so depleted of power. This was almost getting dull.

He shook his head and breathed again—aimed at the air over her head. Tiny bits of ice this time, barely visible to the naked eye, but just as sharp as the magic she aimed at him, pattered down on her. She flipped her hands, palms up over her head. The shards hit the magic and sizzled to nothing but steam.

She smiled at him, victory shining from her eyes.

He sighed and sat, waited for her to realize this time he'd done the outwitting.

Watching him from the corner of her eye, she scrambled to a stand. Her golden hair fell over her face. She flipped it over her shoulder with an impatient flick of her wrist. Then she faced him, one hand wrapped around the chain that connected them, the other held out toward him.

"Release me," she ordered.

"I could," he replied, but made no move to do so.

She rubbed her fingers together, seemed to be checking for something. Doubt flickered deep in her eyes, but she covered the emotion quickly. "Release me," she repeated. "Or I will do it myself."

He tilted his head. "Go ahead."

Her fingers glowed…pure white light poured from their tips. With an arrogant glance in his direction, she wrapped her hand around the chain. The metal glowed as power poured from Amma into it. Her eyes closed; lines formed on her forehead.

Joarr flicked his tail through the dirt while he waited. He wished she would hurry. In his dragon form the room was confining. The entire thing was just uncomfortable.

Her brows pulled together. Joarr flicked his tail again.

It was obvious the task was draining her. Of course, that had been Joarr's intention. He yawned, wondered how much longer it could possibly take for her to realize her folly.

As magic continued to leak into the metal, the links swelled, until they had doubled in size. Amma seemed unaware of their change, bending at the waist from their increased weight but not halting what she was doing. As the chain swelled more, she stumbled and fell onto the floor.

Joarr took a step forward. "Are you done?" Steam shot from his nostrils. Tired of the games, he didn't wait for her response; he shifted back to his human form and clothing. Unlike less magical forandre, he was able to create clothing with his shifts. He dressed himself in his favorite color, white—suit pants and a crisp cotton shirt.

After smoothing a wrinkle, this one out of his pants, he bent and scooped the exhausted witch from the floor. She was looking frail and innocent again. His heart tightened, but he kept his voice terse. "You don't think I wouldn't consider you in my plans, do you? I do know you are a witch. Even fully recovered, your magic won't break the cuffs or the chain that connects them. It will strengthen them actually. The elves built the manacles to work like a witch—magic directly applied to any part of them is absorbed. Ingenious idea, don't you think?" He didn't expect or wait for a response. He jostled her in his arms, so her head fell against his shoulder.

He continued talking as he carried her from the back room into the main part of his cavern. She didn't reply and didn't struggle, leaving him to wonder if she was even awake.

On reaching the main room, he got his answer. "How about you, dragon? Do you absorb power now, too?" she hissed. Her body was limp. She had managed to drain herself thoroughly. But her voice was strong and her cornflower eyes were hard, like cold jewels.

He released the arm that held her legs and let her body slide down his form, felt every inch of her as it pressed against him. She didn't resist. She seemed to enjoy the slow trip down his body as much as he did. Her eyes glowing with challenge, she stared at him.

"It would take more than one little witch to fell me, no matter how fully charged her battery," he murmured.

Amma's gaze grew sharper. He could see she wanted

to say something, rebuff his words, but she stopped herself.

"But, just in case you are thinking you can…remember these." He held up his wrist, the one connected to hers. "Dragons convert to their dragon state when they die. If you plan to kill me, best work that into the equation, too. And what you saw back there—" he jerked his head toward the back room "—was not my full form, just a modified version. Trust me, you would not be making a quick getaway. In fact I doubt you'd get away at all."

Her eyes shuttered off. She crossed her arms over her chest and turned away, or tried to. Their connected state stopped her from completing either act entirely.

Tired of their standoff, Joarr bent forward and flung her over his shoulder. She elbowed him in the head.

His ears rang from the blow, but he kept walking. "I'm taking us to the portal. Once there you can tell me what else you remember. As long as you keep your word, I'll keep mine. We will be free of each other in no time."

Chapter 5

The trip to the portal was uncomfortable. The dragon insisted on making the journey in his human form despite Amma's efforts to convince him flying would be more efficient. If he had shifted, magic would have leaked out of him like water through a sieve. Amma suspected that would be the best time to pull his power. She had messed up before by trying to pull the energy she needed while he was standing still and easily able to sense what she was doing. Of course, she had thought he was occupied with more base things—enough heat had been pouring out of him. She knew he was attracted to her. She had thought that attraction would be enough to distract him. But it hadn't been, or perhaps he'd been playing her all along, pretending attraction to get her to show her hand.

The last thought was annoying. He was annoying… and appealing. She ran her fingers over her lips. She had been tempted by his kiss, tempted to wait before stealing his power. It had been so long since she had been able to feel anything, then to be thrown into the depths of sensation the dragon offered…

It was like resisting a promise from the gods.

But hard as it had been, she had resisted.

And then he had shocked her by somehow shutting off her attempts to drain his magic. A skill she hadn't realized dragons had, but now that she did, she would be smarter and not let any opportunity slip by. If only she had been thinking when he had shifted in the cavern.

He might be able to stop her from pulling power when he was steady in one form, but while he was shifting? Too much magic was released then. There was no way he could keep her from gathering energy.

So, while her goal was to escape him altogether, until then she had to get him to shift as frequently as possible, and she would soak up the resulting magic like a sponge, silent and unobtrusive. She would stay that way until she was so full of energy her hair sizzled with it.

He had no idea who she was or what she was capable of.

He also had no idea what was at stake for her.

She placed a hand on her abdomen. The dragon couldn't learn her secret. Couldn't learn she'd found a way to get the family she craved…and how he had helped.

The bar was located about ten miles from the dragon stronghold. They had ridden a motorcycle down the steep mountain, the engine roaring in Amma's ears and Joarr somehow steering with one hand. The entire thing had been both unsettling and exhilarating—a bit like the dragon himself.

Joarr parked the machine in the bar's huge gravel lot. The squat building of white stone looked out of place here—as if it had been plopped down from the sky. It was little more than a way station. Most in-between places the size of the dragons' home didn't warrant a portal this size, but no other in-between place was home to all of the nine worlds' male dragons. And although dragons didn't need portals—in their dragon forms they could fly anywhere they liked—they used them. Flying meant arriving in their dragon form, taking away any element of surprise.

As they approached the bar that held the portal, Joarr wove his fingers between hers. "No reason to advertise our connected state," he murmured.

She didn't argue. The garm who ran portals in most parts of the nine worlds were no friends of hers. She had no friends, no one, except her sisters, whom she wouldn't exactly term as friends.

Although the noise coming from inside the bar signaled the portal was doing booming business, the parking lot was empty.

A few feet from the door, Joarr stopped. "Do you hear that?"

Thinking he was referring to the clamor behind the door, Amma shrugged. Who couldn't hear that? But before she could voice the sarcastic thought something small and dark dropped from the roof.

Joarr looked up. Three small bodies flipped off the roof and landed on the gravel beside him. He grabbed

Amma and twirled her body toward his, so her face was pressed against his chest and his arm was wrapped around her. Bound together it was the best he could do.

She mumbled something and tried to shove herself away, but he held firm. With her protected as best he could, he assessed his attackers.

Short and stocky.

Dwarves.

All three were dressed in head-to-toe black with their faces covered. Each carried a short blade, a typical dwarf weapon. One dwarf, who in addition to the blade carried some kind of glass-and-metal flask, made a subtle hand signal to the others. The pair spread out, leaving about six feet between them.

Still struggling, Amma managed to pull her face free. "What do they want?" she muttered.

"Nothing good, I think." Joarr jerked her more closely against his body and let his gaze dance over the group. The leader lifted one finger, and as a unit, the three leaped.

Joarr blasted them with ice, or tried to. In his human form the spray was much narrower than when he shifted. He concentrated on the leader and hit him square in the chest. The dwarf was knocked back against the bar's rock wall.

The others paused and exchanged glances. They hadn't expected his attack, or perhaps it was the ice they hadn't expected. Very few dragons could produce ice and even fewer could produce both fire and ice. Enemy expectations, or lack of them, could work to his advantage. Something he needed to remember during this quest.

As the thought was racing through his head, he attacked again. Sticking to ice, he targeted a second dwarf. This time, however, the small being was prepared. He dropped and rolled. The stream of ice shot over his head and smashed into the bar. The building shook, and the noise inside ceased. No one, however, opened the door or peered out a window.

Beings who congregated in portal bars were not the type to get involved in others' arguments.

"Give me power." Amma stared up at him, anger clear in her eyes. "Let me fight."

He didn't have time to argue with her or even acknowledge her demand. The third dwarf was charging toward them, blade drawn. Joarr turned his ice on him, but this time aimed for the dwarf's feet. The dwarf stumbled and fell forward, catching himself on his hands to keep from colliding with the ground. His ungraceful posture worked in Joarr's favor. The ice solidified as the dwarf fell, locking his ankles and wrists to the ground.

His posture would have been comical, if the other two dwarves hadn't chosen then to attack in unison.

They raced forward, both with their blades drawn. The second dwarf, the one not carrying the flask, had added an ax to his attack.

Joarr pulled in a breath and again discharged a flow of ice. He shot for their feet this time, too, but the pair jumped, landing on gravel untouched by Joarr's attempts. They rolled, each going a different direction.

Joarr spun, pulling Amma with him. He shot ice at one dwarf then the other. Each time they leaped, avoiding his attack.

"Enough! Give me power," Amma muttered through gritted teeth. "Or shift."

She was right. In his human form, with one arm tied to her, he was at a distinct disadvantage. They could be here fighting the three for hours.

He did not have the patience for that. He shifted, and he didn't hold back. His body filled the parking lot. Beside him, Amma's eyes rounded, but only for a second. She quickly began to pull power. He could feel it being siphoned from him, but he couldn't worry about the witch now.

He had dwarves to flatten.

Joarr nudged Amma with his foot, warning her that he was about to move. Without pausing in what she was doing, the witch wrapped her body around his leg and held on.

He smiled. Amma as an adornment. He liked it.

The dwarves had freed their companion from the ice. Now all three faced him again. He opened his jaws, ready to lay a coating of ice so thick across the landscape that those in the bar would be trapped and the dwarves outside converted into instant ice sculptures.

Two blades flew toward him, aimed at his front leg, the one without the witch. Surprised his attackers would pick a place sure to do him little damage, Joarr hesitated. Perhaps he'd overestimated the group.

The blades struck home, painful, but no more so than a mosquito bite would have been in his human form. He shook his leg, dislodging both knives. Then eyed the dwarves again. The followers stood back. They seemed to be waiting for something, but the leader ran straight at him. The dwarf's blade was sheathed but his flask was still in his hand.

He landed on Joarr's leg near the spot where the other dwarves' knives had struck. Joarr could feel him there, like a tick or other small pest. He shook his leg, but the dwarf hung tight.

Amma yelled, but Joarr couldn't hear her words. Then she cursed loud and clear, and magic, white-hot, seared into the leg the dwarf clung to.

He glanced down. Amma stood with her feet wedged against his leg. Her bound arm was extended so the chain that connected them was taut and her body was angled away from his. Her golden hair streamed from behind her and silvery power flew from her free hand. Power that was directed at his other leg…or the dwarf; he couldn't be sure which.

There was another curse, this one from the dwarf. He jerked his ax free. Without pausing to aim, he threw the weapon. It whirled end over end toward Amma. The witch didn't move, didn't try to stop the deadly missile flying toward her. She simply fired off another attack of her own.

Both struck. The chain snapped, cut by the ax, and Amma and the dwarf both fell to the ground, leaving Joarr shocked and unable to process what had happened for a second. Then as he stared at Amma's body tumbled like a broken doll onto the gravel, it all set in.

He roared.

Fire erupted from Joarr's belly and flew from his lips. In seconds all three dwarves were nothing but ash. A cold wind blew from behind him, scattering the residue over the previously white portal building, coating it with gray.

A hollow feeling of defeat, despite his victory, settled in Joarr's stomach. His gaze fixed on the witch, he shifted.

He walked to her, not bothering to create clothing for himself as he did. He didn't feel the cold; he could survive in an ice storm or a river of lava completely bare. Blood trickled down his arm, the wounds from the dwarves' blades already healing. He knelt beside Amma and brushed her hair from her face.

Her skin was pale and her eyes closed. He scooped her up and held her against his chest. She was cold, too cold for any being except a dragon.

He lowered his lips to hers and breathed hot, rejuvenating air into her lungs.

Her body shuddered and her eyelids fluttered. She looked up at him, her eyes as clear and blue as they ever had been, and groaned. "Damn. Why did I do that?" She flexed her fingers. Hair-thin lines of power sizzled from her fingertips. "All of it gone."

Joarr smiled, then turned his head, hiding his relief at finding her well. His arm still supporting her around the waist, Joarr lowered her feet to the ground. Amma leaned against him, shaking her head and mumbling to herself. As she gathered herself, he created clothing in his mind—his standby favorite: white pants and shirt.

Dressed and his emotions under control, he tipped up her chin, so he could stare into her face. "What did you do?"

She shoved her hand against his chest. He loosened his hold, allowing a few inches of space between them.

"Saved you, I'd guess." She pointed at what was left of the dwarves—their blades, axes and the strange flask. As she moved, the chain that had connected them swung free, knocking into Joarr's side.

He grabbed hold of the end and wrapped it around his fist, letting her know with his body language that he still had control.

She narrowed her eyes. "I saved you."

"Really?" He gripped the chain tighter. "Convenient how the dwarf's ax hit this chain and not you."

"Would you prefer it had hit me?" she asked, her eyes wide and innocent.

Joarr growled. He didn't and she knew it. Why he didn't, he wasn't sure. He shouldn't care. She was a thief, and though she said she had saved him, she had actually freed herself.

He didn't trust her. Didn't trust that she wasn't behind the dwarves' attack in the first place. The whole thing was too convenient for her.

Her jaw jutted to the side. "The chain is severed. Am I sad? No. But am I free? No." She shook her head. "I should have let him do whatever he was doing." She gestured to the flask.

Curious now, Joarr walked toward the object, tugging her along as he did.

The flask lay on the ground. Its stopper was out and a half inch of what Joarr recognized as blood lay congealing on the bottom. He picked up the flask and held it to the light. He tipped it side to side. The liquid inside moved but slowly, confirming his guess that the blood came from his own body. Dragon blood was much thicker than any other beings', smelled and tasted of metals. He raised the flask to his nose and inhaled.

"Mine, or some other dragon's, but considering the circumstances I'll go with mine." He held the open flask to Amma.

She took a whiff, her expression turning analytical. "Any legends regarding dragon blood?" she asked.

Joarr tapped the glass against his palm. "Not that I can think of."

Amma reached for the flask.

Joarr pulled it back. "How about you? Know any legends regarding dragon blood?" he asked. "Or potions perhaps?"

She lowered her brows. "No."

"And you'd tell me if you did?"

She shrugged. "Not if I'd sent the crazed dwarf ninja contingent."

He smiled and handed her the flask.

She ran her fingers over the metal decorating the glass. "Strange a dwarf would carry a glass bottle. They're all about metal."

She was right. The flask hadn't been created by a dwarf. Given a choice, a dwarf would make everything out of metal—could make almost anything out of metal. So, there had to be a reason this flask wasn't. Like maybe it was created with a specific purpose in mind— to collect dragon blood perhaps, to keep the minerals from a metal container from mingling with the already metallic blood?

He took the flask back and, after some consideration, tucked it into his pocket. It might become useful.

It might help him discover why the three dwarves had attacked.

"What about this?" Amma pulled on the chain he still held fisted in his hand.

Yes. What about it? Joarr frowned. It would mean finding an elf to have it repaired properly, and he didn't think Rike or the other Ormar would appreciate the detour.

"If you run, I'll find you," he said.

Amma angled her head. "And if I don't?"

He stepped closer and ran the back of his finger down her cheek. "Ah, you think I should trust you?"

She raised one brow. "What choice do you have?"

He stared at the metal links in his hand. The magic was broken; there was no way for him to repair that, but there was also no reason for Amma to realize that. He grabbed the last link and slipped it back through the loop still attached to the manacle on his wrist, then shoved them back together.

"There," he said. "All better."

"Impressive." Her tone was dry and her expression less than thrilled.

He wove his fingers through hers and pulled her hand up to his mouth. After placing a kiss on her knuckles, he gestured toward the bar. "Show me I can trust you and maybe I'll change my mind."

"Change your mind and maybe next time I won't let the dwarf bleed you dry," she replied.

"Ah, sweet Amma, how could I risk the loss of your company?" With a laugh, he opened the bar door and tugged her inside with him.

Chapter 6

The bar was like every other portal bar Amma had been through—dirty and crowded with customers lacking the most basic of personal hygiene. And not one of them looked up when she and Joarr walked in. If anything they took an extreme interest in whatever drink sat before them.

Joarr was tall, broad-shouldered and, by his size alone, intimidating. Impossible to miss. There was no way the other occupants hadn't noticed his entrance.

Joarr, she guessed, knew this, too. He glanced around with the brazen confidence she'd come to expect from him. Then gestured toward a booth already occupied by two elves. As she and Joarr approached, they both grabbed their beers and scuttled to the back.

"Friends of yours?" she asked, her tone dry.

"Dragons, I'm afraid, have few friends." Joarr motioned for her to enter first, then slid onto the seat beside her. "It takes a special confidence to be friends with a dragon." He fingered the hand-crocheted lace that decorated her blouse. "Are you confident, Amma?"

Joarr seemed to dominate the booth. Amma resisted the urge to put space between them. There was really nowhere for her to go. Instead, her eyes wide, she replied, "Are you asking me to be your friend, Joarr? How…sweet."

He tilted his lips in a smile that made her wiggle in her seat and her heart race. "Friends? No, that's not how I see us."

The bartender's approach saved her from having to form a coherent answer.

Not surprisingly, the bartender was a garm, a wolf-shape-shifter. Garm ran all of the portals Amma had been through. This one stood beside the table, silent, a white bar cloth tossed over his shoulder. When Joarr didn't look at him immediately, he turned to go back to the bar.

"Have any dwarves through today?" Joarr called.

The garm turned back. "I'm not in the information business. You want a drink or to buy passage somewhere, let me know." His hand touched the towel on his shoulder, a simple gesture, but the tension in his body was clear.

"Drinks would be good." Joarr glanced at Amma. "Don't you think?"

Not knowing what game he was playing, she didn't reply. In fact she wasn't even sure why they were at the portal. She had expected Joarr to ask her where she had gone to sell the chalice, but he hadn't. Perhaps he'd intended to, but the dwarves' attack had changed that plan.

The chain rested heavy on her leg. With her free hand she reached down and touched it. Joarr had bent it back into place, but she was no fool. She knew more about magic than any dragon could. Whatever power had been embedded into the metal couldn't be repaired so easily. Her guess was the thing was nothing more than a simple shackle at the moment. Meaning if she could regain her power, she could escape the binds.

But that didn't mean she could escape the dragon— not without killing him, and she didn't think she could do that, not alone. And not with the low amount of power she had at the moment.

Joarr glanced at her, suspicion clear in his gaze.

She smiled. "An itch."

He cocked a brow then looked back at the garm. "Two waters."

His face impassive, the garm walked back to the bar.

"So, what's so important about this chalice, any-way?" Amma had heard the conversation between Joarr and the other dragon, but it had left a lot of questions in her mind. Number one being if she had made a huge mistake by selling the thing in the first place. The in-formation she'd got for it certainly hadn't led to any-thing good, and as important as it seemed to be to the dragons…

A waitress appeared at the table with waters. She slid them in front of them and left.

Joarr took a sip, his gaze wandering over the bar's occupants. "It isn't."

Amma twirled her glass in a slow circle. "There

were a lot of threats coming from your friend back at your house for something that isn't important."

"Just because someone believes in something doesn't make it real."

"Are you saying the chalice isn't real?"

He took a drink and set the glass down with a thump. "Exactly."

The table was damp where Amma's glass had sat. She ran her finger through the moisture, drawing a cup, then wings. "So, since it isn't important, you wouldn't mind telling what it's supposed to do."

Joarr stared at her, his eyes so blue and intense she shivered. Then he smiled. "Why not? You should know what you held in your hands, what you flittered away. At least I suppose you flittered it away. You don't seem to have anything to show for it." There was a question in his gaze; Amma ignored it. She had no desire to reveal anything about herself and the folly that had led her to where she was.

"The chalice—" Joarr's tone changed and became "official," as if he was presiding over some ancient ceremony "—is the heart of the dragons' power, the key to our vitality. With it under our control, in our stronghold, we stay strong, maintain our rightful position as the most powerful of all the nine worlds' beings. Without it, we will fade. Others will prey on us, our species will fail and we will fall into oblivion."

He held her gaze for a second, then took another sip of water. "Or not."

"You don't believe it." It was a statement. It was obvious Joarr didn't believe what he had said, no matter how official his words had sounded.

"It didn't protect my father," he replied. "And he was the Keeper."

"He was killed?" she asked.

"By a hero." Joarr placed his palm flat over the top of his glass.

"So, why do the other dragons believe in it?" Amma twisted her lips to the side, her mind racing. What would happen if word got out dragons could be defeated? How many opportunists would descend on them looking for trophies? Her stomach constricted. Would dragons be like hellhounds, hunted and caged to serve others? Her sister owned hellhounds; she had got them young, stolen them from their mothers. Why would dragons be any different? They wouldn't—except they'd be rarer, even more desired. They would be stolen, too; it only made sense.

Her fingernails scraped over her skirt.

"Heroes are considered the exception—they are born heroes, marked at birth by the Norn. They are beyond the chalice's magic, but they are also very rare." He drained the last of his water, set his glass down, then looked around as if expecting someone.

He seemed done with their conversation; Amma, however, wasn't. "You said 'under our control.' What does that mean?"

Joarr sighed. "When the chalice is in the Keeper's possession in the stronghold, all the dragons in the stronghold share its protection."

"What about dragons not in the stronghold?" Her fingers twitched, brushing over her stomach.

Joarr shrugged. "There aren't any—no males, anyway. I'm not sure how the legend affects females. I assume they have some talisman of their own." He waved his hand in the air, as if brushing the possibilities aside.

"But what if there was? Would he be protected, too?"

Joarr studied her. "Why do you care?"

She dropped her gaze to the drawing she'd made with the water. "I don't. I'm just trying to make sense of it, that's all."

"There is no sense." He picked up his empty glass and sat it back down. "Actually, the Ormar use the story of the chalice to keep the young ones from roaming for too long." He paused, his gaze resting on the glass. "Another reason they want the chalice back I'd guess. Without it, there is no threat, no way to keep dragons from dispersing and the Ormar losing all of their control. That—" he shook his head "—would kill them."

While Joarr seemed to mull over this new thought, Amma stopped listening. Her child was half dragon. She hadn't thought of what that might mean before this except knowing she didn't want Joarr to learn of his existence. But now she realized she needed to. If the Ormar were right, if the chalice truly had the powers they claimed, raising her child away from it would make him a target for beings like her sister who got joy in owning others, especially others with rare power they could use for their own gain.

Which meant he would either have to be raised in the stronghold with the chalice or perhaps... A new thought forming in her head, she said, "You mentioned a Keeper. Your father was one? What does that mean?"

Joarr's expression was strained. "The Keeper is in

charge of the chalice. He's the only dragon allowed to handle the chalice."

"Why?"

The dragon shrugged. "Who knows? There might be a reason, but my guess is it's just tradition."

"But when your father died, the chalice kept working."

At Joarr's skeptical expression, she added, "If you believe in it."

He tilted his head in acquiescence. "True, but the job is hereditary. So, when my father died, there still was a Keeper—me."

"Oh." Amma sat back against the cushion. And when Joarr died, her son would take the role. So, he could possess the chalice and keep himself safe simply by owning it.

Joarr turned his gaze to the bar. He wasn't sure why Amma had developed such an interest in the chalice. He had assumed she'd known what she was stealing, would have researched the thing before she stole it, or at least before she sold it. Perhaps after the attack outside she was feeling regret… He shook his head, silently laughing at himself. If Amma felt regret, it was most likely for not asking enough for the item.

A couple paid the garm and made their way through the portal. Dark elves. Joarr watched, half expecting a troop of dwarves to flow through the portal before the garm stepped away, but no one appeared.

With the portal closed and the garm back behind the bar, he let his thoughts wander back to the chalice and Amma. The cup's true value only existed for another male dragon, and as he'd already told the witch, no males of his species existed outside the stronghold. Which meant she must have sold the thing based on its outward appearance alone, unless…?

He glanced at her. "This dwarf you sold the chalice to, what did he want with it?"

She jumped, as if she'd been lost in her thoughts.

He repeated the question.

She released a breath. "I told you, he collects things."

"He didn't mention dragons?"

"No. He didn't mention anything. He had something I wanted or I thought I wanted, and I asked what it would take to get it. I'd been in your cavern and seen your treasure. I thought I could buy him off with some gold, but he wanted something special. After I described the chalice, he asked for it." She shrugged. "Simple as that."

"Simple as that," Joarr repeated. And now two dragons had died and one was missing. And after receiving a note to come to the portal, he'd been attacked outside by three dwarves. Somehow it all had to fit together.

Amma tapped a finger against her glass. "Why are we here?"

"Good question." Joarr stood, then held out his hand to Amma. They had been sitting for half an hour. If the note's writer was here, he should have approached them by now.

She slid out of the booth and dropped her hand to her side.

"Don't be shy." He wove his fingers through hers. "People will think you don't like me."

With a laugh, he led her toward the bar. The garm

watched them approach. He didn't look as if he was watching, but he was. He stood a little too still as he bent over to select a beer from the cooler and turned a little too slowly as he twisted off its lid and slid the bottle to the dark elf who had ordered it.

Once at the bar, Joarr waited.

The garm messed with something under the counter for a few minutes before looking up.

He was playing with Joarr, trying to establish dominance that would never exist.

Behind them a Svartalfar, a dark elf, who had entered the bar after Amma and Joarr, brushed up against the witch, copping a feel as he did. She spun, her hands opening and closing, reaching for magic no doubt. Thin lines sputtered from her fingertips. She stopped abruptly, cursing.

She glared at Joarr, no doubt letting him know she regretted using the magic she'd gained to help him fight the dwarves. Joarr hadn't figured out that move yet himself. She could have joined with the dwarves, or at least ran while they kept him occupied, but instead she'd used the bit of magic she'd siphoned to save him.

It didn't make him trust her. If anything it made him wonder about her even more. He couldn't take her actions as what they appeared—support. She'd tricked him before; he wouldn't let her again. And the coincidences…her saying she'd sold the chalice to a dwarf, then three dwarves attacking… It was a puzzle that was fitting together too neatly to be ignored.

Still dealing with the dark elf, Amma squared her shoulders and faced the drunken male head-on. Her hands were balled into fists at her sides, making Joarr guess she'd given up on magic for a more basic defense.

Pretending he was oblivious to what was happening, he watched the pair from the corner of his eye.

The Svartalfar made a purring noise deep in his throat. "What type of being be you, pretty?" He held up a hand. Joarr stiffened, thinking the dark elf was going to touch her...or try to. But instead something silver, a bracelet, glittered from his fingers. "A little gift," he whispered.

Beings in the nine worlds, especially those who frequented portals, didn't give gifts, not any without strings...sometimes deadly ones.

Amma made a sound of disinterest deep in her throat and turned. As she did, the dark elf moved closer. Another flash of silver, a weapon this time hidden in the Svartalfar's hand. Bait and switch.

Too bad for the drunken dark elf, he hadn't paid attention to what else lurked in the waters.

Joarr shoved Amma to the floor and shot frigid air over her head. The dark elf was so focused on Amma, so focused on whatever plans he had for her, he didn't see the blast coming. He was still there, his hand still outstretched, the bracelet still dangling from his fingers, but now he was encased in solid ice.

Joarr ran two fingers along the sides of his mouth, knocking ice crystals to the floor beside her. "To stop any further confusion. This pretty is mine."

Amma lay on the floor, shivering. From the beer-soaked wooden planks, she stared up at Joarr, then glanced to her right where the dark elf had been standing.

Joarr couldn't tell if she was pleased or not.

Around them, the room cleared. Every patron took a step back or turned to study their drinks, the floor, anything except Joarr. He glanced around the room, checking for any other challengers.

If losing the chalice had weakened the dragons, these beings didn't realize it. None even met his gaze.

He held out a hand to Amma. She ignored it, instead choosing to scramble to a stand by herself. Almost upright, she slipped and was forced to lean against him. He slid his arm around her, supporting her weight despite her sounds of protest. She was soft and warm. For a second, he forgot his suspicions.

Then he glanced down and saw the shine of silver in her hand—the dark elf's weapon.

Chapter 7

The object was cold and heavy in Amma's hand. She'd
felt it beneath her when she fell and picked it up without
thinking. Now she realized what it was—a weapon that
the Svartalfar had been going to use against her—and
why Joarr had shoved her to the ground.

She ran her thumb over the object's smooth, round
top. Thoughts raced through her head. Joarr had saved
her, but she had saved him before, and if he hadn't
dragged her here, hadn't refused to release a tiny bit
of magic to her, she wouldn't have needed saving at
all. She felt a tiny knob, like the tip of a toothpick, protruding from the metal canister. Forcing herself not to
think any more, not to let herself weaken, she pointed
the object at Joarr.

Then she remembered the chalice. If she attacked
Joarr, he would never trust her. She would never get

close enough to the chalice to steal it and save it for her child.

She opened her palm and held out the weapon. "Thank you," she said.

Joarr started, surprise clear in his eyes. But before he could reply, or move to take the weapon, the garm leaned across the bar and plucked it from her palm.

"No weapons near the portal." He pulled out a bin and tossed the thing inside.

Joarr still watched her. She folded her hand closed and tapped her knuckles against her leg. She'd given up the weapon to buy his trust—that was all. Still, his analysis made her uncomfortable; she shifted her gaze to the end of the bar. A dwarf sat there, a hat pulled low over his face. She stiffened, and then forced herself to relax. Thousands of dwarves had to be traveling through the portal system; it made sense some would be here. It didn't mean he was with the group that had attacked them.

Still, she kept track of him from the corner of her eye. When she looked back at Joarr, the dragon was watching her, then without warning he moved. She tensed, afraid he'd somehow read her motive, but he just reached past her and grabbed the bracelet from the frozen dark elf's fingers. With a twist, he snapped it free. With one finger he coaxed her fist open and laid the silver bauble on top of her open palm. "He doesn't need it."

Amma stared at the jewelry, then back at the dragon. She couldn't decide if she was angry or pleased. If he wanted to give her a gift, unlocking the manacles or letting go of a little magic would have been a lot more practical. And she had always prided herself on being practical. Still…she weighed the bracelet in her hand…no one had ever given her such a purely girly gift before. Her fingers folded closed over the bracelet, seemed unwilling to loosen. She told herself to toss the thing on the ground, but her fingers wouldn't open. Annoyed with her reaction, she stared at her closed fist, but still couldn't make herself let go of the bracelet.

Deciding to wait to decipher her emotions, she slipped the object into her pocket.

"Do you have business here?" the garm asked Joarr. The wolf-shape-shifter had waited patiently, bored really, while Joarr had disposed of the dark elf, only showing life when he took the weapon. Now he looked annoyed and suspicious…and his gaze was on Amma.

Realizing this was an opportunity, she stepped forward. "I do." She glanced at Joarr, pretending to ask his permission. He raised a brow, but didn't stop her. She leaned across the bar and whispered into the garm's ear the coordinates for the portal that led to one of her sister's homes.

The garm tilted his head and studied her for a second. "I can send you, but the place is empty. The witch that lived there disappeared, and her hellhounds are roaming free. Where have you been that you didn't hear of it?"

Amma clamped her teeth together, hiding her shock.

"Really?" Joarr glanced at her. "Does this witch have any dwarf companions?"

Amma's fingers tangled in her skirt. Her sister Lusse was missing, her hellhounds released. Something horrible had to have happened. Lusse would never have abandoned her kennel.

She stared at Joarr, keeping her gaze blank, although her mind was scrambling. Her other sister, the third in their triad, didn't have a settled home like Lusse. Amma had no idea how to contact her, not one hundred years since their last meeting. Besides, while Lusse had never been exactly warm and loving, Huld was the definition of cold and calculating. She would, Amma had no doubt, sell Amma's every secret for the smallest of profit.

If Lusse was missing, Amma truly had no one— except her secret. Her hand drifted back to her abdomen.

Joarr continued to watch her, his gaze hard.

To divert attention, she stiffened her shoulders and forced a scowl onto her face. "We were attacked outside, then again in here. You always run your portal like this?" She raised a brow.

The garm seemed unimpressed. "I thought I made it clear—I serve drinks and operate the portal. You're worried about your safety, you should stay tucked in your little bed." He turned back to Joarr. "You have another destination?"

After one last thoughtful glance at Amma, Joarr replied, "I thought perhaps you might have one for me. Is someone, somewhere, looking for a dragon?"

The garm cocked his head. "Dragons haven't frequented the portals lately."

Joarr sighed. "Not my older and wiser betters perhaps…but me? How could I resist all this charm?" He motioned to the room behind him and the disheveled patrons nursing their drinks.

The garm pulled a mug out from under the counter and filled it with beer. Without looking, he slid it down the length of the bar to the dwarf whom Amma had noticed earlier. If Joarr noticed the small being, he made no sign.

Looking back at Joarr, he said, "I don't believe you've paid for your water yet, and a tip for the service. I'm sure you wouldn't want to forget that."

Joarr pulled a small sack from his pants pocket and slid it onto the bar.

The garm eyed the bag for a second, distrust clear on his face. After a sideways glance at the dragon, he pulled the tie loose and poured out the contents. Gold powder spilled across the wood. Surprise rounded his eyes. "This looks like—"

Joarr sighed. "Treasure. Yes, I'm sure it does. And being a dragon and all, I really shouldn't part with it. Greed. Our fatal flaw, etcetera, etcetera." He placed both hands flat on the bar top and leaned forward, pulling Amma forward, too, and revealing the manacles that attached them.

The garm glanced at the cuffs, but his expression gave away none of his thoughts.

Joarr tapped one finger on the wood. "So, are there any destinations I might be interested in visiting?"

The portal guardian turned his body to the side, blocking the dwarf's view. "As it happens, something came across yesterday. Free passage for any dragon. You think you'd like to visit?"

Joarr smiled and reached for Amma's hand.

The garm held up one hand. "This offer, it was for a dragon traveling alone—no other dragons, no…companions."

The dragon's eyes glittered. The scent of warm spice, a mix of cinnamon and clove, rolled off him, but he smiled and pulled out a second bag of gold.

The garm glanced at the bribe, but made no move to take it. "Being a portal guardian is an important role. I take it seriously—if I don't there are a hundred other garm ready to step into my place."

Joarr's eyes flickered.

The garm crossed his arms over his chest. "Of course, this destination, it isn't off-limits to anyone. Someone could come along and ask to go there, pay and I'd have to send him—" he glanced at Amma "—or her."

Joarr made a growling noise deep in his throat. "And where would this destination be?"

The garm walked a few feet to his right and grabbed a dirty beer mug. "Now, that would fall under 'restricted information.'"

"Then how—?" Joarr's hand tightened around Amma's; heat flowed from his palm. But his face remained calm and his posture relaxed. Still, she could feel an eruption coming.

"Perhaps," she jumped in, "someone might say, send me where he went. Don't change that dial, follow that horse, whatever verbiage she chose?"

The garm smiled. "Yes, I think that would work."

He reached for the gold and dropped it into a drawer.

Joarr wrapped his fingers around Amma's hand but made no move to walk around the bar to the portal.

Amma could sense tension thrumming through Joarr's body. She knew the garm's game had pushed him. She placed her hand on the dragon's arm, then immediately, surprised at her own actions, pulled it away.

Her touch, however, seemed to calm him. He pulled another bag from his pocket.

He stepped forward, until he was staring directly into the garm's eyes. "Are you sure this is the only option?"

The garm picked up his towel and tossed it on the bar top. "Completely."

Joarr turned to Amma, his gaze sharp.

She held up her wrist, the one with the manacle. "You realize this wasn't keeping me with you, don't you? I am a witch. I know enough about magic to know that its spell was broken out there." She nodded toward the door, to where they had fought off the dwarves. "You don't fix that by bending a little metal."

He frowned, and she smiled in return. He hadn't repaired the magic in the shackles. In other words he'd underestimated her—always a good thing, for her.

Joarr turned back to the garm. "If you know dragons at all, you know I won't need the portal to get back to you."

The garm's lips lifted on one side. "Are you insinuating I might cheat you? That there might be some reason you'd want to find me later?"

Joarr's fingers tightened around Amma's hand. "I've found it pays to be untrusting." He tossed the bag of gold onto the bar. "Make sure she follows."

The cold band of metal still around her wrist, Amma waited. She was afraid if she offered her hand to Joarr, acted too interested in having the manacle removed, he would change his mind and come up with some other way to get to wherever it was they were going.

Finally, when the garm was positioned next to the portal and Joarr was ready to step through, he grabbed her hand. "Will you run?" he asked.

"Perhaps," she whispered. She didn't know what made the truth fall from her lips. She hadn't decided. She wanted the chalice, wanted anything that could insure her child's safety, but Joarr scared her. The fact that she had passed up two opportunities to attack him and leave scared her.

He brushed her hair from her face and bent to whisper in her ear. "If you don't, if you follow me and help me, we can work out a deal." He blew hot then cool breath against her neck, sending shivers down her body. "I can make your time worth your while," he finished.

He grabbed the chain in both hands and jerked it into two pieces.

Amma was free. She wrapped her fingers around the length of chain that hung from her wrist and watched Joarr walk through the portal, his head high and his shoulders square. She waited, expecting him to look back, but he just moved forward in total confidence.

When he was gone, when the portal had converted back to nothing but a mundane doorway, the garm looked at her. "Your passage is paid. Where would you like to go?"

She gripped the chain until her fingers ached, and stared at the doorway.

Where would she like to go?

* * *

Joarr stepped through the portal alone. It opened onto a dark street lined with blinking neon signs that advertised cheap rooms and all-nude dancers. The temperature was cool but not cold, and the pavement beneath his feet was wet.

Could be any number of worlds or in-between places. But something fairly well populated.

He sniffed the air. The distinct scent of human came back to him.

Interesting. He had been to the human world only a few months earlier, but aside from that it wasn't a place he'd visited much. There really wasn't much here for a dragon. Actually, the place made him uncomfortable. It was the only one of the nine worlds where he was expected to hide his powers. It was a bit of an unspoken law—hiding from humans the existence of the other eight worlds and the beings that populated them.

He found it tiresome.

With a resolved sigh, he stepped onto the sidewalk and leaned against a deserted brick building. If Amma was going to follow, she would be along soon.

If she wasn't… He twisted his lips to the side. Where would she go? And did it matter? As he'd admitted to himself earlier, he didn't need her, not with someone offering to hand over the chalice. But he'd gone to so much trouble to catch her, letting her go had seemed wrong.

Something gouged into his back—a rock that had been embedded in the concrete to add decoration to the building. He adjusted his stance and resisted the urge to calculate how long he had been waiting.

If she came through the portal, would that mean he should trust her, or question her motives all the more?

Something flickered, a flash in the darkness and a faint whirring noise. The portal, surely.

Joarr tensed but didn't move. He didn't want the witch to think he was eager to see her—but he was. With that disturbing realization weighing on him, he waited for Amma to appear.

Someone short and dressed in black stepped into the street. Glancing from side to side, scanning the area for something or someone, the being stepped forward. A neon sign that had previously seemed dead flashed to life, catching the all-too-clear profile of a dwarf in its glow.

A trap. The witch had tricked him.

Amma stepped through the portal. She hoped she'd made the right decision. She had waited until it was almost too late, until two elves had approached and asked for passage. The garm had given her a now-or-never look, forcing her to stop thinking and just move.

As her foot landed on wet pavement, something hit her from the side, knocking her to her knees. She cursed and pulled the tiny reserve of power she'd gathered into her hands. Arms wrapped around her, shoving her to the ground. A hand covered her mouth. She cursed again, then unwilling to let go of her magic until absolutely necessary, she found bare skin and bit down.

Joarr hissed against her ear. "Surely you can do better than that. Call off your partners or I'll blow an arctic wind through your skull."

She twisted her head to the side, pulling her face

free from the dragon's now-bleeding palm. His blood clung, thick and warm, to her lips. She rubbed her mouth across her shoulder. "What is wrong with you? I thought you wanted me to follow you. Is this how you make it worth my while?"

"Don't play games. You fooled me once—you won't again."

Something whizzed overhead.

His hand on the back of her neck now, he shoved her lower. "I don't know what deal you've made, who you are working with or why, but you might want to rethink your partnership. They seem as willing to take you out as me."

"Maybe because I have no partners." She flung back an elbow, hitting Joarr in the gut. "I'm here of my own free will, to work with you…for pay."

He raised his head. Cold air flowed from his mouth and with it, balls of ice that smacked into a metal trash can a few feet away.

Three bodies rushed forward. They were short and dressed in black and in their hands were axes and swords.

"Dwarves," she muttered.

"Yes, dwarves. What else?" His hand moved to her back and with a hard thrust pushed her flat on the ground. Above her she heard a roar, then crackles. The temperature soared. A few feet away there were screams. Then the unmistakable stench of burning flesh. The dwarves were toast.

She pressed her palms onto the pavement and pushed herself up. Joarr didn't stop her.

But once she was on her feet he watched her. Suspicion shone from his eyes.

"Why should I trust you?" he asked.

Her shirt and skirt were wet. The thin cotton of her blouse clung to her breasts and tiny bits of gravel had embedded themselves into her skin. She brushed her hands over her body, knocking as many free as she could and then stared at him. "I can leave."

"Yes, you can. So, why are you here? What do you hope to gain?"

She gritted her teeth. He said he wanted her to follow him, then when she did… She turned on her heel and started to walk away.

He grabbed her by the arm and twirled her back around. "Talk to me."

His voice was at least low now, encouraging rather than demanding.

She swallowed. She wouldn't tell him the truth, that she wasn't sure why she had followed him, or even a partial truth, that she wanted the chalice for herself. Instead she'd stick with the lie she'd concocted at the bar.

"You said you'd make it worth my while. I've been locked out of my body for one hundred years. Anything I had is long gone. I have nothing."

"What about your home?" He'd moved to the side. His face was lost in shadows, but his tone sounded concerned. It stopped her for a moment, made her wonder again if she should have run.

"I don't have a home. I never did. I just stayed with one sister or the other, and only one of them had a real home. The other roamed, and not to nice places."

"The witch with the hellhounds, the one that is missing."

She nodded. "With her gone…" She let her words drift away. Her position was evident and what she had said was horribly true. She had nowhere to go. Wherever she went from here, wherever she wound up calling home now, would have to be of her own creation. She dropped her gaze. She hadn't considered her situation before, not really.

She had no one and nowhere to go.

Joarr sniffed the air. "Humans," he announced. "Have you been here before?" He moved out of the shadows; the fingers of one hand twisted the manacle that still hung from his other wrist.

Amma let out a breath. "When you—" She motioned with her hand. Joarr and his hellhound friend had captured her in the human world.

"Before that."

"Do you mean, is this where I sold the chalice?" She shook her head. "No, I went to Nidavellir." The underground world of the dwarves. She had expected to hate the land, but to her surprise, the small, twisting tunnels had made her feel safe, perhaps even bold. "A cave, far underground. It wasn't exactly on the main path. Wasn't a place I could find again."

"You went by portal?" he asked.

She ran her hands up her arms and nodded. "But like our trip here, it was prepaid and I wasn't given a location. I could just tell it was somewhere in Nidavellir." The land of the dwarves was hard to mistake for any other place.

Joarr's gaze flickered and he stepped closer. He looked as if he was about to say something.

A man half of Joarr's height, dressed in stained sweats and reeking of grain alcohol, staggered past.

He brushed against Joarr. The dragon grabbed Amma and pulled her tight against him.

As the man continued on his drunken wanderings, Amma looked up. Her tone dry, she said, "How gallant."

Joarr squeezed her upper arm. "I could call him back if you like." When she didn't reply, he said, "So, I'm preferable to something."

"Not much," she murmured, but low. She wanted him to hear, wanted herself to hear, too—needed to remind herself that she and Joarr weren't on the same side. No one was on her side, no one ever had been, not really.

Joarr smiled and his fingers danced across her middle. Her loose top slipped up, and his fingers found the bare skin revealed there. She shivered. He leaned down and whispered in her ear. "Oh, I think you find me preferable to many things. Perhaps we should find a room and discuss just how many."

Amma flicked a cigarette butt off the stained bedcover and into the equally stained wall. The room Joarr had booked for the night defined the human term *seedy*. In fact she was positive all things vile were growing in the carpet.

The dragon, however, seemed impervious to it all. She slanted her eyes toward him. He was lying on the bed next to her, a soda can balanced on his table-flat stomach and the TV remote in his hand.

After his less-than-veiled comments at the portal, she had really thought he had something more exciting planned than this.

Not that she would have agreed to anything…personal…but this… His unexplainable fascination with a documentary on the sinking of some city in Jamaica almost two hundred years earlier was just insulting.

As the camera panned over a pile of riches pulled out from under the sea, Joarr shook his head and murmured to himself. Amma threw herself back against the disgusting motel-supplied pillow with a huff.

"What are we waiting on?" she asked, lifting her hand. The manacle still shone back at her; she twirled it around and around. She was beginning to like it. Although she could do without the extra length of chain.

Without removing his gaze from the television, Joarr replied, "For something to happen."

She dropped her free arm over her forehead and stared at the ceiling. She wasn't good at waiting. "Of course," she murmured to herself.

There was noise outside the door. Someone was leaning against it.

Joarr turned to glance at her, his eyes bright in his face, telling her to be quiet. He leaped up, his feet landing on the indoor/outdoor carpet with just a whisper of sound.

Something white appeared in the gap between the door and the jamb. Joarr waited, tense. Then suddenly he was gone. One second he was Joarr the man, broad-shouldered and sexy in his all-white outfit, the next he was a dragon. His scales shone silver so bright Amma could see the dingy room reflected off them. He raised his wings, cutting her off from the room's entrance. To stop her escape, she thought at first, but when he kept his gaze on the door, she realized instead he was protecting her, shielding her like he had in the cavern. Of course then he had caused her sphere to shatter, to spray its magic over them.

Magic. Late, but not too late, she remembered the magic. Power still hung in the room, like smoke in a bar. With Joarr's attention on the door, she began pulling it in. She had just started to feel rejuvenated when he changed again, picked something up from the floor and turned back to her. Her face innocent and expectant, she redoubled her efforts while taking care to target only the magic that floated freely, to not draw any directly from the male in front of her. He didn't seem to notice; he was too focused on the sheet of paper in his hand.

The cloud of magic gone, Amma closed her eyes for a second and wiggled the fingers of her free hand behind her back. Magic zipped through her, sizzled at her fingertips. Opening her eyes, she smiled. The power felt good, but it wasn't enough, not to take care of herself, much less challenge Joarr. Still, it was a start, and she was fairly certain the dragon hadn't even noticed what she had done. She had to keep it that way. She nodded to the paper in his hand. "What is it?" she asked.

He held it out to her. "Look familiar?"

It was an advertisement for a nightclub, Tunnels. She

frowned. "I haven't exactly been doing a lot of party-ing."

He stared at her, then reached for the door. "Let's go."

"Wait." She shook her head. "It's just a flyer. It was probably shoved under every door here."

He glanced at the paper in his hand. "I don't think so. I think it's an invitation."

"To what?" She sat up on the mattress and draped the chain attached to her manacle across her lap. "We need to talk. I told you my situation, and you promised to make it worth my while if I stayed with you and helped you find the chalice." She paused. "I'm not even sure why I'm here, what you expect from me."

He dropped the flyer onto the bed beside her. "You've seen the Collector. You'll know him if we see him again."

"So, we're looking for the Collector? Then why come here? I told you I met him in Nidavellir."

"We aren't looking for him. I just want to know if we meet him." He turned; the bit of chain still attached to his wrist knocked against a table. He grabbed the end and held it as he paced.

She could see now that his time lying on the bed, appearing nearly comatose, had been an act. He moved like an animal trapped too long in a cage. "Back at my home, there was a note—did you see it?"

She shook her head; she'd seen that there was a note, but her lantern hadn't been positioned so she could read it.

"It was from someone claiming to have the chalice. It's why we went to the portal."

"Where we were attacked," she murmured.

"And from there we came here, to the human world."

"Where we were attacked," she couldn't keep from repeating.

Joarr stopped, dropping his hold on the chain. It swung back and forth, seemed to hold the same energy she could see waiting coiled inside the dragon. "By dwarves."

"Like the Collector." She sighed. "So, what do you think is happening? Why would the Collector buy the chalice from me, then send the dragons a note saying he has it? And why would he attack us?"

"I don't know." The chain swung again. This time Joarr reached down and snapped off the extra length, let it drop onto the floor.

She thrust her arm into the air. "If you want me to help, you have to give me something. Removing this would be a good start."

He stepped forward and grabbed hold of the chain. She thought he was going to do as he had done to his own, simply twist it off. Instead he used it to pull her to her feet. With it wrapped around his fist, he stared down at her. "I kind of like it on you." His eyes warmed; something inside Amma warmed, too, but she kept her desire off her face.

"This is the human world. People do not walk around with shackles on their wrists and a chain dangling down their arm. They have laws, police."

He tilted his head to the side. "And this should concern me, why?"

"Because they will think I've escaped from some prison—or crazed kidnapper. This—" she shook her wrist, making the chain rattle "—is not an everyday accessory in the human world."

He stroked her cheek. "Maybe you just don't hang out in the right circles. The desk clerk didn't seem to care when he checked us in. In fact he offered to 'add to the party.'"

Amma tilted her chin. She had heard the tiny man's whispers and seen his leers. Although her fingers had twitched with the need for magic, she had suppressed her natural reaction to blow him to bits. He was only a human, after all—and she'd had so little magic to waste.

"Not many humans are as open-minded as our dear friend Carl," she replied.

Joarr grinned. "I take it you weren't interested?" he asked.

Her eyes flared.

A low chuckle rolled from Joarr's throat. He leaned down and brushed her lips with his. "Don't worry. I share my treasure with no one."

As Joarr prepared to kiss the intriguing witch, she pulled back and held up her wrist.

He sighed. He did enjoy the chain hanging from her wrist; it was convenient. He held the manacle in one hand and pulled the chain tight with the other. "Just the chain, or the bracelet, too?"

She angled her head as if considering the question. "Just the chain. I'll keep the manacle to remind me of our past." Emotion flickered behind her eyes.

He ran his finger under the shackle. Her skin was

soft and her pulse jumped under his touch. "And I'll keep mine. I think we both need reminding."

Her expression sweet, she replied, "Great minds."

He twisted the metal and the chain fell to the floor. She bent to retrieve it. With it slung over one shoulder, she returned to the bed.

He sat beside her.

She looked at him from the corner of her eye. "Now we need to work out the details of our deal." She leaned toward him. The chain fell onto the mattress between them. "I've proven myself, and I didn't run when I had the chance. So tell me, dragon, what will you give me to stay and identify the Collector?" Her arms pressed against the sides of her breasts, causing them to jut up over the top of her shirt.

He ran the backs of his fingers down her cheek and leaned down to whisper in her ear. "A good deal goes two ways. What do you offer me?"

Her skin had a glow to it he hadn't noticed earlier—the magic she'd taken. He'd felt her drawing power during his last shift. It made her more alluring, made him want to give her a little more. He stroked her cheek, inhaled her scent...the earth again, hot from the sun.

"I'll help you find the Collector," she murmured. "I found him once before. I can do it again, but you have to give me something in return."

His hand stilled. "I shouldn't have to pay you for helping to retrieve what you stole from me."

"Yes, well. If you want me to cooperate freely, you will." Her chin was squared, determined.

Once again he analyzed how much he needed her help. Again he came up with the same answer—not a lot, not really. It would be useful to have someone who could identify the Collector, and if she could actually contact the dwarf, change their position from mouse to cat, that would certainly be useful, but completely boiled down, he didn't need Amma's help; he did, however, want it. He wanted her.

He shook his hand, the one wearing the cuff. The metal slipped down his wrist, over the top of his hand. Amma waited, moving her own cuff in short, angry twists as she did.

Her anger, the fire in her, was irresistible.

"I think we can work out a deal."

She raised her eyebrows. He'd surprised her.

"I..." He let his fingers drift from her cheek to the side of her neck, continued to move his touch lower... He cupped his hand over her shoulder, then onto her back. His fingers splayed over the center of her back, and he whispered, "I'm sure we can work something out."

He let her absorb that for a second, then stood. "But perhaps not now."

She jerked as if wakened suddenly from sleep. Frustration showed on her face. Then she scowled.

Joarr hid a frustrated scowl of his own. She didn't appreciate his games; that was clear. But she hadn't realized yet why it was important he play, why he had to make her think it was nothing but a game. He wanted to share the fire that flamed in both of them way too much.

Both hands dropped to his sides, he studied her. "What is your price now? And how do I know you will honor our deal?"

Her eyes darted back and forth in her face. The wheels were turning in her head; he was instantly alert.

"Treasure, of course. Lots of it. You gave the portal guardian two bags. I'll need…" Her lips parted. She was searching for a sum. The question was, was she looking for one he would pay or one so high he would refuse? Joarr couldn't figure the witch out, couldn't guess her motivation. "One thousand," she finished.

Was that high to her or low? Joarr couldn't decide. He had probably a million such little bags of gold lying around somewhere. Of course, each was very precious to him. High, he decided.

"Too much," he declared and waited to see what she would do next. This really was very entertaining and kept him diverted from thinking of other entertaining things they could be doing together. He settled in for a long match of parrying.

A tiny line formed between her brows as she twisted her lips to the side. It was obvious she was trying to look annoyed, but the flame he so loved was missing. The act confirmed what he had guessed; her first offer had been a ploy. Now she would ask for what she really wanted.

His face lacking expression, he waited.

She pressed two fingers to her brow. "One thing, then," she said. "Is that too much to ask? One thing, my choice of everything you own."

"Of everything I own?" He shook his head. "That hardly sounds like a smart deal on my part. You could name my house or cavern, or somehow twist them together and take both. Then I'd be no better off than what I face with the Ormar if I fail altogether."

Eagerness shone from her eyes. She was fully engaged in their negotiations now. "A size limit, then. Nothing bigger, say, than…you."

"Than me?" He frowned; as he'd already told her, in his dragon form he was huge. He wasn't comfortable with this deal. He narrowed his eyes. "Than you. Nothing bigger than you." She was tiny, maybe a little over one hundred pounds. He could afford to lose one hundred pounds of treasure. And there was nothing in his house he valued that wasn't larger than that. Even his favorite chair outweighed her. Confident in his choice, he nodded. "You help me find the Collector and to get the chalice back, into my hands, and I give you one object I own that is no larger than you."

She smiled and held out her hand. "Deal."

He stared at her hand for a second. The temptation was too great. Slowly he wrapped his fingers around hers and pulled her closer. "Surely you can think of a better way to seal our bargain than this." He brushed his lips over her hair. "I know I can."

Chapter 8

Riding high on her victory, Amma hadn't noticed how close she was standing to Joarr. Not until she felt heat seeping from his hand into her body, warming her inside and out. She curled her toes into the soles of her shoes and tried to keep her mind focused on the deal they had made—and what it meant to her.

Unknown to Joarr, he'd just agreed to give her everything she wanted.

All she had to do was help him find the chalice and their baby was hers. Joarr had just agreed to give up any claim of ownership he had to his child.

And if she chose, if she decided the legend of the chalice was true, she could do as she had done before—trick the dragon into trusting her so she could steal the cup, this time for herself and her child. She had only agreed to help Joarr retrieve the chalice. She hadn't said she wouldn't steal it again right afterward.

So two options. Two good ones.

Amma watched Joarr as if she held some secret, like every hero in every tale who had ever outwitted the dragon—or thought he had. Sometimes, though, the dragon came back. Sometimes he gobbled down the hero, leaving nothing behind but an over-glorified sword and a distraught village. Amma would do well to remember that.

Joarr stepped back, so he could study the witch. She moved to the side, watching him, too. They were like two cats deciding when to pounce.

He held out his hand. "In the human world, I believe they would shake now."

She glanced at him from the corner of her eye. "Seems like overkill."

He took a step forward. His knee pressed against hers. "Humor me."

She tilted her chin. "I could, I suppose."

"Well, then…" He leaned down and plucked her hand from her lap, stroked his fingers over the fine bones visible beneath her skin. "So soft. You're exactly as you were when I last saw you."

"As are you."

It was both compliment and insult on both of their parts. Joarr smiled. Then he leaned down to capture her lips with his.

He expected her to resist, or at least play at resisting, but instead she grabbed him by the back of the head and jerked him onto the bed beside her.

He didn't object.

Her lips pressed against his. He opened his mouth and let her tongue find his, while his hands roamed her body. Her loose shirt gaped around her shoulders. He pulled it down, baring the tops of her breasts. He moved his lips from hers to her neck, flicked his tongue out, tasting her. Her skin was warm now. The glow that he'd noticed on her face seemed to cover her body. Her scent was stronger, too. He inhaled, wondering how she could smell so fresh after days in his cavern followed by hours here in this dingy room.

The bed beneath them creaked, as if reminding him where they were and how bad the conditions were. He pulled her against him and turned onto his back so she was shielded from the questionable linens by his body. Her skirt bunched around her waist; she straddled him. Her golden hair hung like a curtain over one shoulder and touched the mattress beside his face.

She ran her hands over his shirt and slipped the tiny buttons from their holes. "Can you remove them yourself?" she asked.

Without shifting, she meant. He shook his head no, and shoved her shirt up and over her head. Her skin was smooth and pale, but with the glow he'd noticed earlier—almost as if someone had sprinkled a bag of his gold dust over her body. And her breasts…were perfect. Round with peach tips and a tiny mole that lay just on the inside of one, the left one…over her heart. He leaned up and kissed it.

She laughed. "My flaw. You found it."

He kissed it again. "A pearl is a flaw to the oyster."

He tugged her hips closer, sitting up as he did. She was facing him now, her eyes staring directly into his.

She draped her arms over his shoulders. "I don't think you believe that."

He paused, surprised. "Of course I do. I value everything."

"Then why is your treasure all gold and jewels?"

He cocked his head, not understanding her at first. "My treasure is everything I own. You only saw the gold and jewels. The rest, the stone from a Svartalfaheim mine, the brick from a human street, even the leg from a dwarf's discarded chair—I value them all. All are my treasure. Dragons may be greedy, but we value each thing for what it has to offer—not what some world or being says it is worth."

"Worth is in the eye of the beholder?" she murmured.

"Of course, and I see worth in everything, beauty in everything. Why else would it be so hard to let anything go?"

Joarr's words disturbed Amma. She'd been half joking when she'd mentioned her mole, and half not. Neither of her sisters had any imperfections—not a mole, a wrinkle, not even a freckle. They were perfect from head to toe.

The mole that he had kissed had been one cause of her great quest, one reason she'd stolen his chalice and traded it to the Collector. It had been one of the signs that she wasn't like her sisters, wasn't perfect. One more reason to find out who she was and where she'd come from.

She'd hoped she'd find something great, something that made up for the ruthless determination and sense of self her sisters had and she lacked.

But she hadn't. She'd found nothing but outrage and hurt.

As if sensing her distress, Joarr pushed his fingers into her hair, lifting it off her skin. Then trailed kisses down her neck. "I love your mole," he murmured. "I have never seen anything more perfect unless—" he kissed the hollow of her throat "—it would be your skin. Or perhaps—" he trailed his lips up her neck, pressed a tiny kiss, no more than a peck, against the corner of her mouth "—your lips. But then there are your eyes."

She closed her eyes. He kissed each closed lid. "They are like nothing I've ever seen before, and your hair." He wound the locks around one hand and stared at them as if they had turned to pure gold under his touch. "I would trade a mine filled with gold for such treasure."

Her gaze darted over his face, not sure if he was playing with her or was serious, but when he turned his blue gaze toward her she saw the truth in his eyes. There was no lie there, not even a tease. Just pure admiration.

She blew out a breath, placed her hands on his shoulders and shoved him backward onto the bed. "Enough talking," she murmured.

His shirt was completely open now. She pushed it to the side and ran her palm over the hard muscles of his chest. She had been with a number of males, both magical and mundane, but she had never been with anyone who excited her as much as the dragon. He was attractive, of course. She had never met a forandre who wasn't. But Joarr also oozed power, and not just magical. He had a confidence that could only come with being one of the oldest, most revered beings that existed.

Who didn't want to capture a dragon? Who wouldn't love to bed one?

But Amma's attraction to Joarr went past that, or she was beginning to believe it did. He talked of treasure and that is how he made her feel—rare, special, like no other female existed who could compete with her. And while she told herself the same, there was something about the glow in Joarr's eyes that made her actually believe it.

Her hands on either side of him, she leaned down and twirled her tongue around his nipple. His hands moved to her back, his thumbs ran along her rib cage until he found the undersides of her breasts.

She breathed out, warm air on the skin she'd just moistened. He placed his hand behind her head and pulled her lips to his. His lips firm, his kiss was strong and possessive. Heat shot through Amma. She trailed her fingers down his chest, her nails scraping his skin.

His dress pants were already undone, but her skirt was still wrapped around her legs, constricting her movement. She jerked the tie at her waist loose and wiggled to free herself.

He didn't seem to notice, kept kissing her, his tongue moving slowly and sensuously around her mouth. Then his hands found her breasts. Heat poured from his palms; his thumbs flicked over her nipples. She moaned and squirmed until she'd shoved her skirt off her body and forced her underwear to follow. Still kissing her lips and kneading her breasts, he lifted his hips. She tugged his pants free, too. He wore no underwear; she wasn't surprised. The skin beneath his pants was smooth and radiated heat like a fire burned inside him. Which she supposed it did. She didn't understand where dragons got their fire, if they stored it like she stored magic or created it as the need arose.

Right now she didn't care. She was only interested in having him inside her—warm and pulsing. Pulling in and out, driving her passion to the point where she might explode.

And magic—there would be magic. She should siphon what she could; caught up in their lovemaking, Joarr wouldn't notice. He would be too lost in the pleasure.

But as he moved his mouth from hers, placed his lips over her breast and rolled his tongue over her nipple, she realized she was lost already. She didn't care about pulling magic. That would have to wait. All she cared about right now was being with Joarr and experiencing the magic of the moment, not stealing some to use later.

When they both were naked, he ran his hands up her sides. His warmth seeped into her. Without thinking, she returned the favor, slid her hands down his, over his arms and onto his chest, power flowing from her palms as she did. She didn't have fire to offer like he did, but she had the magic she'd pulled earlier. It seemed natural to share. She formed it into something soft and warm in her mind. Surprise lit his face; he smiled and his blue eyes darkened.

His entire body radiated heat. Sweat trickled between her breasts. He lapped at it. A new bead formed; he lapped at it, too, lifting her up so he could trace its path down her torso. As he held her almost overhead, he buried his face in the curls that covered her sex and breathed into her core.

His breath filled her, teased and tickled her all at the same time. She squirmed, the feeling so intense it made her uncomfortable—too intense. Her breasts tingled; her sex tightened. He swirled his tongue over the nub that was hidden there and blew again. Her head fell back and her back arched. Caught up in pleasure, she couldn't hold on to him any longer, was dependent on his strength keeping her in place—and he didn't weaken, kept her there, his face pressed against her sex, his breath filling and teasing until her own breaths came in fast puffs and her heart thumped inside her chest.

Hot and wet and desperate for him to fill her, she let her head fall forward and thrust her hands into his hair.

"Joarr," she rasped.

He didn't stop. Another wave rolled over her. She squirmed against him. "Joarr." Again and again, he flicked his tongue over her. Then as she quivered with release, he lowered her down, positioned her so she was poised above his rigid sex.

Struggling to gain control of her pounding heart, she pulled in breaths and knelt over him. He grabbed her by the hips and positioned her body so the tip of his sex brushed hers. Then slowly he edged inside her.

Her body tingled…with magic. As their arousal grew, magic swelled around them. It was everywhere.

With each breath, she pulled it into her lungs. As he slid deeper inside her, it touched her there, too. Caused her body to quiver and her hands to shake. She didn't have to pull power. Their union seemed to be making it; for the first time in her life, Amma felt as if she were creating magic, not just stealing another's.

She felt strong. Stronger than she had ever felt before, even when her stores were full. This new sensation, from creating rather than stealing…she'd never imagined how incredible it would feel. She'd never imagined it was even possible.

How was it possible? The question tickled at the edge of her consciousness. Perhaps it was just a trick of her mind, swathed in so much pleasure she couldn't discern where Joarr's actions left off and hers began.

Beneath her, Joarr moved and the question was quickly forgotten. He was fully inside her now. She pressed her palms into his chest and concentrated on moving her body up and down, on the delicious slide of his sex in and out.

Power sizzled against her palms. She released it as heat…fire. She could see her palms glowing red, but felt no pain, and Joarr didn't seem to, either. Instead he seemed impassioned. His tempo increased, the blaze in his eyes burning so bright Amma couldn't look away.

"Let it go," he murmured. "Don't hold back."

Without asking she knew what he meant. He wanted her magic, wanted her to unleash whatever she still held inside.

She shouldn't; she needed it if she wanted to escape him. She bit her lip, one tiny bit of logic holding out, screaming at her not to give in.

He lifted her, then lowered her again. Her body fully encased his length, and she knew she couldn't resist, knew her orgasm was upon her. It was now or never. She had to choose. Logic or passion.

With a scream, she chose. She unleashed every bit of magic that had built up inside her. Twin streams, red then blue, poured from her palms into his chest. Her body quivered, her back arched and Joarr's did the same.

Together they found their release. Joarr poured out his heat while Amma let her magic flow. Pleasure swirled around her, pounded into her, so intense it verged on pain. Then when they both were physically and magically spent, she collapsed on top of him, her heart beating loudly and her magic completely drained.

She closed her eyes and folded her fingers against her palms.

Stupid. So stupid.

Joarr reached up to stroke her hair, then pulled it back from her face. She couldn't look at him; she was too overwhelmed, didn't understand what had happened, why she had lost herself, how she had given up her goal so easily.

"You shared your fire," he murmured. "I didn't know…" He ran his fingers down her arm. She pressed her face against his chest, wished she could pull her hair back over her face, hide. She'd never felt so exposed. "Thank you," he finished. Then he leaned up and pressed a kiss to her forehead.

Amma froze. *Thank you.* She'd never had anyone thank her for anything before. Maybe because she had never done anything for anyone before. She and her sisters took. They didn't give or ask. But she realized, not anymore. She'd broken that pattern.

She placed a hand over her mole. Her sisters would never understand this.

Her face pressed against Joarr's chest, she breathed in his spicy scent. Funny, even though she knew she had just wasted all the magic she had struggled to store, she didn't feel as if she'd lost anything. This seemed to be becoming a trend when she was around Joarr. One she needed to break.

Joarr wrapped his arm around her, his hand cupping her hip. And she relaxed against him. She stopped her mind from wandering to her sisters and what they would think, stopped her mind from wandering at all. She just enjoyed where she was and the heat that still wrapped around her and Joarr like a cocoon.

Joarr lay on the stained bedclothes with Amma draped across his body. She had shared her magic. He was shocked. He'd wanted it, but hadn't expected it. He would never have dreamed this witch, who had only stolen from him and lied to him before, would do such a thing. Magic was precious to a witch—much more precious than a dragon's heat or cold.

A dragon could produce new fire and ice on a whim, but magic for a witch? Especially a witch in Amma's position who had been completely drained…

Sharing her magic was a gift. A gift she had chosen to give him. It swirled inside him, stoking his fires to degrees he'd never reached before.

With Amma's magic pouring into him, he could have

melted rock, turned the world around them into molten lava. Or frozen the boiling pits of Muspelheim.

With Amma's magic pouring into him, he could do anything.

Did she realize that?

He doubted it, but still, the sharing had made the sex into more than just an act. Made it into a true union, a melding of their powers, something only dragons did as far as he knew.

He ran his fingers down her spine. She shivered. Without stopping his movements, he raised the temperature of the fire inside him and warmed her with his body. She sighed and relaxed against him.

He realized then she wasn't just quiet; she was asleep. For how long? And once she awoke, then what? Would they discuss what had happened? Or pretend it hadn't?

Did the sharing mean as much to her as it did to a dragon?

He knew she wouldn't tell him, not unless he asked. And he wouldn't.

Because he didn't want to say it out loud, didn't want the rule of the Ormar hanging over them. Melding was yet another thing regulated by the dragon army. The power it created was too intense and made the dragons involved too strong. Because of that, dragons melded only once and then they separated. Any children that came from the union were divided—boys to the males, girls to the females—and the adults, the lovers, were never allowed to be together again.

He could have kept Amma before. The thought had occurred to him—that he could lock her in his cavern and cherish her like the prize she was, but not now. The Ormar would smell the meld on both of them and Amma would be banished, perhaps Joarr, too, for trying to trick the dragon army.

His fingers tangled in Amma's hair. He held them up and admired the golden threads that clung to his knuckles.

No, this treasure wasn't his to keep. He needed to remember that.

Chapter 9

Fafnir leaned back in the velvet recliner he kept in his office. It was a little after midnight. He'd had his drink and for once his brother had agreed to watch the door. A rare night off.

He ran his tongue over his lips. The taste of dragon blood still clung to them. He pulled his lower lip into his mouth and dragged his front teeth across it, scraping off any remaining molecules.

Dragon blood was thick with a metallic hue. The first dragon he'd bled had spilled coppery liquid into his cup; the second and third had offered more of a steely shade. But as the blood aged, the punch lessened. It was disappointing at best. He tapped his fingers on his chair's arm.

How many shades, varieties and tastes of dragon blood were there to choose from? He longed to learn.

Saliva filled his mouth at the idea.

The chalice had limits—only one sip a day. He needed more than that, needed to drink his fill. A dragon's worth.

And he could, he realized, if not from the chalice, then from another cup or flask. The blood he had was old, anyway—why limit himself as he had been?

Fafnir placed his hands together, as if he were praying, and tapped his finger pads against each other. He hadn't been back to the building since he'd locked the last dragon's corpse there. He hadn't wanted to risk his father or brother following him. But the blood he'd brought to the bar was running out. He needed more, if not from a live dragon then blood from the dead one he had stored would have to do.

He frowned. Across the room, the mirror reflected his image back at him. Same stout dwarf that he'd always been, with shaggy brows forming a V in the center of his forehead. He lowered them more, concentrated on looking his most ferocious. Intimidating to some perhaps, but not at first pass, not to humans at least.

He was tired of dealing with the drones that occupied this world. They assumed because of his size he was no threat. He had taught many of them differently, but he was tired of that game, too. He wanted to see the fear and awe he deserved when they first lay eyes on him.

Fear, respect—that was what he deserved and humans were too stupid to see it.

His hand dropped to his ax. The wood was worn, but the edge was still sharp. Even after slicing into the necks of three dragons, the metal held.

He picked it up and let the light from the candle he'd

lit play along the blade. Then he stared at the flame. Lost in its flickering beauty, a new idea occurred to him. Until now he'd filled his cup and released the dragons. He'd drugged each before slicing into their neck. Some herb the dark elf who'd educated him on the cup had sold him. It was like catnip for dragons. They spaced out on the stuff until they lost all sense of what was going on around them.

He did his job and moved on. Their wounds healed quickly, more quickly than any being he'd known. So, when they awoke they had no idea they'd been harmed. They left—all except the last one—nice, tidy and easy.

Maybe too easy. Took some of the fun out of the act.

But now that he was so close to getting full dragon powers, he didn't need to be so cautious. He could trap a dragon and keep him. Drink his blood, as much as he liked, every day until the supply in the chalice was gone. Then he could refill a different cup and keep drinking—a never-ending supply of fresh, power-filled blood.

And he wouldn't have to hide what he was doing from the dragon—because he would never escape, never be a threat.

It was perfect...a dream.

He sat back against his chair and imagined a dragon, the mightiest of all beings, staring down at Fafnir, his face hollow with defeat.

He leaned forward and jerked his cell phone out of his desk drawer. It took five rings for his agent to answer.

"Did one come?"

The dwarf he'd sent to the portal nearest the Ormar

landholdings hemmed and hawed, saying he'd found the dragon and done as Fafnir had asked.

"When? If you'd done your job he'd be here. Why don't I have my blood?"

At the agent's claim that the dragon had a female with him and might have had help in the attack, Fafnir's interest flared. "A female dragon?" He'd never seen a female dragon. Dragon females did not stay with the males; they didn't raise their young, either, at least not the male children. And as rare as it was to see a male dragon out in the nine worlds, spotting a female was unheard of. Fafnir didn't even know where they lived or if they lived together as the males did.

Two dragons, a male and a female. The thought of such bounty was mind-boggling.

"…not a dragon…" his agent muttered.

"What? But that's what I sent you to find." Fafnir slammed his ax into the four-foot-wide piece of log he kept beside his desk. The blade slipped through the ancient wood like a heated knife through butter. He picked it up and studied the edge. Still perfect.

"No, the male is a dragon. The female is not."

"Hmm." Fafnir placed the ax head on the floor and leaned on the handle. "What is she, then?"

When the agent stuttered for an answer, Fafnir cut him off. "Doesn't matter. My plans have changed. I need the dragon, the whole dragon, alive. Get him to the bar. Tell him about the treasure. Tell him I'm willing to give it to him in exchange for…" Fafnir searched for something a dragon might be willing to part with. "The female."

He smiled. Perfect. If the dragon and the female had

already done what Fafnir suspected, the dragon would have no further need for her. He would expect her to leave him, anyway. Why not trade her for treasure? "Tell him I will trade my father's hoard for the female."

Thrilled with his new plan, Fafnir punched the end button and tossed his phone back into the drawer.

Now to make good use of his time off and visit the dragon he did have. He went to gather some flasks.

An hour had passed since Amma had awakened. She'd found herself draped across Joarr's body. He'd been awake and watching her. She peeled her body off his and rolled over onto the mattress. Something flittered in her stomach—nerves.

She couldn't believe what she had done.

Sex, fine. But what had happened between her and Joarr had gone past that. She had felt something, something beyond the physical. But then, was that bad? Was it wrong to feel something for the dragon? She stared at the ceiling and tried to puzzle through the thoughts pinging around her brain.

"What are you thinking?" Joarr asked. His question was casual, but it sent a frisson of alarm through Amma.

She plucked at the rumpled cover beside her. "Nothing. You?"

He ran a finger down her shoulder, sending tingles over the rest of her.

She was weakening, warming to the idea that maybe feeling something for this dragon wouldn't be bad... might even be good.

She cleared her throat. "Back at your house, that other dragon, he mentioned you were an orphan."

Joarr placed a light kiss against her shoulder. "My father died when I was little more than a hatchling."

"And your mother? What about her?"

Joarr's lips stilled. He pulled back and stared at the far wall. "I never knew her."

"She is dead?" Amma's heart thumped. She'd heard tales about dragons—that the males raised the males, kept the babies from their mothers. She hadn't questioned it before, hadn't cared before because she'd had no intention of telling Joarr about their child, but now... maybe she'd been wrong...

He shook his head. "No, she's alive, at least as far as I know."

Amma's skin turned cold. "But then you aren't an orphan."

He looked at her then, surprise in his eyes. "Of course I am. My father died. In the dragon world that makes me an orphan. Since I was male, my mother had no claim on me." His gaze went distant again. "Not that she would have wanted one."

Amma couldn't listen to any more. She had to get off this bed and away from Joarr. She'd almost... She'd wanted... She jumped up, naked, and with her eyes carefully averted from his, she walked to the bathroom.

He didn't say a word as she trekked toward the bathroom, but she felt his eyes on her back like stones. She couldn't shake the feeling that he knew why she was asking the questions, knew her secret and was already planning on how he'd take her child away from her.

With the door closed behind her, she turned on the

shower and then leaned against the wall, her eyes shut, wondering what in hell was happening to her.

She had considered telling Joarr about her baby, staying with Joarr. She had come dangerously close to losing all she had. When she was so close to gaining everything she had wanted.

She couldn't let herself be taken in. He was the dragon. She was supposed to outwit him, not fall for him like some bubbleheaded princess who was too stupid to see she was dinner.

She stared at the cracked vinyl and let the room fill up with steam. The humid air activated Joarr's scent that clung to her skin. Angry with herself and him, she jerked open the shower curtain and stepped inside.

With the water pounding on her face, she closed her eyes and placed her hand on her stomach. She forced herself to think logically. She'd come close to screwing up, but she hadn't—not irreparably. She'd had sex with him, but she hadn't said anything stupid. She hadn't made any kind of declaration. He was a male; odds were to him what had passed between them had been nothing more than an especially sweet orgasm. And she had not in any way let him know she was pregnant.

There was no reason for him to realize she had felt more, given that she never had before. So, for all practical purposes it hadn't happened. If she was the only one to realize the significance of what she had done, she had shown no weakness.

She slicked her hands over her face and stared at the pink tile. She just had to let him know that handing out magic was meaningless to her, common even. She rolled her eyes at the thought.

She grabbed the white packet of soap and ripped off its paper wrapping. As she lathered up, as she washed off Joarr's scent, sanity returned. She had to do what she had done before—let Joarr think she was taken in by him, had fallen for him. With his guard lowered, stealing the chalice for herself and her child would be easy—just as easy as it was the first time.

She slid the curtain open and stepped onto the vinyl, water puddling around her feet.

This dragon tale would have a whole new ending— with no prince to save her, the princess would save herself and take the treasure.

Calm again, she rubbed her legs with the rough towel she'd found hanging from the towel bar. A light rap sounded from the hall outside their room. She moved to the bathroom door and pressed her ear against the crack where the flimsy barrier didn't quite meet the jamb.

"Are you alone?" The voice was rough with an accent Amma recognized instantly—dwarf. Gunngar, where she had spent the past one hundred years, had been lousy with dwarves. She had no issue with dwarves, but she didn't trust them, either, especially after being attacked twice.

Joarr didn't reply, but he must have moved aside for the dwarf to enter their room because the next time Amma heard the accented voice it was louder, closer.

"The female, is she here?"

Amma raised both brows. The dwarf had been watching them. Following them? Had he been with one of the groups who had attacked them, or was he perhaps the dwarf she'd noticed at the portal bar? Either way, she knew Joarr was savvy enough not to trust him.

"Why do you ask?" Joarr this time, sounding bored. The dragon had made an art of appearing disinterested, but she had spent enough time with him that she could discern the act. And he was definitely acting now.

"I come with an offer that I don't want to fall on other ears."

Joarr must have made some nonverbal sign for the dwarf to continue. There was a pause, then the dwarf's voice.

"My employer is interested in acquiring—" his voice lowered "—your companion."

Amma stiffened.

The rustling of paper followed. "Come here tonight, ask for Fafnir. He'll give you the details."

"And why would I do that? Why would this employer think I'd be interested in whatever deal he has in mind?" Amma could almost see Joarr standing over the much shorter dwarf, looking down at him, letting him know the dragon wasn't amused.

"Treasure," the dwarf hissed. "Lots of it, like you've never seen. Objects gathered from all over the nine worlds for a century. A magical item gone missing? The Collector most likely has it."

At the Collector's name, Amma pulled back, catching her towel on the doorknob. The knob rattled and all sound in the room outside the bathroom stopped.

Amma held her breath, waiting, hoping the dwarf would go on. After a few seconds, she called out. "Damn. I dropped my…towel." As the word left her lips, she cursed, realizing how that had sounded. "I mean I slipped on the soap and the towel is wet."

There was movement outside the bathroom, the sound of the motel room's door opening and closing. Amma leaned against the sink, her eyes staring blindly at the pink tile. The Collector wanted her? Why? Did he think she'd cheated him in some way? She hadn't. She'd given him exactly what he'd requested, and in return he'd given her information that led her to Alfheim, and eventually the horrible fate of losing her body. If anyone should be angry it was her. And how did he know she was here? He must have been involved in everything that had happened. But again, why?

The bathroom door moved, opened a crack.

"Did you want me to dry you?" Joarr purred. It was the only way she could describe the sensual way the words left his throat.

The door swung open and Joarr stood in the doorway, his eyes glimmering like sapphires.

Chapter 10

The witch was naked and damp. Joarr didn't hide his interest; he let his gaze roam her body.

Amma jerked a scrap of a towel around herself. It barely met over her breasts and gaped outrageously at the side, revealing her hip, thigh and calf.

He stepped into the tiny bathroom. She stepped backward until her body was wedged between the toilet and the sink. His hands pressed against the tile wall behind her, he looked down.

"If you need drying, I'd be happy to help."

Her gaze flitted to the side, as if she was trying to see around him—reinforcing his suspicion that she had been eavesdropping.

With that in mind, he stepped back and held out the paper his unexpected visitor had given him. "We have an invitation, a direct one this time," he murmured. The fact that the Collector's name was mentioned and he apparently wanted Amma aroused every suspicion Joarr had had toward the witch.

He would show her the paper, but not mention what the dwarf had said, at least not yet.

Her head jerked back toward him. There was surprise in her eyes. She hadn't expected him to tell her about the dwarf's visit. This was good; it would help build her trust in him. "Is this address familiar?" He knew it had to be. He'd recognized it instantly, but it was time for Amma to give him something, to show she was going to work with him to regain the chalice. Otherwise, despite his conflicted feelings toward her, he might be tempted to take the dwarf up on his offer, assuming the offer was real. Joarr had his doubts.

The note was really more of a ticket, a backstage pass of sorts identifying the holder as a VIP to a club called Tunnels. The paper was made to look aged and a red wax seal had kept it closed until Joarr had broken it.

One hand pinching the ends of the towel together, Amma reached to take the paper. Joarr loosened his grip on the invitation and relaxed his posture, leaning one hip against the sink. The bathroom was steamy, and smelled of generic cheap soap and shampoo. But as the steam cleared from the air, Amma's scent broke through. He inhaled, but kept his face neutral, showing no sign of his appreciation for the female trapped in the tiny room with him.

As she studied the note, a thin line formed between her brows. Joarr was interested in her response, but interested in other things, too. He blew cool air above her head, pushing the steam faster from the space and causing the tiny hairs of Amma's arms and shoulders to rise.

She glanced at him. He closed his lips, pretended he'd only been standing, waiting.

A shiver shook her body. "The bar... It's the same as the flyer."

"Is it?"

She nodded; her towel slipped. She grabbed for it, managing to keep it from falling to the ground—much to his regret. He blew a second breath over her head. Another shiver passed over her and she glanced around as if looking for the source of the breeze.

When she looked up, he held out his hand. "How observant of you." Her fingers shaking, she extended the note toward him. He let it fall from his fingers and float toward the floor.

"How clumsy of me..." He bent, brushing against her and the towel she was struggling to keep wrapped around her body. He managed to subtly give the thin cloth a tug; it slipped from her grasp and joined the note on the dirty vinyl floor. He scooped it up along with the note.

She didn't cover her breasts; he appreciated that. She also didn't look as if she were fooled by his act. She jerked the towel from his hand. "You did that on purpose." Pushing him to the side, she grabbed her clothes, which were piled in the corner. Then she moved with the clear intention of leaving the room.

He wrapped his fingers around her arm and let his thumb drift over her skin, soft and still a little damp. When she looked up at him, her eyes glittering, he whispered, "Would you rather I didn't care? That what you hid beneath that scrap of cloth held no interest for me?"

She blinked.

With a low chuckle, he released his hold and she walked on past.

As he watched her hips sway back and forth, watched her walk naked and unintimidated to the other side of the bed, he whispered to himself, "No worries there, my treasure. No worries there."

The streets were busy in a scurrying, don't-make-eye-contact kind of way. As Amma stepped over a drunk passed out on a piece of cardboard, she wondered how much of the human world was like this. She'd only been to a few parts of this world. Before her entrapment, she'd spent most of her time with her sisters, Lusse mainly. But both gravitated to stopping points carved out of in-between places—lands not connected to any of the major worlds. Lusse had preferred a place not all that different from the land the dragons called home—stark but beautiful with mountains and snow. Her oldest sister was drawn to the underground. Lived most of her time like a dwarf in some dark cave...or like a dragon. Amma hadn't realized until now how both of her sisters had homes similar in some way to the dragons'.

Maybe that was why she was attracted to Joarr.

He stepped over the drunk she'd just passed. Joarr was wearing white again, a new outfit he'd got from somewhere. He'd had clothes delivered for both of them, paid with another bag of his gold dust. She didn't know why he'd ordered clothes for himself and not just magicked them as he did when he shifted. Perhaps because he realized she needed something other than her filthy skirt and peasant blouse to go to the Collector's club or perhaps he realized shifting around her gave her access to his magic.

He'd left off a jacket this time, wearing just a close-fitting sweater that showed off his muscled chest, and wool pants. Even his shoes were white, but with a hint of metallic.

On anyone else the outfit would have looked outlandish, but on Joarr...it just emphasized how masculine he was. Honestly, she couldn't imagine him any other way, except maybe with no clothing at all.

She laughed. No, Joarr's choice in clothing had nothing to do with her attraction to him. Damn him.

She smoothed the skirt of the dress that he'd chosen for her. It was white, too. Not a choice she would have made for visiting a place that promised danger. Something dark that would blend into the night or club crowd would have been her preference. But she had to appreciate Joarr's brazen confidence.

She adjusted the bracelet he'd taken from the dark elf at the portal. She'd added it to her outfit. She still wore the manacle, too. Somehow the two seemed appropriate, one reminding her why she was here and the other... She fingered the silver chain. She wasn't sure why she wore it, didn't want to analyze her motive too closely; it had just seemed right.

She tightened her grip on the tiny silver purse that Joarr had also supplied. She was on edge and overthinking things. She didn't like being hunted, especially by an unseen adversary.

They were only a few yards from the address now. All around them were three-story buildings, old warehouses. There was no sign advertising which building might be the bar, but the line snaking from a basement entrance left no doubt where they should go.

Joarr pulled the invitation from his pocket and checked the address, anyway. "Looks like this is it." He glanced around, obviously looking for the sign Amma had already noted was missing.

A group of female humans dressed in thigh-high boots and skirts that barely covered their asses sashayed past them. One turned and raised an eyebrow at Joarr. Amma slipped her arm through his and raised an eyebrow back.

The human tossed her head and laughed—as if she were a match for Amma.

Amma opened her fingers, instinctively reaching for power, only to once again realize she had none.

"Interesting clientele." Joarr's gaze wandered from the female who was now traipsing down the stairs to the club's door and over a mixed group of dwarves and Svartalfars, dark elves.

It was obvious to Amma, and she was sure to Joarr, too, that the dwarves and Svartalfars were fully armed. The wooden handle of an ax poked out from under one dwarf's jacket and the dark elves' pockets were bursting. Dark elves were known for strange and destructive weaponry.

She placed a hand on Joarr's sleeve. "Do you think this is smart?"

He glanced at her, surprised. "This is where the chalice is—or where the person who sent the invitation has directed us."

As he said the words, she realized her instincts were right. "Where the person who sent the invitation wants us to be."

Joarr smiled. "Yes. Good point."

They stood for a second, both staring at the crowd milling toward the bar.

One of the Svartalfars brushed up against the female human who had eyed Joarr. She shot him a contemptuous stare. Amma paused, hoping for some reaction that would induce the dark elf to produce whatever toy he had hidden in his pocket. Unfortunately, he only leaned closer to the woman and whispered something in her ear.

The woman grabbed her friend's arm and stomped away—obviously outraged—but her response was nowhere near what Amma had hoped for. Disappointed, she turned back to the job at hand.

If they wanted to get in the bar unseen, they needed a diversion or a disguise, probably both.

"We need to change." She tapped her purse against her thigh. "If the Collector is behind all this, he'll recognize me, and you…" She turned her gaze onto Joarr, steady and direct. Then shook her head. "You just stand out."

He tilted his head, his brows lifting in surprise. "Dragons like to stand out. It's kind of a goal of ours."

She huffed out a breath. "One that will get you killed or at the very least cost you the chalice—and me my pick of your treasure."

"You're very take-charge all of a sudden." He leaned

down and breathed against her lips. The night was chilly and he'd selected no coats for either of them. But the air he blew on her was warm and sparkled with magic. It made her want to open her lips and suck it in. She found herself leaning toward him, her breasts resting on his forearm. "I like it," he finished. Then smiled, his lips almost touching hers.

For a second she stood there, unable to react. Then she jerked back and stared at the building in front of her. Her voice cool, completely hiding the emotions swirling inside her, she said, "You can do your thing and change, but—" she pulled at her skirt with two fingers "—I'm a different story."

He pulled her hand, which she had dropped to her side, back through his arm. "I am a dragon. We don't hide well. We don't hide at all. Our power is in others knowing what we are, fearing us, not acting like we are something else."

His answer was cocky, frustrating and likely to get him the same fate that had befallen two, perhaps three, dragons before. She opened her mouth to tell him so, then snapped her lips shut. Some things just called for action.

He patted her hand, the one looped through his arm. "Your concern is touching. You keep up with it and I might just start to believe you care."

When she didn't reply, he continued, "Just do as you promised—help me retrieve the chalice. For now that means coming with me and not worrying about what my plan is." He led her into the crowd, then down the first step that led to the bar's door. Not prepared for the move, Amma wobbled. She grabbed hold of the iron banister that was mounted on the concrete wall beside her to keep from falling. Joarr stopped, too, just as suddenly, and reached out to grab her. She held on to the railing, determined not to have him touch her again, no more than she had to. Every touch and she got a little more confused, forgot she had an ulterior motive for her part in this fool's errand.

"Hey, you're blocking the road," someone called from behind. A hand shoved her squarely in the back. Even with both hands on the banister, she fell...or almost did. Joarr thrust out his arm, catching her. Then twirled her toward him, as if they were performing some fancy dance move, and just as quickly, he pivoted on his foot to stare down the human couple who stood behind them.

It was obvious the female half of the pair had shoved Amma. Her arms were crossed over a strategically torn T-shirt and her overly made-up face was sullen. And Amma couldn't help but notice they were the same height and weight. It gave her an idea.

She eyed the woman's companion. He was almost as tall as Joarr, but skinnier. Plus his dark pants didn't look as if they would stretch, and his shirt barely fit him. In other words—not a match.

But the pair could still be useful.

She pulled on Joarr's arm until he leaned so she could whisper in his ear. "You asked for my help. Either take it, or I leave, now."

His eyes grew round. She expected him to argue, or offer some other bit of dragons-the-invincible wisdom, but instead he made a sweeping "go ahead" motion with his hand.

She used the banister to pull herself forward and squeezed her way past Joarr. Standing next to the over-confident human, she raised a brow. "I'm sure that was an accident," she said.

The woman's chest threatened to explode from her T-shirt; she puffed it out further. "We're regulars here. I don't think you want to make trouble with us."

Oh, but Amma did. She really, really did. She flexed her fingers.

Joarr slipped his hand around hers; warmth poured into her, but no magic. She growled.

He seemed to sense her meaning; his fingers pressed into her back and this time she felt it, the sweet release of magic, dragon magic. Her face showing nothing of what was going on, she soaked up every bit of power he offered.

"Regulars? What kind of place is this?" Joarr managed to look intimidating and encouraging at the same time.

The woman turned her black-lined eyes away from Amma. When her gaze hit Joarr, her mouth formed a perfect circle and an "ooh" sound escaped her pinup-girl red lips.

The man beside her, however, did not seem similarly impressed. He jerked her by the arm. "Fafnir's on the door. Be nice this time." He held up a hand and called to the dwarf who had appeared in the bar's now-open doorway.

Joarr's fingers tightened. He, like she, recognized the name. Now crackling with power, Amma grabbed the woman by the forearm. She jerked, but Amma didn't let go. "Don't tell me you go in this way? Don't you know the VIP entrance is on the other side?"

The woman's eyes narrowed, but her insecurity was easily visible.

Amma motioned with her head. "Come on. We'll show you." She turned just as the dwarf glanced in their direction. She pulled on Joarr, warning him to keep his back turned, too.

The woman's companion waved his hand and jumped, obviously struggling to gain Fafnir's attention, but the dwarf barely looked their way.

She pulled on Joarr's sleeve. "Give me the invitation."

He handed it to her.

She dangled it between two fingers. "Well, if you don't want to go to the VIP door with us, I guess I understand, but I hate to see you standing out here while others—" she made a sniffing noise as the stocky dwarf gestured the first group of annoying humans they'd encountered into the club "—waltz inside. Here." She held out the note as if it was a golden ticket—which it was. She was sure it would guarantee admittance. Of course, once Fafnir realized the bearer wasn't the dragon or the witch he was most certainly expecting, things might go decidedly south. A problem that most definitely wasn't hers.

The raccoon-eyed wannabe eyed the note with suspicion. Amma started to pull it back. "Of course, if you think—"

"No." The woman snatched it from her fingers.

The light by the bar entrance didn't make it to where they were. The woman flipped open her cell phone and used its light to study the piece of paper. "Huh." She twisted her lips to the side. "Kind of strange."

"Well, I'm sure—" Amma's fingers grazed the edge of the note.

The woman jerked it out of her reach. She punched her companion in the arm. "Let's go. Dolly's been inside an hour. She'll never let us hear the end of it."

The woman shot one last suspicious glance at Amma. Then the couple tromped down the stairs.

"Come on, over here." Amma pulled on Joarr, until they were both deep enough in the crowd Fafnir wouldn't spot them.

The couple elbowed their way to the front, the woman waving the note like a flag. "Let us pass. We're here by special invitation."

Fafnir looked up. Even from this distance, Amma could see the excitement flash behind his eyes. He rubbed his hands together, and as he spotted the woman's companion, he licked his lips.

Amma frowned. Fafnir's reaction was disturbing. Obviously, he'd been expecting someone to arrive with the note, but there was something about the way he looked… She glanced at Joarr, wondering if he had noticed.

Fafnir slammed a board down, cutting off the entrance. Mutters and angry looks traveled through the waiting crowd. He stepped forward, hands on his hips, and motioned to the couple waving the note, pushing other patrons who had been about to enter to the side.

Amma could see his lips move, could see whatever he said to his aspiring customers was far from polite.

The couple disappeared through the doorway. Fafnir followed close behind, slamming the door shut behind him.

Chaos broke out immediately.

Joarr looked down at Amma. "And that helped, how?"

"Excuse me." Two women and a man, girls and a boy actually—Amma doubted they were out of their teens—tapped on her arm. "Did we hear you say there's another way in?"

The three looked at Amma expectantly.

She glanced at Joarr and didn't even try to hide the victory she knew shone from her eyes.

It took approximately two minutes to lead the three to the alley behind the bar and zap them with enough magic to knock them unconscious. As Amma pulled on the smallest girl's thigh-high boots, she muttered to their inanimate forms. "Good lesson for you. Don't be walking off with strangers. When you wake up, remember that." She squatted next to the second girl and shuffled through her bag.

A few feet away Joarr was holding the boy's pants. "Is this necessary?" he asked.

"Put them on or magic something like them yourself." She turned back to the bag.

Ten minutes later, they were both dressed and sporting black eyeliner.

"Open your eyes," she told Joarr. She held a ball of power in her hand; it felt good to be able to use magic on something so small again, to not feel as if she had to hoard it like a dragon did his gold.

Joarr stared down at his black fingernail polish. "This is not my normal style."

"Exactly the point. Even as big as you are, they'd never expect a dragon to look like this." She held the ball low, checking his appearance from the tip of his black leather boots, up the skintight pants, and onto the gray snakeskin jacket and old concert T-shirt.

He ran his hand over the jacket. He had objected as soon as he noticed the scales. "Is this necessary?"

A smart reply on her lips, she held the ball up to illuminate his face. The words froze in her throat. Her whole body froze. Joarr's eyes were always intense, always made her feel as if he could see inside of her, but now, surrounded by the black eye makeup... She swallowed.

"What?" he asked.

"You..." She closed her fist over the ball, extinguishing its light. "You look good, totally believable."

Five minutes later they were back by the club entrance. A new dwarf was at the door. "Who's that?" she asked a girl dressed in ankle boots and torn hosiery.

The female glanced at her and apparently finding her acceptable replied, "Regin. He doesn't usually work the door, but Fafnir disappeared a while back. The door was closed down for hours."

More like half an hour, Amma calculated. Long enough for Fafnir to have discovered her and Joarr's trick. They needed to get inside fast. Her hand wrapped around Joarr's arm, she dived into the crowd.

Chapter 11

Fafnir placed his hand on the handle of his ax. The worn wood protruded from his belt; the head was encased in its leather sheath. A "safeguard" his father forced upon him. Couldn't let the humans see the blade. Might cause a panic. Might start talk.

He flicked his thumbnail over his finger, imagined he was unsnapping the sheath...running the pad of his thumb over the blade, preparing to slice into the dragon's neck. In his mind, he could smell the blood. Dragon blood... It smelled like the deepest part of a cave, where the dirt was thick with minerals, where you would find the strongest, most rare of metals. His mouth watered and his fingers trembled.

The dragon, his hand covering the female's, placed his foot on the next step. He glanced at Fafnir and hesitated, suspicion fluttering across his face. Fafnir stepped back and yelled at a bartender who was oblivious to the dark elf leaning across one of the club's many bars, trying to fill his mug for free from a beer tap.

When he looked back, the dragon had climbed two more steps. He was almost to the main floor now. Fafnir rolled up onto his toes, fighting to keep his excitement hidden and his face blank. He didn't have his prize yet. Once the dragon was in the main club Fafnir would have to get him into a private room without his brother seeing.

Regin was already suspicious. If he learned a fourth dragon had arrived at the club, he would feel the need to shove his way into Fafnir's business. Maybe even steal the dragon away. Fafnir couldn't have that.

He ran his thumb in a circular motion over the ax's handle. How to hide a dragon? It shouldn't be hard— not with this one. He frowned.

This dragon was different from the others…weaker, paler. He sighed; he guessed it made sense. Dragons like any species had to have good and bad, strong and weak. Unfortunately he'd hit upon the latter. He could only hope his blood was as thick and strong as the others' had been. Not watered-down and anemic as this dragon appeared.

He sighed. At least his plan had worked; he'd attracted a dragon. His spies had followed the male from the dragon-stronghold portal. No one except dragons lived there. So, weak as this male appeared, he had to be a dragon.

Concentrating on that, Fafnir watched the dragon and his companion step onto the main club floor. He glanced around, looking for Regin or his father. Neither was in sight. He released a breath and began shoving his way through the crowd, leading the pair to the closest bar. Behind it was a small seating area—not as private as the rooms overhead, but a place to stash the dragon while he located his family and retrieved the dragon's bane from his office. Once he knew his family was occupied and wouldn't see what he was doing, he'd get the dragon onto the boards and into one of the rooms. There he'd slip the bane into the dragon's drink. Then, he'd be set.

A dwarf stumbled into his path and fell onto the floor. Fafnir kicked him out of his way. The dwarf spun across the polished concrete floor like a hockey puck. Fafnir kept going.

Nothing and nobody was going to make him lose this dragon.

A human, knocked off balance by the spinning dwarf, teetered close. Fafnir elbowed him, knocking him into the crowd.

Nothing could stop him from getting his dragon blood now, and the gods protect any who tried.

Joarr followed the witch through the press of humans. She blended in now, as much as a witch determined to get somewhere or something could. The short skirt she'd stolen from one of the girls they'd ambushed clung to her ass. The shirt clung to everything.

He smiled. It was a whole new look from the loose peasant top she'd worn earlier. Still, while this outfit, dark and in-your-face, was undeniably sexy, Joarr preferred the juxtaposition of her angelic wardrobe with her determined reality. He wasn't sure the human males eyeing her from all angles agreed, however.

One ran a hand down Amma's bare shoulder as she passed. Joarr paused to stare at him, let a little fire flicker in his eyes. The male stepped back, startled.

Amma, realizing Joarr had stopped, jerked on his arm. With one last flickering gaze at the male, he followed her.

There was a throng jammed in front of the door. The dwarf standing beside it seemed little interested in managing the scene. A fight broke out to their right; the dwarf simply moved to the left, stepping in front of a group seconds from entering. Another fight erupted.

The dwarf tapped a wooden rod he held against his palm.

"He's getting ready to shut it down," Amma called. "Follow me."

Suddenly the crowd in front of them parted, magically. Literally. As Amma approached the humans blocking her way she tapped them lightly with her finger, and each jumped and moved from her path.

Joarr leaned down. "Is that wise?"

She shrugged. "They're lucky I'm being careful." She zapped another group.

Within seconds they were in front of the door and stepping over the threshold.

"Now what?" Joarr asked. The interior was dark, but no challenge at all for his eyesight. Many dragons chose to live most of their lives underground. Light was optional.

"We find Fafnir." Amma moved forward with ease and grace, as if she, too, had no difficulty with the dark. He admired her for that, for her sudden desire to take charge, too. Not that she was in charge, but for now he was happy to let things play out as she chose.

Still, he did need to remind her whose mission they were on. He grabbed her by the arm, slowing her pace. "Moving a little fast, don't you think?" he asked, moving casually as if they were strolling through an art gallery absorbing all the sights, instead of winding through a narrow hallway where the only adornment on the walls was an occasional hole in the drywall or smear where a drink had been sloshed. "Lovely place," he murmured.

"There has to be more," she replied. And she was right. A few moments later the hallway opened into a bigger room. It was still dark, but a few dim lights revealed a bar in the back. Beside it were stairs going up. They had also found the crowd, or part of it. As they approached the stairs the noise level multiplied.

"The main club must be up here." Amma already had her foot on the first step.

Slipping her hand back through his arm, Joarr joined her.

At the top of the stairs was another room—a room that gave Joarr pause.

Somehow the dwarves, or whoever ran the place, had opened up the center of the building—no second or third floor, not really at least. Instead there were swinging boards that only dwarves, elves and billy goats could cross easily…and dragons, but only in their dragon form, complete with wings. These strange road-ways led to what appeared to be private rooms located on what should have been the second and third floors. They jutted out over the main club, like jagged hunks of rock that at any minute might tumble down and crush the partyers below.

There were three bars in this room, each constructed of stalagmite-like structures. Water dripped from the ceiling in spots and a small stream wound its way through the center of the room. And it was dark, not cave-dark, but close.

"Interesting," Amma murmured. "It's like…"

"Being inside a cavern," Joarr finished for her.

"They brought a little Nidavellir here to the human world."

Joarr brought her fingers to his lips. "Sweet, isn't it?"

Across the room he spotted Fafnir. He was still with the humans. He had them in the back by a small bar cut off a bit from the main room. Joarr nodded toward them, and he and Amma wove their way through the crowd.

He bent and whispered in her ear. "Did I tell you the dwarf who brought the note asked about you? He offered treasure in trade for you. Any idea why?"

She stiffened, but he kept moving, sliding the pair of them between groups, smiling and blending as best they could.

Amma's fingers dug into his arm. "Did you explain to him that I'm not yours to trade?"

He patted her hand, nodded at a woman who turned as they approached. "Didn't occur to me."

Amma looked to the side, as if bored. But he knew she wasn't. He knew the dwarf's offer was like a stick jabbing her squarely in the back. It was wrong of him to poke her with it, but then, he was a dragon. They liked to poke things, and he, in particular, liked to get Amma fired up.

"Perhaps he doesn't realize how much more rare you are than me. Perhaps he'd be more interested in acquiring his own dragon for a pet," she replied, smiling at a few patrons herself.

"Hmm." He pretended to consider her suggestion. "It would make sense. Witches...so common, but a dragon? Yes, you are right. I am the far more valuable catch."

Throughout their sparring they had continued to close the distance between themselves and Fafnir. The couple was sitting on a gray couch. Fafnir stood in front of them, his back to Joarr and Amma.

A waitress arrived with drinks, but as she held a glass out to the girl, Fafnir knocked it out of her hand. "Where did you get the note?" he shrieked.

The girl paled and shrank toward the male sitting beside her. His arm was around her, but he looked none too sure, either.

"A woman gave it to us. She said it would get us in—"

"A woman—was there a male with her? What did they look like?" The dwarf bounded onto the couch beside them, then jumped onto the sofa's arm. He peered down at them like a bird of prey calculating when to make his strike.

"I don't know. They were old—her, anyway—and average."

A dagger appeared in Fafnir's hand, matching the ones that had appeared in Amma's eyes at the woman's comment. He plunged the blade into the back of the couch, inches from the girl's head. A lock of her hair fell onto her lap. She stared at it stupidly. The male, however, came to life. "Hey, you can't—" He reached for the girl and started to stand.

Fafnir lifted a hand. Three dwarves all bearing daggers appeared as if from the shadows. The couple sat back down.

Their fear was palpable. The girl clung to the boy, her dark nails digging into his skin.

Fafnir, however, took on a new appearance of calm. "I asked what they looked like. Are they in the bar now? Did they follow you or leave?"

"I—I don't... I didn't see them behind us," the girl replied, her gaze darting over the crowd.

Joarr pulled Amma against him, kept them both shielded behind a stalagmite protruding from the floor.

Suddenly, the girl's head snapped back toward Fafnir. "White. They were both wearing white—all white, even their shoes."

She glanced around again; lines of desperation surrounded her eyes. "There!" Her hand rose and she pointed.

Joarr pulled in a breath, automatically preparing to shift, but Fafnir and the couple were looking past him to the stairs he and Amma had walked up minutes before.

"Oh, not good for them," Amma muttered. The two girls and the boy whose clothing Joarr and Amma had stolen walked into the main bar, one of the girls in Amma's white dress, the boy in Joarr's jacket and pants.

Fafnir jerked his dagger from the couch and motioned to the three dwarves. They moved closer, their daggers obvious to Joarr, but hidden from the other patrons.

Fafnir slipped his dagger into his sleeve and hopped off the couch. Without a backward glance at the couple he'd just terrorized, he stomped toward his new target.

In the center of the room, he stepped on one of the boards that lowered and rose from the ceiling. It lifted him until he was ten feet above the crowd. He stood there, his gaze locked on the unknowing trio—the pulsing lights of the club making him look bigger somehow, darker and much more dangerous than Amma would ever have thought possible.

Amma squeezed Joarr's arm. "I don't like this."

He tilted his head toward hers, surprised that she would show concern for the humans that outside she'd seemed so willing to sacrifice for her own gain. His expression calm, as if discussing what drinks they were about to order, he replied, "Of course not. The dwarf means to harm them—thinking them you and I." He nodded toward the couch where the first couple was still trapped, then glanced back at the dwarf. "The question is, do we interfere? And if so, for whom?"

Amma stilled, only her eyes giving away the emotion battling inside her. Finally, she glanced at the couch. The couple was standing now. One dwarf stood behind them and one on each side. They were obviously being herded somewhere—somewhere from which Joarr doubted they'd ever appear again.

Amma hated what she was thinking. Hated what she knew she was about to do. The human female had shoved her in the back, treated her with disdain, even called her old when describing her to Fafnir.

Three solid reasons to let whatever the dwarves had planned for her and her companion unfold undisturbed. Her sisters certainly wouldn't have interfered with their plans.

But there it was again—she wasn't her sisters.

She looked up at Joarr. "I'll take care of them." She nodded to the couple. "You watch Fafnir." Then with her silver purse, which she had not given up in the name of a disguise, tucked under her arm, she strolled with deadly intent toward the couch.

As she got closer, her decision felt better. Power simmered under her palms. What she'd done outside, zapping a few humans to get them to move, even knocking the three teenagers unconscious for a while, had been completely unsatisfactory. It had only whetted her desire to battle for real. It had been so long...too long.

Of course, unfortunately, unless she could get the dwarves away from the room filled with humans she would still have to hold back. She and Joarr, while having decided to save the humans who had fumbled into this mess, weren't ready to reveal themselves to the dwarf.

So, her fun would have to be contained somewhat, yet again.

She sighed, but didn't let the realization totally fade her anticipation. A fight was a fight, after all.

Her bag open and her hand fumbling inside as if searching for a lipstick, she stopped directly in the group's path.

"Move," one of the dwarves grunted, and he slammed his shoulder into her hip.

She looked to the side. "That," she said, "was rude. Very, very rude." She placed her hand on his forehead and zapped him with as big a stream of power as she could get away with without drawing the attention of every being in the bar. He stopped, his mouth already open to utter some insulting comment back. His eyes widened, then fluttered. And without another noise, his eyes rolled back in his head and he fell backward with a rewarding thump.

The human couple jumped and stared down at the dwarf who had just landed on their toes.

The other two dwarves blinked and glanced at each other.

Amma smiled and tucked her purse back under her arm. "I hope it wasn't anything I said." Then before the remaining dwarves could move, she zapped them, too.

Three down—just two very stupid humans left. Amma flipped her hair over her shoulder and stared at the girl who had shoved and insulted her. "Remember me?"

The girl took a step back. Amma took a step forward. The heel of her boot caught on one of the downed dwarves' arms. That reminded her why she was here, and that the human, annoying as she was, was not her intended victim.

She sighed and pointed toward the stairs. "Now would be a good time to leave."

The female grabbed the man and they scurried for the exit. As they wove through the crowd, Amma scanned the room searching for Joarr. He was only a few feet from the trio now. Even in his dark clothes he stood out. He was taller and broader in the shoulders than any other male here, but it was more than that. Power, now that he'd loosened the control he kept on it, flowed from him. It was tangible. Amma could feel it, taste it, even smell it, and it attracted her like iron files to a magnet.

Her mouth suddenly dry, she went to join him.

She had no idea how the dwarves, how any of the beings in the room, could look at Joarr and not realize what he was. There, quite simply, was no one else to compare to him...in this room, in this world, anywhere.

Her fingers tightened around her bag, and she swallowed hard. Unhappy with the direction her thoughts had taken, she focused instead on Fafnir. He was still on his board, but it was lower now, hanging directly over the trio's heads, almost over Joarr's. He stood that close. The two girls and the boy were looking up at the dwarf talking and by the expression on their faces all at least seemed well.

But Amma knew that couldn't last. Intent on getting close before she missed out on any fun, she began weaving her way through the crowd.

Chapter 12

Joarr kept his head turned, watching the dwarf from the corner of his eye. Fafnir squatted on a board overhead, eyeing the man and woman who were dressed in Joarr's and Amma's discarded clothes. The girl who had been with them outside had been approached by a dark elf and gone off to dance. Leaving the pair alone with the dwarf and, based on the smiles on their faces, completely unaware of the potential danger.

Fafnir fingered his sleeve, where Joarr knew the dwarf had stored his blade. "What brings you to Tunnels?" he asked. He seemed to be more careful with this couple, more suspicious. He sniffed loudly and frowned. A furrow between his brows, his gaze darted over the crowd surrounding the couple.

Joarr tensed. Dwarves didn't have a sensitive sense of smell, not like forandre. There was no reason to believe Fafnir could discover that Joarr, a dragon, was hiding in plain sight so close by—but there was something about the way the little male twitched, the way his interest in the couple immediately began to fade, that made Joarr distinctly uncomfortable. Actually, there was something about the dwarf in general that didn't seem right. As a dragon, Joarr did have a good sense of smell and there was an odor, a brackish edge to the dwarf's scent, that did not fit.

Concentrating on the dwarf, Joarr didn't see Amma approach. He did, however, feel her. He turned, moving so his back was to Fafnir, blocking the dwarf's view of the witch. "All well?" he asked.

She tilted her head. "Could have been better, but yes, I guess it went well." Her gaze jumped to the dwarf. She frowned.

Joarr looked behind her, to the couch where he had left her. A group was gathering. A few knelt; the rest stared down as if something or someone lay on the ground. "You left them there?" he asked.

She shrugged. "Incinerating them was my first choice, but with the humans…" She made an annoyed motion with her hand.

He slid his arm around her waist. "Well, let's just hope our dwarf friend makes his move soon." He angled his head toward Fafnir, but she was already looking at him, the frown firmly in place.

The dwarf was standing again and scowling. "You're no dragon. Who are you?" he asked the male half of the couple.

"Dragon, dude. I am." The man lifted Joarr's shirt, revealing a dragon tattoo that wrapped around his torso. "Got it three weeks ago."

Fafnir's blade appeared in his hand. He swung his board forward and grabbed the man with stubby but powerful fingers by the back of his head. With the tip of his knife shoved under the man's chin, he said, "Who gave you my invitation?"

"Invitation?" The man's eyes had grown huge. His hand dropped, but his shirt stayed up, the tattooed dragon's head leering into the crowd. "What invitation?"

"There is something about him…" Amma shook her head, then held out one hand.

Joarr could tell she was doing something…feeling for something.

Wondering if what she had noticed was related to the dwarf's strange scent, Joarr waited for her to continue, but after a few seconds she shook her head and lowered her hand.

The dwarf pricked the skin under the man's chin with his blade. Blood ran down the man's neck. He yelped and jumped, but the dwarf held steady. His gaze locked on the tip of his blade, Fafnir held the knife up and studied how the blood ran down the metal. Then carefully, as if afraid to waste even a drop, he touched it to his tongue.

Fafnir spat. "Human." He twisted the man's hair and shoved the blade back against his throat. "You are no dragon."

This time the man didn't reply. Blood flowed down his neck and soaked into his white shirt, forming a red, glaring stain. His hands were at his sides and he rose on his tiptoes to keep Fafnir's blade from digging deeper into his skin.

"Should we...do something?" Amma murmured.

Joarr had been wondering the same thing. After stealing the couple's clothing, it hardly seemed right to let Fafnir dice them into tiny pieces.

"Fafnir!" A second dwarf stood on another hanging board, this one halfway across the bar, but in his hands were opera glasses and they were pointed at Fafnir.

Fafnir cursed and dropped his hold on the man's head. He wiped his knife on his pants and slipped it back into his sleeve in one easy movement. Without so much as a scowl at the man he'd almost skewered, he flipped off the board he'd been standing on and onto another. He repeated the move three more times before landing on the top of a bar at the back of the room.

The second dwarf yelled again, but Fafnir continued his trek, scurrying down the bar's length. A group of dark elves pulled back, sacrificing their beers as the dwarf kicked full mugs out of his way.

As he dropped to the ground behind a group of stalagmites, Joarr grabbed Amma by the hand, and with Amma clearing the way, they made their way through the crowd.

"What now?" They were next to the bar. One of the dark elves lay across the top, refilling his and his companions' mugs from the tap. When the human bartender approached, electricity flashed from the dark elf's hand. The bartender's gaze zipped to the weapon, then with studious care, his face went blank. He stared over the crowd—as if he couldn't see the one-hundred-fifty-pound male stretched across his bar, stealing the club's beer.

"Wonder what else he has learned to ignore?" Amma murmured.

"Hopefully, guests disappearing out the side door." Joarr held open a metal door that had been painted to match the stone-gray walls. "Fafnir must have gone out here."

The door opened and closed without so much as a click. And they were outside in what appeared to be an alley—dark, narrow and stinking of trash.

The door Joarr had opened led to an unlit alley. Amma glanced around, surprised her eyes had adjusted so quickly. Of course, it had been dark in the bar, so not that much of an adjustment. Still, it was a relief to be able to make out more than just shapes. She could see both Joarr in his dark clothes and the wheeled Dumpster that sat a few feet away.

Perhaps pregnancy was affecting her skills. If so she hoped this lasted past birth. She placed her hand on her stomach.

"Are you feeling well?" Joarr asked.

She started. "Yes, why?"

He shook his head. "Nothing, just…" He touched his own stomach with two fingers. "You do that a lot."

A lump formed in her throat. She laughed, low, little more than an expulsion of air. "Nervous habit."

There was a clank in the distance, then cursing. They both froze. Then without speaking they crept toward the noise.

Twenty feet down the alley there was another door. This one stood open. From inside there were more noises—someone rustling around.

"Has to be one. Has to be," Fafnir mumbled to himself.

Amma looked at Joarr. "What?" she mouthed.

He motioned her to the side, where a concrete portion of the building jutted out. Behind it, standing perfectly still, she would be invisible to the dwarf. She nodded and took her position. Beside her, Joarr disappeared—literally and suddenly. Her shock must have shown on her face. A hand grabbed hers, warm and full of power—dragon power. Joarr. He was still beside her; she just couldn't see him.

Another dragon skill she hadn't known of. She squeezed his hand, even as her mind whirred, and she wondered what other talents the dragon had—what he could possibly be capable of that she had yet to discover. She licked her lips and stared at the spot she knew Joarr had to be. She could see him then. He was still beside her, not invisible but just shrouded in fog that blended with the night, hid him from her and, hopefully, the dwarf's view.

He smiled and pointed upward.

For flying, he meant. How dragons managed to fly in their dragon forms without those below seeing them.

There was another crash from where Fafnir stood just out of view. "Damn Regin," the dwarf muttered. A can filled with what sounded like nails rolled out the doorway, followed by another can that fell open. The smell of wet paint filled the alley. A few seconds later, Fafnir appeared, a knapsack over one shoulder. He kicked both cans back in through the door and clicked the door closed. Then with the knapsack hitched higher on his shoulder, he took off down the alley. His short legs moved at a steady pace, but he didn't run.

Joarr and Amma waited, silently agreeing to let the dwarf get far enough ahead he wouldn't notice them behind him. When he was again twenty feet ahead, and his mumbles could only barely be heard, they stepped out of hiding.

"Are we still following?" Amma asked. Her instinct said they should, but she realized it was Joarr's game. And the dwarf was not acting as she'd expected—not that she knew what she'd expected, but this…mumbling to himself while rooting around in a dark alley…was definitely not anything she would have foreseen.

And while she wasn't sure it had registered with Joarr, she'd seen the dwarf's face when he'd gouged the human male in the neck with his knife, seen him lick the blade and heard his disgust when he had declared the male was not a dragon. She pressed her palms against her legs and darted her gaze around the alley. Fafnir had been alone, but she couldn't shake a growing feeling of unease.

None of this was normal. None of this made sense. And she was beginning to suspect none of it had anything to do with the chalice—but had everything to do with dragons and whatever the dwarf's plans were for them.

"We could go back to the club," she suggested, her voice low. "We didn't look around. I didn't get a chance to look for the Collector—if he's there, this—" she gestured to the end of the alley where Fafnir had disappeared from sight "—may all be unrelated and unnecessary."

Joarr cupped her chin in his hand. "Unrelated perhaps, but I doubt it. The dwarf is up to something."

Heat radiated from his hand into her body. She didn't know if he did it on purpose, or if it was something he couldn't control without concentrating. Either way, it relaxed her, like sinking into a tub filled with hot, scented water.

"And, I think he has a bit too much interest in dragons for me to stop now." Joarr leaned forward and breathed on her lips. She breathed in, pulled his heat and magic into her lungs. Joarr spoke again. "You, however, are right. I don't know where he is headed, but I doubt it is to this Collector. There's no reason for you to continue. Go back to the hotel. Wait for me."

Amma's knees weakened and her head nodded. Languid and content, she wanted nothing more than to go back to the hotel and curl up on the bed. His lips hovered over hers. "Go," he whispered.

She closed her eyes, almost drifting off for a second. "You want me to wait there?" she asked.

"Very much." His mouth was over hers now. Her head tilted toward him and her lips opened.

Wait. She could wait. Her body swayed and she could feel herself turning, or being turned. Being turned. The dragon was using his fire somehow to seduce her. Suddenly aware of what was happening, she jerked and stepped back, away from his touch and his heat.

She turned her back on him and walked away—following the dwarf.

Behind her, Joarr cursed.

Within seconds, he was beside her. "You don't have to go," he muttered. "This isn't your problem."

She didn't reply. Her steps quiet but determined, they walked on, leaving the alley and turning onto a street.

There were streetlights now, but they were dimmed by the mist that had clouded down around them. Amma's clothes clung to her; she was cold and damp.

Joarr snagged her hand as it swung at her side and wove his fingers through hers.

The heat was back, just as strong, just as relaxing, but this time confidence instead of languor came with it. He pressed his fingers against the back of her hand, and she pressed back.

It might not seem like her problem. Fafnir might not be heading toward the chalice or the Collector. But there was no way she was turning back, no way she was leaving Joarr to discover what the dwarf was up to alone.

Chapter 13

A light above them hissed and went out. A rat scurried across their path.

Joarr gripped Amma's hand tighter. There was no reason for the witch to be here, but despite his efforts to get her to leave, to go back to the hotel and be safe, she'd insisted on staying with him.

And for now, he wasn't going to question her motive. He was just going to concentrate on doing what she wouldn't do for herself—keeping her safe—and on discovering what the dwarf was up to.

Joarr had no idea what they were walking into. He believed the dwarf didn't know they were behind them, just as he believed what he had told Amma—that whatever the dwarf was up to it didn't involve her. It did, however, involve dragons.

He was beginning to suspect both notes—not just the one delivered to their hotel room, but the original one that Rike had shown him, as well—were nothing but a ruse. A trick to lure a dragon to the dwarf.

If so, why?

He was fairly sure he was about to find out.

Amma and Joarr had followed the dwarf through the streets for ten minutes now, keeping far enough back so Fafnir wouldn't hear or see them. Their caution, however, seemed unnecessary. Fafnir didn't look anywhere but straight ahead, not even when a cat jumped in front of him and knocked over a metal trash can. He was focused, one-hundred-percent focused, on wherever he was going.

In the ten minutes of walking, the scenery hadn't changed a lot. Old warehouses still lined the streets. They were newer, however, than the building that had been converted into the bar. These weren't brick, but were constructed instead from some human-made prefab material.

Fafnir stopped in front of one and glanced around. Still, the caution seemed at most cursory. He pulled a key from his pocket, approached a dented metal door and jiggled the key in the lock. With a creak the door opened and Fafnir disappeared inside.

"Follow or wait?" Amma asked. Her fingers dug into Joarr's arm. He could feel her tension.

He was tense, too, with anticipation. It was obvious the dwarf was hiding something here, something he didn't even want the other dwarves from the bar to discover.

"Follow," Joarr said. "But quietly." The last was an unnecessary add-on, but he didn't want the dwarf to discover them yet. Not because he was afraid—that idea was ludicrous—but because he didn't know yet if his quest stopped here. If as Joarr expected the chalice wasn't inside, he would still need to watch the dwarf without Fafnir realizing it. No matter what he found inside this warehouse, Rike and the Ormar would still be expecting Joarr to return with the chalice.

The door opened into a small room that looked like a reception area. There were offices, constructed of thin partitions, off to one side. A few yards ahead of them, out of Joarr's sight, another door opened and started to creak closed. With Amma close behind, he followed, managing to shove his foot in the still-open doorway before it clicked shut. He and Amma slipped inside the room. Then he guided the door to make sure it eased closed silently.

Once it was shut behind them, they assessed their surroundings.

The space was huge and open, like an airplane hangar. It was obviously the main room of the ware-house, but there were no shelves, no boxes—nothing but the little dwarf and the prone form of a full-size dragon.

"Fuck," Amma swore, but in a whisper.

Joarr couldn't even say that. He was too shocked, too appalled and too aware that the dragon was not only dead, he was Rike's missing nephew.

Fafnir turned.

Joarr pushed Amma toward the ground. They crouched behind a forgotten forklift.

Fafnir pulled a battery-powered lantern from his pack and set it on the concrete floor. Then he bent to shuffle inside some more. When he stood, he held a dagger and a flask—just like the one the dwarf outside the portal had carried.

Fafnir stepped forward and ran his hand over the fallen dragon's skin.

"Is he…?" Amma whispered.

"He's dead," Joarr confirmed. "Dragons don't decompose like other beings when they die. We don't decompose at all."

"So, how do you…?"

"Fire. Dragons' funerals are all rites of fire." The words were solemn; Joarr was solemn. He'd known dragons had died recently, known this one was missing, but seeing him lying there forgotten—for how long?—made it all real. Bile rose in his throat.

"What's the dwarf doing?" Amma wiggled on her heels, apparently trying to get a better view of Fafnir from behind the forklift.

The dwarf was done stroking the boy's form. He held his dagger now, tip down, and thrust it into his flesh. The smell of blood, thick with metals, filled Joarr's senses.

"He's…" Amma turned her head and closed her eyes.

Joarr glanced back at the dwarf. He stood with his lips pressed against the wound he'd created. His tongue curled out again and again, lapping at the blood that oozed from the dragon's body.

"He's drinking it…" Joarr didn't move. He'd never imagined this. He'd seen Fafnir taste the human's blood at the bar, seen his anger when the dwarf realized the man wasn't a dragon, but it hadn't occurred to him—

"Why? Why would he do that? I've never heard…

Do beings do that? Do they drink dragon blood?" The horror was clear in Amma's voice.

Joarr shook his head. "Not that I've heard of, but then, the chalice…"

"Protected you," Amma finished.

"No." Joarr shook his head. He'd been thinking the same thing, but he wouldn't…couldn't believe it. The legend of the chalice wasn't true. If the dwarf had developed a taste for dragon blood it wasn't because the dragons had lost the chalice; it was simply bad timing.

"What's he doing now?" she asked.

"Filling the flask." Joarr's fingers tightened on the forklift's metal body. He wanted to stop the dwarf. Stop the sacrilege his fellow dragon was being submitted to, but he knew Rike's nephew was past feeling, past caring, and to honor his memory Joarr had to keep his head, had to do what Rike had asked of him. He had to find the chalice. Suddenly the job seemed real and important.

It took the dwarf a half hour to fill his flask; the blood flowed slowly. When he was done, he screwed on the lid and carefully, lovingly placed it inside his bag. Then with one last lick of his tongue over the gash he'd created in the dragon's skin, he walked out the door.

Joarr and Amma stayed behind the forklift until they heard the door bang closed and the key turn in the lock.

Amma stepped out first. She glanced toward the dragon's corpse, but seemed unwilling to move closer. "Is that… Do you think Fafnir sent those dwarves? Were they trying to gather your blood?"

Staring at the body and thinking of how he would

tell Rike, it took Joarr a moment to answer. "So it would seem."

"So, the chalice… Is it all coincidence? Is it not here at all?" Amma rubbed her hands over her arms as if she was cold, which she very likely was, dressed as she was in the skimpy skirt and shirt of the club girl.

Joarr closed the space between them and pulled her into his arms. Then he stood there, heat flowing from his body into hers, silence settling around them. She pressed her face into his chest and her heart beat against him. It was good, having her there with him. He didn't want to be alone right then; didn't know if he could do what had to be done without her by him.

He sighed, then tilted her face up so he could stare into her eyes. "I can't leave him here like this, not for the dwarf to feed on again. Will you help me?"

Her lips parted; she thought to say no. He could see that the events had shaken her, would have shaken anyone…they were that unnatural. But she nodded. "Just tell me what to do."

First they examined the body. It was difficult, both physically and emotionally. But it had to be done. Joarr needed to know what had killed the young male. Unfortunately after studying every inch of the dragon's body, they could find nothing more than a few old battle scars and the wound Fafnir had inflicted on the body as they watched.

"So, what killed him?" Amma asked.

Joarr didn't answer. There was no answer. It was exactly as Rike had told him. No mark of a hero's sword, no sign of being blasted by some as-yet-unknown force—nothing. The dragon was just dead. But dragons didn't just die—they hadn't, until now.

With a shake of his head, he waved off Amma's question and concentrated instead on what little he could do to provide the boy's family with comfort.

He couldn't haul the boy home, but he could save him from further insult at the dwarf's...or anyone else's...hands. He could perform the burial ceremony himself—or try to.

Joarr didn't have the firepower to incinerate an entire dragon alone. Feeling both tired and antsy, he explained to Amma that she would have to convert her magic to fire, too. Together they would convert the boy's body to nothing but ash—hopefully without destroying the human neighborhood around them.

Amma didn't hesitate. She nodded her head and waited expectantly. He led her to the dragon's middle, where the boy's own fire should still be stored. He placed her hand on the body's stomach, where he wanted her to aim her power. They stood there for a second, the silence in the warehouse seeming to grow around them, swallow them. Then he stepped back.

Amma's magic would act as an igniter while Joarr actually set other parts of the body aflame.

With Amma waiting, he converted to dragon form. He towered over her, barely fitting inside the huge open space. She looked small and fragile. Seeing her standing by the dead boy sent a chill through Joarr. Dragons weren't supposed to die... If something had downed this strong, healthy male, how could the witch be safe? He wished she'd listened to him and gone back to the hotel...but he needed her, too, needed her power to do what had to be done, needed her support to get through finding the boy like this.

He straightened his wings and fought the need to shriek his anger and outrage.

Now he knew why the dwarf had a brackish scent, knew the source—dragon blood. There was no telling how much the dwarf had consumed.

Was Rike's nephew the first? Or were the other two boys this dwarf's victims, too?

Joarr couldn't sort it out now—but he would. His mission had changed, grown bigger. He didn't just need the chalice. He needed revenge, too.

He flapped his wings. His feet lifted slightly off the floor. He hung there and pulled air into his lungs, held it until he saw that Amma was ready.

Together, they let loose with their powers. Fire burned from Joarr's lungs, up his throat and out of his lips—fire hotter than any he had ever created before. As it burst from inside him, he realized the danger— that Amma wasn't a dragon, that he had no idea what temperatures her body could withstand. Panic flashed. His eyes darted toward her, but she stood strong, magic flowing from her palms and not so much as a bead of sweat forming on her brow.

White, then blue magic streamed out of her. She kept her attention directed where Joarr had told her—at the dragon's center, his core where he created fire, where hopefully pure magic like the witch's would ignite the dormant flames.

The boy's tail took fire first; the skin was dry there. It crackled up his spine, creeping toward his center where Amma waited.

Joarr tensed, but Amma seemed unaware, was too focused on her part of the job to sense things might soon shift out of control. Her magic continued to pound into the boy's core, didn't seem to weaken and neither did she. Her feet were braced and her face was determined.

She wouldn't stop, not until the job was done; Joarr could sense that—but he'd let her do enough, let her risk enough. He wouldn't risk any more. He rose on his wings, as high as the building's roof would allow him, and bent down toward her. His feet wrapped around her middle.

She glanced up. Surprise was clear on her face. He curled his legs, held her safe and hidden beneath his body. Then, cloaking himself in clouds, he rose and crashed through the roof. Below, the boy's body glowed. Amma's magic was doing its job; the fire in the boy's belly was obvious now. It burned like a hot coal. But it wasn't enough, not quick enough.

Amma still held safe against his stomach, Joarr dived headfirst toward the building. Fire shooting out of his throat, he targeted the boy's core like a laser.

Without warning, before Joarr could pull back, the boy's body erupted into one massive explosion of heat and fire.

Amma felt Joarr dive, felt the heat as it flew from his throat. She clung to his feet, strong and wiry, like a bird. She wasn't afraid. She should be. She'd always had an aversion to heights, but she knew the dragon wouldn't drop her and wouldn't allow her to burn. With

Joarr holding her, no matter what happened around them, she knew she would be safe.

There was a roar. Joarr, she thought at first, then no, she realized it was the dragon they'd left behind, his body, anyway. With Joarr's last dive, he'd pushed the heat building in the corpse over the edge. The body exploded, the heat so intense there was nothing but heat… and fire. She could see it shooting around her, could feel waves lapping at her.

It should have hurt, should have scorched her lungs as she breathed in, but it didn't. Instead it felt right— as if she belonged here in the middle of the firestorm, riding the waves of heat like a surfer mastering the ocean.

Joarr listed to the side, but quickly righted himself. They circled, hidden she knew by the clouds. He stayed there hidden, flying above the city, watching the fire burn.

"It's beautiful," Amma thought to herself.

"But deadly." Joarr's voice was in her mind.

She started, although she shouldn't have. All forandre could speak telepathically when not in human form. But, this was more—he'd answered her, too. Answered words she hadn't spoken.

Joarr smiled; she could feel the smile as if that, too, had been projected into her mind. "The last of my secrets, witch. How about you—do you have any to share?"

Amma's eyes rounded. Her secret… She clamped down on her thoughts, concentrated on the fire, only the fire.

"Hmm," the dragon whispered in her mind. "What are you hiding?"

Thankfully, at that moment, sirens filled the night. Joarr shifted again, flew lower, closer rather than farther from the fire. He tilted so his head was again pointed at the ground. "What do you see, Amma? Is it safe to put out our fire?"

Their fire—and it was. They had created this together. A sense of pride washed over Amma. She had never created something this big, this astounding before.

"The humans are almost here. Let's hope our creation has done enough." Joarr opened his jaws again; cold air filled the space over the warehouse. Joarr flipped again, shot upward, then righted them both so Amma could see what was happening below.

The cloud of icy air hit the hot cloud billowing from the fire. Rain erupted—big, fat drops that drenched the warehouse and its neighboring buildings. Fire engines shrieked to a stop on the street beside it. Firemen scrambled from their trucks like bright yellow ants, jerking equipment and yelling orders—but the fire was already under control and the dragon who had lain inside the building nothing but ash.

Joarr turned and soared over the city. The night was almost over; the first tinges of morning showed on the horizon.

"Where to now, witch?"

Where to... She was comfortable right here, flying above the city, confident that Joarr wouldn't let her fall.

"The hotel or your home? I've asked enough of you.

You've done enough. I'll find the Collector and the chalice on my own."

Without allowing herself to think, she replied, "I have no home. I told you that."

"That you did. So, where?" There was tension in his voice, as if her answer was important to him, as if she would be making a declaration or a choice when she made it.

And maybe she was.

"The hotel, but a new one without visiting dwarves."

Joarr laughed. "Yes, I agree. I'm done with dwarves... for tonight."

For tonight. She was done with them, too. Done with everything except Joarr. Tomorrow things might be different. They might be back where they were before, but for now, for tonight, it was just about her and her dragon.

Chapter 14

Back in his human form, Joarr checked them into a hotel—one he had located while flying over the city. Unlike the last place, paying by the hour wasn't an option and the desk clerk didn't talk to him through a glass window. The clerk did, however, stare past him at Amma still in her club-girl outfit with a look of distaste on his face.

When he shifted, Joarr had replaced his tight dark outfit with his normal wardrobe—all white pants, shirt and shoes. He hadn't been sorry to see the other clothes go, but now seeing how the desk clerk looked at Amma, he wished he'd stayed in them.

Joarr leaned forward, his palm on the reception desk's marble top. "Is there a problem?" he asked. He held the man's gaze, dared him to challenge him.

Fear darted through the clerk's eyes. He shook his

head and gazed down, sliding two key cards toward the dragon.

With the cards in his pocket, Joarr slid his arm around Amma's waist and led her onto the elevator.

Joarr's arm ran around Amma's back, his skin touching hers where her shirt rode up. Two women, obviously fresh back from a jog, entered the elevator with them—right before the doors slid closed.

Amma bit her lip and tried not to look at them. Tried to keep herself from thinking too much about what she was doing and feeling.

While she and Joarr had flown over the city, she'd felt nothing but elation. She'd known she wanted nothing but to be with him, didn't care what else was going on, what she had to lose.

But now, after being left alone for even a few seconds in the hotel's cold lobby, feeling the desk clerk's judgmental gaze, reality was crashing back around her.

She was crazy. What she was feeling was crazy. Yes, she might want Joarr physically, find him powerful and exciting, but that was it—and was that worth risking her secret?

He could read thoughts. She went cold. Could he read them now? He'd said it was only when in his dragon form, but what if he had lied? And even if that were true, he could shift without warning, could read her mind and discover why she'd agreed to help him—exactly what treasure she wanted from him in payment.

And then what? He wouldn't just walk away from... She stopped herself from thinking the word. He wouldn't. Not with his past. Her secret. He would want it as his own, and the entire dragon army would support his claim—unless she could find the chalice and officially have Joarr declare the pick of his treasure was hers.

The elevator doors opened and the women walked off.

Joarr spun her in his arms.

"You didn't leave," he murmured.

"I couldn't." It was the truth—she didn't know why, but she couldn't leave him.

"And the fire didn't burn you." He ran his hands down her face, his thumbs brushing over her cheekbones. "Maybe you truly are indestructible."

He was referring to everything the elves had done to her body, when they tried to destroy it—but he was wrong, she wasn't indestructible. At least not all of her. She suddenly realized just how vulnerable part of her was.

Her mind swirling, she tried to step away, but he stopped her, placed a hand on each side of her head and stared down into her eyes. "You didn't run before. Why would you now?"

This time he was right. As much as she knew she should, she couldn't run from him, not now. She placed her hands on his chest and stared up at him. Without shifting his gaze from hers, he reached out and flipped the elevator to off. An alarm squealed.

He leaned down and blew hot air over her neck. Then ran his hand down her shoulder. The torn T-shirt slipped lower, baring her collarbone. He traced it with his tongue.

The alarm blared again.

"Maybe we should…" He leaned as if to switch the elevator back on, but Amma grabbed his arm, stopping him.

"No. I have a better idea." Power flowed from her palm; she blasted the switch. When the noise didn't stop, she aimed her hand right then left, taking out the entire panel.

Silence—sweet, golden silence—followed.

"Now." She turned back to Joarr. "What were we doing?"

Joarr pulled Amma back into his arms, and ran his hands over her back and down her hips. With her against him, held tight, he let his magic and fire flow. He stared into her eyes, snapping now with power. "This," he said. Then he closed his eyes and lowered his lips to hers.

She moved against him, her hands wandering over his chest, pulling his shirt free from his pants. Her movements were quick, almost frenzied, but he felt the need, too, knew if she had let him flip that switch, restart the elevator, he would have died, or at least alarmed a few hotel guests. He couldn't have waited to get to their room to touch her.

"I stopped the alarm, but someone's going to notice the elevator isn't working," she murmured against his lips.

"Let them notice," he replied. His fingers found the bottom of her skirt, which barely covered her butt. He pulled it up, baring more skin. There were mirrors on the walls and ceiling; even the polished metal doors reflected their image back at him, giving him a full view of skin and the white lace panties that barely covered any of it. He cupped her buttocks, kneaded them, his gaze never leaving her reflection.

Her skin was soft, her butt firm. He loved that, loved feeling the power in her whether from magic or muscle. His erection did, too; already painfully hard, it shifted in appreciation.

"You look so helpless, but you're not. You know that?" he whispered against her ear.

He expected her to agree, to claim it all was an act that she'd perfected over time, but she didn't reply. Instead she shook her head as if shaking some thought from her brain, then her hands flat on his chest, she shoved him against the elevator wall and pulled at his clothes. Buttons popped off his crisp shirt and pinged against the mirrors.

She pushed his shirt open and shoved it off his shoulders. He was forced to release her, but only for the second it took to jerk his arms free of the sleeves. Then his hands were back on her hips, pulling her higher so her sex rubbed against his and his tongue tangled with hers.

Her arms went around his neck and he shifted his hands, too—to push her shirt up and over her head. He dropped it onto the floor, waited as she reached behind her back and unsnapped her bra. He stood still, his back pressed against the corner of the car, his hands on the metal bar that circled the small room—like a fighter waiting for his turn in the ring.

Her bra fell forward; her breasts, ivory mounds tipped with rose, tumbled out. She held the strip of white lace and elastic to the side, then dropped it to join her shirt on the floor.

She ran her hands up her own stomach and over her breasts, stretching as she touched herself, as if offering herself to him. Her nipples peeking through her open fingers, she looked at him. Her eyes were wide and innocent, but what she offered was so obviously not.

He groaned and his erection jumped.

She licked two fingers, then touched her nipples again, caused the tips to harden.

He hardened, too—even more, so much that he couldn't move, could only stand there waiting for her to come closer.

With a smile she did, her hips swaying—reminding him what was under that skirt, how much he wanted to remove it, see her in her delicate lace panties, her borrowed kick-ass boots and nothing more. As if reading his thoughts, she stopped and placed her thumbs under the waistband. She wiggled, causing the skirt to slip down and her breasts to bounce.

He swallowed. Fire was building inside him; he fought to keep it contained. One building incinerated today was enough.

She wiggled again; the skirt inched lower. He could see the curve of her stomach and the strip of lace that kept her panties in place. Another wiggle and the skirt fell. She stepped free, then turned and bent over slowly to pick it up. Giving him a clear view of ass, thigh and boot.

He grabbed onto the polished steel bar. Heat from his fingers softened the metal; he could feel it crimping and didn't care. Still bent over, Amma looked up.

She caught his gaze in the mirror across from him, then stood, her hands again caressing her own curves.

Her hands at her sides, she turned and walked toward him—strong and confident in nothing but that tiny slip of white lace and black thigh-high boots.

"How do I look now?" she asked.

He didn't answer. There were no words. Instead he grabbed her by the ass and spun, sat her in the corner propped on the bar. She draped her arms over his shoulders and stared into his eyes.

He kissed her. Heat exploded inside him, roared. His tongue tangled with hers and she fought back, shoved her fingers into his hair and leaned closer. His hands cupped her breasts, his thumbs caressing the nipples she'd touched and teased him with.

She ran her fingers down his back, her nails scratching, her power snapping.

He pulled his lips from hers and found her breasts. He pulled her nipple into his mouth and flicked his tongue over it. A shudder passed through her body; she dug her nails into his back. A hiss escaped her lips. He moved to the side, repeated his attentions on the other breast. Still perched on the bar, she wiggled. Her sex, concealed by nothing but the thin lace, brushed against him. Her hand lowered, found the bulge threatening to burst through his pants. She stroked him through the material. He sucked in a breath and pressed against her. She moved her lips to his ear, nibbled his lobe and blew hot, almost fiery breath along his neck.

Not magic. Fire. She had fire. The thought barely had time to form. Her fingers found the zipper of his pants and his sex sprang forward. She wrapped her fingers around him, rubbed his tip against the rough lace that concealed her core.

He sucked in a breath, let the fire that had been building in him grow even more. He reached for her panties, jerked the tiny strip of cloth free so she was naked, open and ready.

He shifted so he could stroke her folds with his fingers, test the intensity of her heat. She was wet and hot. Dragon-hot.

She murmured and moved, her shoulders pressing against the wall, her breasts jutting upward. In the mirror above he could see her, all of her—breasts, her stomach and the curls that covered her sex. He stroked her there, watched as she twisted in pleasure. Her breasts were flushed, her curls damp. The scent of their lovemaking filled the small room.

He shoved three fingers inside her and brushed his thumb over her nub. She grabbed the bar then his shoulders and called out. Her eyes flew open—blue and intense with emotion, pleasure, fear... He couldn't read them all. She turned her head to the side and wiggled again, reached down and stroked his hand. Touched herself, too.

His sex jumped. He shoved his pants to the floor and stepped back. Let her look at him as he had looked at her. Her hands clung to the smooth walls; her feet still encased in the high-heeled boots were braced on the wall below the bar—keeping her naked form pushed against the corner.

Her legs open, she touched herself again. Her fingers brushed over her curls, parted them. Moisture glistened on her skin. She stroked her folds, dipped deeper and circled the nub. Her lips parted, moist, too. Her eyes widened, and still stroking herself, she held out her free hand, called for him to come and join her.

She didn't need to ask twice. Standing close, he swept his hand down her body. She radiated heat. He responded, releasing new heat of his own. Her legs wrapped around his waist, the leather of her boots cool against his backside. His sex nudged against hers, and unable to wait, he positioned himself to plunge inside her.

She clung to his shoulders. He placed his hands under her thighs, but she did the work, raising and lowering her body. She pressed her face against his neck and flicked tongue over his skin, tasting him. He wanted to taste her, too. He swirled his tongue over the skin between her breasts, savored the saltiness of it. He inhaled; she still smelled of spring—of sun-warmed earth.

He slid his hands up and down her thighs, encouraging her as she moved. Her speed increased; their fire increased. And the fire was theirs this time, something they had created together. There was no sharing; they were past that. This heat was from both of them and from neither of them—it was just theirs.

Her speed increased and he helped her along, raising and lowering his arms to increase the depth of each plunge. Ragged breaths left her lips; puffs of smoke escaped his. Fire tickled at his throat, threatened to erupt.

Her head fell back and her body arched. The walls inside her constricted, hugging him with such sweet pressure he did explode. She shuddered again and again. His arms trembled; his body trembled. Then when he knew his fire was exhausted, they were exhausted, he pulled her tight against him and enveloped her in heat.

Chapter 15

Amma didn't want to move. Being curled around Joarr's body felt right, more right than anywhere she had ever been. Even naked, except for her borrowed thigh-high boots, in an elevator, she felt good.

Still, she had to move. This moment couldn't last. She couldn't pretend forever, couldn't block out reality forever.

Joarr pressed a kiss against her shoulder. A sweet touch of his lips. So in contrast to the frenzied way she'd attacked him. She smiled.

He'd said she looked delicate, although he knew she wasn't. It was a compliment, she supposed, but it had lit something inside her, a need to show how strong and unrepentant she could be. She'd wanted him, and she'd let him know. She wanted her baby and she would have him. Him she could keep, but only if she kept his existence from Joarr.

Joarr she could only have for now, and she'd decided to make the most of it.

He lifted her off the bar she'd been perched on. Her legs slid down his hips and thighs until her feet touched the ground.

From somewhere above them there was a bang, then someone pounding—with the flat of their hand against the closed elevator shaft's door.

"They found us," Joarr murmured.

"Yes." Amma sighed and bent to retrieve her clothing. Without glancing at Joarr, she pulled them on—except the panties. They were nothing but a scrap now. She tucked them into her bra. When she looked back, Joarr was dressed, too, or as dressed as he could get without shifting and creating a new wardrobe. With buttons littering the floor, his shirt hung open.

He looked wild and raw—not at all the under-control male he normally presented himself as. His hair was ruffled and she could see the muscles of his chest. She wanted to touch them—again. But she folded her hand closed and forced herself to keep it at her side.

His pants, she realized, weren't completely closed, either. The button that had joined the waistband had disappeared, too, revealing a V of skin. Hair that was sprinkled across his chest condensed into a line there— like an arrow pointing lower, reminding her what they had done and with how much abandon she had embraced the act.

There was another noise, louder than those before, then voices.

"Are you okay down there? We'll have you out in a jiffy."

She looked at Joarr. His eyes were shadowed, unsure. He held out a hand.

She stared at it for a second; after what they had shared, taking his hand, accepting his support should have been nothing, but it wasn't. Somehow it was far more intimate than anything else they had done in this space.

There was a jolt of movement, then a grinding noise. The car jerked, then jerked again. Amma teetered on her borrowed heels. Joarr's hand stayed where it had been, his offer apparently still open.

Another jerk and she laid her palm against his.

Slowly, he pulled her against his chest, and the heat, sweet, welcoming heat, was back.

She sighed and relaxed against him.

It was just for a few minutes. It didn't mean she was falling for him, didn't mean it would hurt when she had to walk away.

After the elevator was ratcheted up even with the floor and the door pried open, Joarr had led Amma through the waiting crowd of workmen and hotel employees. He'd waved aside the manager, whose practice at hiding his true thoughts showed as he apologized for the inconvenience and insisted both lunch in their room and the room itself were free.

Once past the gaping humans, Joarr had lifted Amma into his arms and taken the stairs to their floor. She hadn't objected. In fact since her reluctance to take his hand in the elevator, she'd done nothing but snuggle closer to him. He enjoyed the feeling of her clasped against his body, enjoyed warming her with his heat.

But he also knew something besides sex had happened in that elevator. She'd gone into the act with complete abandon, then stared at his offered hand, her eyes wide with fear. Of him? Of the people waiting? Or of what had passed between them?

He guessed the latter, because it had shaken him, too. Amma shook him. He had never felt this way before—didn't think he was supposed to feel this way.

Dragons didn't take mates. He knew other forandre did, but dragons didn't. It was unheard of, but he couldn't imagine walking away and leaving Amma—not now.

Joarr had rebelled before. Hell, he was known for it, but this? The Ormar wouldn't stand for it. Male and female dragons did not live together, did not make lives together.

If he tried to, the Ormar would do what Rike had threatened, take everything—his home, his cavern and his treasure— doom him to life as a wyrm. Would Amma want him then? He knew the answer.

Inside the room now, he set Amma down. She didn't look at him. She wandered to the window instead and looked out.

"It's a nicer part of town at least," she murmured.

"Yes."

"I'll need clothes."

"Yes."

Silence settled around them.

Amma pulled her hand away from the curtain and ran a hand through her hair.

It was wild and golden and alive, like the fire he knew was inside her.

Dragon fire. He didn't know how it was possible, but he knew Amma had it. Did she know?

"When you took the chalice, you traded it to the Collector. For what?" He knew the answer. He'd figured it out; after she'd left him she'd gone to Alfheim, claimed to be half elf. They hadn't welcomed her, had actually denied her claims. A war had broken out between her and Alfheim, a war that ended in her being separated from her body and her spirit sent to Gunngar.

"Information," she replied. She wandered to the bed and traced her fingers over the quilted comforter.

"On your family," he added.

She looked up, surprised. "Yes. He gave me their names."

"Did it occur to you he might be lying?"

Her head jerked and her shoulders stiffened. "Why would he do that?"

Joarr shrugged. "Maybe he didn't have the answer." Or maybe he did and was afraid if he told her the truth she wouldn't give him what he wanted—wouldn't give him a chalice tied to the dragons.

Back in his office, Fafnir sat behind his desk and poured the dragon blood he had harvested into a mundane tumbler. He stared at the glass. This was it, the last bit of blood. His flask had been damaged when the warehouse had exploded. He'd lost over half of what he had taken, and all that had still been waiting inside the dragon's corpse. He pressed his index fingers to the bridge of his nose, trying to stop the pain that threatened to split his head in two.

He should ration the blood, but after seeing what

had happened, after being thrown to his knees by the explosion and feeling the heat, he needed the reassuring strength of this drink—more than just the one sip a day he allowed himself from the chalice.

He picked up the glass and sipped.

A smile curved his lips. The taste was the same as from the chalice. He set the glass back down and waited for the warm zing of power to surge through his body.

It didn't. His fingers tightened around the glass and he glanced at the mirror and the safe hidden behind it. The chalice was empty and waiting...and he had blood.

He'd had his sip for the day, but how bad could an extra sip be? Besides, this was old blood. The warning had been for new.

He gritted his teeth. The temptation was like a physical pain, an ache deep in his core.

His fingers tightened even more. The glass cracked, then snapped. Dragon blood spilled over his fingers and onto the papers covering his desk.

He stared at it, horrified. His blood, his glorious blood. It was gone...all of it.

He picked up the empty flask and flung it across the room. The few last drops of blood hidden inside splattered against his wall.

He cursed and swiped his arm across his desk, sent the bloodstained papers and the shards of glass onto the floor.

He couldn't live like this. He had to get more blood—new blood from a new dragon that he could drink from the chalice.

He stalked to the mirror, his hand automatically

reaching for the latch. Then he dropped his hand to his side. First the dragon. He had to find the dragon.

He paced back and forth in the small space between his desk and the mirror.

A dragon had taken his bait, come through the portal into the human world, but then something had gone wrong. It was clear neither of the couples the previous evening had been dragons—they were nothing, humans. He pulled his dagger from his sleeve and slammed it into the back of his office door.

Shaking with frustration, he resumed his pacing. Calm. He needed to calm, needed to think. The dragon was near. He had to be.

And he hadn't got what he'd come for yet—Fafnir still had the chalice. The dwarf glanced at the mirror. He was tempted to check, even though he had looked at the artifact just moments earlier, but he shook his unease off.

He didn't have time for weakness. He needed to find that dragon.

A dragon and a female—where could they be?

Amma awoke, warm and content. She pushed her arm up over her head and stretched. Beside her there was a mumble; then an arm tightened around her waist and pulled her snug against a strong male chest.

She purred and snuggled deeper under the covers, tighter against Joarr...

Joarr.

Amma stiffened, then pulled his arm free of her waist and rolled to her feet beside the bed.

She rubbed her eyes and blinked, earlier events returning to her.

After they'd made their way to the room, she'd been tired and confused. She'd lain down on the bed to give herself time to think, and she must have fallen asleep.

She'd slept soundly, more soundly than she could ever remember sleeping before. And she'd dreamed. She never dreamed, but last night...today—it had been morning by the time she'd fallen asleep—she had. And her dreams had been good, pleasant even. She'd been curled in front of a fire, the heat lapping against her skin. Animal furs, soft and luxurious, had caressed her. The room had been dark, nothing to be seen beyond the light of the fire, but it had smelled of spice, exotic, enticing spice.

A lot, she realized now, like Joarr.

She ran her hands over her arms, tried to wipe away the temptation to crawl back into the bed and under the covers beside him.

She had almost lost the battle when there was a knock on the door.

The dragon didn't stir.

Through the peephole she could see two men in hotel uniforms. One pushing a room-service cart, the other with a hanging bag draped over his arm.

Her magic ready, in case it was a trap, she opened the door and stood to the side for the men to enter. They were in and out within minutes. The entire time the dragon didn't stir, not even when she fumbled through his discarded clothes looking for something she could pass off as a tip.

Two bags of gold powder seemed to do the trick. As

the employees left happy, if confused, she snapped the door shut behind them and hurried back into the room where hopefully new clothing awaited.

Joarr had moved. He was sitting now, propped on a pillow, his chest bare and his gaze following each of her movements. Her hand on the hanging bag, which the valet had left on a chair, she stilled.

"Not hungry?" he asked.

She pushed the cart toward him. "You go ahead. I need to…shower and change." And escape. She needed to escape. Her time with Joarr was changing her, weakening her.

He flung his legs over the side of the bed. They, like his chest, were bare. The covers hid his midsection, keeping her from knowing if the rest of his body was similarly unclothed. She dropped her gaze to the bag's zippered closure. With it open, she pulled new outfits from inside.

Joarr's was white, of course, and of fine material— dress pants and a sweater. She laid them on the foot of the bed and turned back to the bag. She expected another fancy dress, in white, or something else fitting what was obviously Joarr's taste. Instead she found jeans and an embroidered peasant blouse. The material was higher quality than her own had been and the embroidery hand-stitched, but it was her—everything she loved and would have chosen for herself.

She crumpled the clothing in her hands, not sure how to react.

"You didn't seem comfortable in the other," Joarr murmured. "Is this better?"

Better? Perfect.

Amma nodded.

He was out of bed, standing beside her. She hadn't heard him move, but there was no missing him now that he was only inches away.

He ran a hand down her arm. Heat flowed into her, through her. "Go shower. I'll keep your food warm."

And she did. She ran. At least in her mind she was running. She was fairly certain her body left the room at a semi-reasonable pace.

Once inside the bathroom, she turned on the water and willed her mind to slow. It was okay. She could handle this. If she ran away now, she'd leave with Joarr and the dragons still having a claim on her baby.

Perhaps Fafnir didn't have the chalice. Perhaps the notes had just been ploys to lure a dragon to him, but she didn't know that yet. She had to find out.

The image of Fafnir licking blood from the dragon corpse's wound flitted through her mind, causing her to shiver.

It couldn't be safe for Joarr to face the dwarf.

She should convince him to give up, to forget the chalice and return to his stronghold—but he wouldn't. She'd seen his face. It wasn't just about the chalice anymore.

And she still needed the dragons' cup to seal their bargain.

So, what to do? Fafnir was their only lead. She had to talk to him. Then she could leave and let Joarr seek his revenge or not, let him endanger his life or not. She couldn't worry about that, couldn't let herself.

Joarr leaned against the bed's headrest. He'd let Amma talk him into allowing her to go to the club alone tonight—or let her think she had. He, of course, didn't plan to let her visit with Fafnir alone and unprotected.

She'd argued that she could get close to the dwarf without him becoming suspicious, learn if he truly had the chalice and, if not, what his game was.

Her plan was a good one, but it didn't meet with Joarr's satisfaction. Not even slightly.

The dwarf and his dragon-blood-drinking habits were Joarr's problem, his danger to face.

He wouldn't let Amma face the dwarf alone.

But she had been adamant, so adamant, he'd had to wonder at her motive. She'd been with him, seen the dead boy in his dragon form. If the dwarf could down a dragon in his youth, what could he do to a witch?

Unless the witch knew she had nothing to fear... unless she was working with the dwarf.

Despite their lovemaking and despite the fact that he was in danger of falling for her, Joarr couldn't put aside the suspicion. Amma was too eager to get back to the club, too eager to talk with Fafnir. And Joarr couldn't believe winning one piece of his treasure would motivate her that surely.

There had to be something else going on.

And if there was, if he discovered she was involved in the deaths of these dragons...want her or not, love her or not, she would have to be destroyed.

Chapter 16

Dressed in her jeans and peasant top, Amma didn't blend in tonight, but she didn't care. She didn't want to blend in; she wanted the dwarf to spot her.

But he wasn't at the door tonight; the dwarf Regin was. Amma didn't let that stop her, didn't play around like she had the previous evening. Using her magic, she cleared a path through the crowd.

This dwarf was thinner than Fafnir, more wiry, but there was still a resemblance between the two. Brothers, she decided.

She held her hands in front of her and let him see the magic dancing between her fingertips. "I'm here to see…" She hesitated. Who to ask for? Why was she here, really? "The Collector." She locked her gaze onto the dwarf's face, watched for a reaction. The dwarf who had delivered the second note had mentioned the Collector's treasure, but that didn't mean he was here.

If he wasn't, it would up the odds the entire thing was a ruse.

Uncertainty flickered in the dwarf's eyes. He shifted from one foot to the other.

She smiled and lowered her hands, dressed herself in confidence. "We've done business before. I'm thinking perhaps we can again."

The dwarf glanced over his shoulder, into the bar.

Amma tilted her head to the side. "As I said, I'm hoping we can do business again. I have access to a number of rare items. But if you think he wouldn't be interested." She turned as if to leave.

The dwarf jumped in front of her. "No." His eyes shifted from side to side as if searching for his best response. "I mean, I've not heard of this Collector, but if you believe he is here...I can ask."

"That," Amma replied, "would be lovely." She walked past him and into the bar.

He scurried after her.

She didn't speed or slow her pace, just walked confidently toward the stairs. There she waited. "Upstairs?" she asked, once the dwarf had caught up with her.

Looking unsure again, he nodded. "I can take you to a room. Then ask around."

"Yes, that sounds like a plan." Her adrenaline pumping, she followed him up the stairs. Could it be this easy? After all of this, could she simply meet with the Collector and offer him some trade for the cup?

Once on the main floor the dwarf motioned for her to follow him to one of the boards. He signaled to someone Amma couldn't see, and the board lowered.

He hopped onto the narrow piece of wood. Barely

holding on to one of the ropes, he waved for her to follow his lead. Her gaze latched onto the rope and followed it up, to the ceiling three stories above them.

The dwarf frowned. "You want a meeting. You have to go to a room." He pointed to one of the jagged overhangs she'd noticed during her last visit.

Amma shook her head. She wasn't afraid of heights, not anymore. She'd flown with Joarr and been fine, invigorated by it even. But that was different. That had been with Joarr.

The dwarf tapped his foot. "If you won't—" His gaze focused on someone across the room. He cursed.

Amma followed his line of sight. Fafnir stood by one of the bars talking with another dwarf. His hands were moving erratically, and even from this distance, Amma could hear a few of his words.

"Not…enough…need description."

Amma spun, putting her back to Fafnir. Gulping in air, she stepped onto the board.

Joarr stood outside the club. Amma had made it inside easily.

Too easily?

Why had she chosen the direct approach tonight when last night she'd been so insistent on stealth?

As a rule, dragons didn't favor stealth. Yes, sometimes it was necessary to shield themselves in fog so as not to arouse unwanted notice—but in an attack? There was so little to threaten them they almost certainly chose the direct approach.

Of course, perhaps three dragons were dead because of that.

He let out an annoyed breath. He didn't like the direction his thoughts were headed.

If Amma was working with Fafnir, he needed to know. And if he attacked directly, he couldn't. Also, satisfying as storming into the club and blasting the dwarf to roasted bits would be, it would not get him the chalice.

But if Amma was working with the dwarf, Joarr needed a disguise to keep her from spotting him. He glanced at his pristine pants. Fingered the fine wool they were made of.

She would not miss him dressed like this.

With one last sigh, he turned and disappeared back into the alley—to shift and change.

Amma teetered on the narrow board. She was thankful Joarr had thought to include real shoes with her outfit and she wasn't trying this circus trick wearing the high-heeled boots from the night before.

The dwarf beside her had waved for their board to be lifted as soon as she had stepped onto it, but she could tell his attention was still on Fafnir.

"Your brother?" she asked.

He glanced at her, surprised.

"There's a resemblance," she explained, hoping he'd buy her switch from confident wannabe trader to interested patron.

The dwarf grimaced. "It's his job to work the door. He goes missing every time Dad's back is turned."

Dad…the Collector?

She smiled and tried to look trustworthy. "I have sisters. Siblings can be difficult."

He snorted in agreement then without warning picked up one leg and spun out so only one foot was on the board and one hand held the rope. The board turned with him.

"Don't know who he's talking with," he muttered. "If he isn't careful I'll tell Dad what he's been up to when he's out of town. Where I've caught him a time or two."

Clinging to her rope, Amma didn't reply. The floor was far below now. The air was warmer here—heat from all the bodies below rising. Sweat beaded between her breasts. Again she thought of Joarr. When near him she craved heat, but his heat was different, comforting, while this was cloying.

The board jerked and swung another direction. Their upward speed increased. Amma slipped; her arm jerked in its socket as she gripped the rope. Her hand ached.

They were approaching one of the jagged outcroppings now. A few more feet and she'd be able to jump up and grab the edge—not that she would. Her fingers wouldn't release their hold on this rope until the board was squarely sitting on solid ground.

The dwarf waved his hand and the board swung wide, again without warning. It stopped ten feet from the nearest overhang—thirty-some feet above the concrete floor of the club.

Amma swallowed.

Still holding on with only one hand, the dwarf stared at her. There was a new glint in his eyes. "How do I know you've dealt with the Collector before?"

"He... I... Why would I lie?" she asked.

"I don't know, but I have another question for you.

How well do you know my brother?" A short sword had appeared in his hand and it was pointed at Amma's throat.

Like Amma, it had been easy for Joarr to enter the club tonight. No one had been at the door to stop him. He'd just followed the line of humans freely traipsing inside.

As he walked, he listened to the talk around him.

"Better hurry. Fafnir could show up anytime. Or worse, Regin."

Fafnir, Joarr knew. Regin he assumed was another dwarf, most likely the one who had escorted Amma inside.

He tapped on the shoulder of the human who had said the last. "And where would Regin be? Since he isn't at the door?"

The man shrugged. "Beats me. But if you see him coming, go the other way. Fafnir's crazy, but Regin…" He shook his head. "He means business."

A fist grabbed Joarr's heart. "A woman I know was with him, petite, blonde. Did you see her?"

The man's eyes widened. "Regin? Doesn't sound like him. He's all business, man. Your girl have some business with him?"

Did she? That was one reason Joarr was here.

Without replying he made his way to the stairs.

"Your brother? Why would I know your brother? I told you I was here to see the Collector."

The dwarf's blade tapped Amma under the chin; she felt a sting as it sliced into her skin. Her gaze slid to the open space below them; power thrummed through her body, made it hard for her to hold on. Under normal circumstances, she would have blasted the little man, but here, dangling so far above the ground, she was afraid she'd lose her grip and tumble to her death.

He tapped her again. "No one comes here to see the Collector. The Collector doesn't do business here. And I saw you look at my brother. Are you working for him? What have the pair of you plotted?" The sword dug deeper into her flesh. She couldn't swallow, couldn't move. She was barely able to breathe.

She shifted her gaze to the club floor and saw Joarr.

She didn't know how she recognized him. He wasn't dressed like himself at all, wasn't dressed like he had been the night before, either. His hair was blue and he appeared to have put on one hundred pounds.

It was his eyes, she decided. That blue was hard to hide, as was the fire that blazed from behind them.

She smiled. Joarr was here. His appearance, especially in disguise and after acting as if he agreed with her plan to approach Fafnir alone, could mean he didn't trust her. But he was here and suddenly she wasn't afraid any longer.

She let go of the rope and held out both arms. "I said I was here to see the Collector, but if you are going to be difficult about it—" She unloosed two streams of power and blasted the dwarf in the chest.

He saw it coming and lunged toward her, but she stepped backward off the board.

It was an insane thing to do, or would have been, if she hadn't been so inexplicably sure Joarr would keep her safe.

She fell feetfirst, dropped like a torpedo, her hands pointing up above her head. She didn't let herself feel fear. She concentrated on the sensation of falling instead, the power of the wind pulling at her clothes and the screams from the people below. Her eyes were open and she could see the world going by, saw the dwarf who had threatened her grab another board and cling there, his sword still gripped in one hand. The look on his face, shock, made her move worthwhile—or would if things played as her heart told her they would.

Then there was a roar and she closed her eyes. More screams from the humans below and warmth flooded through her. Her feet hit something solid. She bounced onto her side, grabbed with her hands.

Scales.

Joarr. He'd come like she'd known he would. He tilted to the side so her feet landed on his wing. She grabbed ahold of the ridge of hard scales that ran down his spine and pulled herself atop him. Then a leg on each side, her arms wrapped around his neck, she leaned down and pressed her face against his scales.

She'd known he would save her, and he had.

Amma had never trusted in anyone or anything.

And then, with little thought, she'd stepped off a ledge and fallen, known the dragon would catch her.

Her world was turned upside down.

Joarr flew up, then down—shrieked his outrage as he did. He'd seen the dwarf with his blade at Amma's throat and felt fear like he had never felt before.

Dragons didn't fear. Dragons had nothing to fear. But Amma was a witch, not dragon, and it had been too easy to imagine what would happen if she fell, how her body would look lying broken on the concrete floor.

He'd shifted before he'd seen the rest, before Amma had attacked the dwarf and actually fallen. He'd already been in the air, winging toward her.

He'd chosen to take a modified form so he could take wing, not simply fill the building with his mass. And now he didn't want to shift back. He wanted to fly farther and faster, steal the witch away and keep her safe, forget the dwarves, the Ormar and the chalice. Forget why he couldn't do such a thing, why he would have to shift back and then, when this adventure was over, walk away.

Chapter 17

Fafnir's heart leaped to his throat. His pulse pounded so hard in his ears he couldn't hear the terrified screams of the crowd packed into Tunnels. Didn't see them rushing toward the exits or diving behind the bar.

In his world at that moment there was no chaos. There was nothing except the dragon.

A dragon, in dragon form, soaring through his club. Fafnir had never seen anything so majestic.

His mouth watered.

His fingers were wrapped around the wrist of the dwarf beside him—the dwarf who had been assigned to watch the dragon as he came through the portal and deliver Fafnir's message, the dwarf who had lost his quarry, who, until seconds before, Fafnir had intended to skewer like the worthless chicken he was.

But then the dragon had appeared.

The dwarf jerked, tried to follow the others and dive for cover. Fafnir squeezed his wrist harder.

"He's here," he murmured. "Where did he come from?"

The dwarf struggled. Fafnir, his gaze never leaving the dragon, raised his ax and held it to the other male's throat. "See what you almost cost me?"

The dwarf didn't reply. Fafnir didn't bother glancing at him to see his reaction. The spy had failed; he was lucky to be alive.

"The woman, is she the one you told me about? The one who came through the portal, too?"

The dwarf didn't move or make a sound.

Grinding his teeth, Fafnir lowered his ax, but only a hair. "Answer."

"Looks like her."

"Hmm. He seems fond of her—to reveal himself like this he'd have to be." Fafnir mulled the thought around. "What's her story? What is she?"

"Don't know."

The dragon swooped low. The dwarf Fafnir held trembled.

Fafnir lowered his ax and swung it at his side. He could throw the weapon, wound the beast, but he'd still have to collect the blood. Two teams had already failed at that assignment. Time for a new tactic—put away the hammer and use a more delicate approach.

"She was with Regin. He won't talk to me, but he might to you...or one of your females." He prodded the dwarf in the gut with the handle of his ax. "Set it up. Find out whatever you can about this woman."

The dwarf nodded and started to move. Fafnir jerked

him back. "And when the dragon leaves here, have him followed. Pick someone good. If you lose him…" He let the threat hang. The dwarf knew what would happen. Fafnir was tired of waiting. If he couldn't have dragon blood, he just might have to try dwarf next.

He watched the dwarf scurry toward the exit. Most of the club's clientele had left by now or were hidden out of sight. A few dark elves lurked in the shadows, their gazes locked on the dragon. They appreciated what was happening, but were smart enough to know the danger, too.

Dragons were rare, almost a thing of legend.

Fafnir envied their stares, couldn't wait until he could shift, too, become the mighty flying beast. Would he be silver like this male or some other color—perhaps copper like the veins of metal that ran through his father's cavern in Nidavellir?

The dragon shrieked again. The woman who clung to his back seemed to be whispering to him, calming him. His flight slowed, became more of a glide. Ropes hung from his wings where he had flown through them, the sharp edges of his scales slicing them free of their moorings. He tossed his head and a flame flickered in his throat.

Unable to move, Fafnir stood his ground. The dragon could have torched the building around him and the dwarf would have been unable to move. He shifted his hold on his ax, tempted again to fling the thing, but there were still witnesses and the dragon was already on alert.

He had to wait, to be smart.

He lowered the ax to his side and stepped back, into the shadows where the dark elves watched.

The dragon circled once more, then landed softly with only a whisper of sound.

In this form he wouldn't fit through the doors. Fafnir held his breath, hoping the forandre would shift, that he would get a look at the dragon's other form.

A flicker, like a light with a short losing and regaining power, then the dragon was gone—the giant silver beast was gone, anyway. In his place stood a man dressed all in white and in his arms was the woman.

Fafnir froze. His heart thumped. He memorized every nuance of their appearances. They wouldn't slip by him again.

Joarr didn't let Amma down, not at first; he couldn't. And she clung to him, too, just as she had clung to him in his dragon form as he had circled the interior of the club.

A rope was tangled around his leg; he shook it free.

"Fafnir was here, watching," Amma murmured.

Joarr glanced around. He didn't see the dwarf now. There were a few shadows behind the bar and cowering behind the stalagmites. "If he's here, he's hiding," he replied.

"He's seen us now. There's no hiding who we are."

Joarr shrugged. He didn't care about the dwarf or the chalice right then; he only cared about Amma. He walked toward the exit.

Back at the hotel, Amma and Joarr didn't bother with words; words were unnecessary and might bring up issues Amma didn't want to deal with. Instead as soon as the door closed behind them they began undressing each other slowly...lovingly. Their affair might be temporary, but while it lasted, Amma had decided to participate in it fully—emotionally and physically.

They sat on the bed. Amma knelt with her bare feet tucked under her butt. Joarr sat beside her, his body twisted so one foot was on the floor and the other was curled under him, but his torso was facing her.

Joarr pushed Amma's blouse up over her head first. She let it fall onto the bed beside them and shook out her hair. The muscles of her shoulders and neck were tight, as if she was still holding the tension she'd felt while standing on that board considering how far she had to fall. She rolled her head to one side and then the other, her hair brushing over her back as she did.

Joarr watched, but said nothing, didn't make a move to hurry her, either.

Her hands on her thighs, she arched her back and stretched again. Her breasts pushed together, threatened to spill out of her lacy bra. Joarr's attention focused on them; she could feel anticipation building inside him.

She rolled her neck again, took her time enjoying the blue blaze of his eyes. Then her head back upright, she leaned forward and tugged his shirt up and off. She ran her palms over his chest. His skin was smooth and warm; the muscle beneath couldn't be missed. She rose on her knees and trailed her tongue down his pectoral muscles. He tasted of smoke, as if he'd been standing beside a wood fire.

She pulled back, but his hands caught the waist of her jeans. He slipped the button free, and pulled down the zipper. Her panties, what there was of them, matched her bra. He tugged the denim down her hips; she wiggled, willing them to fall lower. He pressed a kiss to her breast and she wrapped her hands around his head, moaned as he used his lips to shove her bra aside and lave his tongue over her nipple.

She reached for his pants and unhooked them in a quick, easy movement. He helped, jerking them from his body and tossing the expensive wool onto the floor. She shoved him back so he fell against the mattress. Still in her bra and panties, she crawled up his body, her hair hanging over one shoulder, sweeping over his skin.

He was completely naked now, while she was still somewhat clothed. It made her feel stronger, as if she was in charge. She lowered her butt and brushed the rough lace over his swollen sex. Straddling him, she lowered her mouth back to his chest and nibbled her way down from his pectorals, to his abs…lower still.

His skin was even warmer now, his heat flowing. She traced her fingers over his shaft, wanted desperately to share their magic, but wouldn't yet, wouldn't deny herself the pleasure of being in control. She darted her tongue over him. His fingers curled into the cover beneath him. Her fingers were on his stomach; she felt his abs tighten.

She laughed and flicked her tongue out again. The taste…smoke and spice. She opened her mouth and slipped her lips over the tip of his shaft, down then back up. Her fingers found his balls. She weighed them lightly then rolled them back and forth as if they were made of crystal.

His lower back left the mattress.

She swirled her tongue over his tip, her fingers continuing to caress his sacs.

He bent forward, placed his hands under her arms and pulled her up flush against his body. Within seconds, she was naked, too, her matching bra and panties tossed on the floor, forgotten.

Her breasts were heavy, her core wet. She hadn't realized how much excitement touching him could bring her.

He thrust a finger inside her; she tightened. He pulled it out and found her nub. He swirled his finger over it. She tensed, her hands against his chest, and cried out. She pulled her legs up, positioning herself to take him inside her.

She rose up, her weight on her hands, and stared down at him.

His eyes were alight with blue flames. There was fire inside her, too. She ached with it, burned to let it free.

He rubbed his sex over hers, finding the place where she so needed him to be.

Then in one quick plunge of her hips she encased him.

Fire raced through her. She could feel it pouring through her, couldn't tell anymore if it was from her or from him. It just was a part of them both.

Magic roared from her palms into his body; heat swirled around them. It was as if she was inside a tornado of fire and magic. Her skin tingled; sweat beaded on her body and Joarr's.

She pulled herself up then shoved herself back down.

Joarr's hands found her breasts; he held her there, massaging and lifting, helping her with the movement of their bodies. Up and down she moved. Her body tightened around his; his hands squeezed her breasts.

She grabbed his wrists, holding his hands against her while using his strength to increase their pace. Her thighs began to shake, the muscles screaming while her mind screamed for more.

Panting, she threw back her head. Fire flickered from inside her. Joarr had leaned forward. His mouth on her nipple, he missed the explosion of flame, but must have felt the heat. He looked up and Amma snapped her lips shut.

Witches didn't breathe fire. Something was happening—something strange and terrifying.

His hands moved to cup her butt. His fingers touched her as she moved. A jolt of pleasure shot through her. She gasped, pulling in air instead of shooting it out. No fire. No smoke. She held her breath or tried to.

He touched her again and her body began to shake, her core to tighten over and over. Spasms of pleasure she couldn't slow buffeted over her. She wrapped her hands around his head and held him against her, then tilted her head to the ceiling and shot pure, hot fire from her throat.

Her eyes widened and she felt his head jerk, knew he'd felt the heat.

Panic replaced pleasure. She tightened her core and let magic flow from deep inside her.

He tensed. His fingers gripped her hips and he urged her up and back down. The pleasure was back, swirling, as the pressure inside her built. She concentrated this time, kept the fire pounding to an almost uncontrollable force hidden inside her.

Magic, fire and pleasure. All three grew until her body pulsed, until she thought she would explode. Joarr cried out and pulled her tight against him. She cried out, too, let go just a little, just enough to let her orgasm wash over her and for a tiny bit of tension to leave her body.

With a sigh, Joarr spooned her body against his, but she couldn't relax, couldn't let go of her magic or her fire. Couldn't risk him realizing she had both.

He brushed her hair away from her neck, pressed a kiss to her skin and drifted into sleep. But she lay there awake and afraid.

What was happening to her?

Chapter 18

The club was a shambles, but for once Fafnir didn't mind doing his brother's grunt work. A rope thrown over his shoulder, he scampered up the scaffolding, looped the ragged end of the rope through one of the pulleys attached to the ceiling and dropped the extra length onto the floor. While there he searched for Regin.

He wasn't doing all of this without an expected payoff. His brother had been talking to the dragon's female. Fafnir needed to know why and about what.

He could see his brother on the ground yelling at the human help who were cleaning up broken glass. Fafnir's spy was beside him, as was one of the female dwarves who worked for him. The female dropped her broom and bent over to pick it up. Regin stopped his yelling.

Smiling, Fafnir grabbed another rope and rappelled

his way back to the bar's floor. His brother and the female had already disappeared from sight.

He picked up the broom the female dwarf had dropped and sauntered over to drop it into a pile of cleaning tools.

Once he knew why the dragon's woman was at the club, he would have a better idea of how to bait his trap. And, if the dwarf did her job right, he should have that information very soon.

Joarr awakened to the ring of the phone. Amma was curled on her side on the bed beside him, naked, not even a sheet covering her. He ran his palm down her shoulder and arm, before reaching for the phone.

The voice on the other end of the line was friendly, but professional. "We have a letter that was left for you at the front desk."

"A letter? From whom?"

The clerk stuttered a bit, then admitted he didn't know. He had gone into the office and returned to find the note, sealed with sealing wax, sitting on the reception desk.

After asking for it to be sent up, Joarr hung up the phone.

Amma rolled over. There were dark smudges under her eyes. Joarr brushed his lips over hers.

"It appears we have another contact."

She didn't reply, just pulled the sheet over her breasts and pushed herself to sit against the headboard. There was a distance in her eyes he hadn't noticed before, and something else… Fear.

He reached out to touch her, but she turned her head, then slid off the bed and headed toward the bathroom.

As the door clicked shut behind her, he curled his fingers back into his palms.

What had happened? The sex had been great, better than great. She'd shared her magic again; he could still feel it roaring through him, making him feel strong and alive. He'd thought she'd felt it, too, for a bit even imagined fire had escaped from her throat.

No beings except dragons harbored fire inside themselves.

There was a knock on the door. Pushing aside his wayward thoughts, he pulled on his pants, then went and answered it.

The note the bellman handed him was just like the first one—same paper, same plain envelope.

After tipping the hotel employee he closed the door and slipped his thumbnail under the seal.

Another invitation, to another bar, but this time in the middle of the day. He glanced at the clock that sat beside the bed. There was only an hour before the meeting. If he was going to make the appointment without shifting and flying, he would have to leave now.

He tapped the edge of the envelope against his palm and stared at the still-closed bathroom door.

"Amma," he called.

The sound of water running was the only response.

He stared at the door again. If he told Amma about the note, she would most likely expect to come with him—their bargain was still in play. She would surely want a chance at getting the chalice and winning the reward.

But, there was also a huge likelihood that this was another trap.

He picked up his jacket and tucked the note into the inside pocket.

He dressed quickly. After finding a piece of stationery in the room's desk, he wrote a note for Amma and left it on her pillow.

As he walked past the bathroom door, he could hear the shower running. He paused one more second, wondering if leaving Amma behind was the right move.

His hand on the doorknob to the hall, he nodded to himself. It might not be fair, cutting her out of what was happening, but it was smart and it would keep her safe.

Fafnir ambled into the hotel lobby. He sniffed the air; the place smelled of humans. He grunted and kept walking. The place was fancy—marble floors, real flowers and plush rugs. Just the kind of place a dragon would choose. The only kind of place Fafnir would choose once his transition was complete.

Sitting against the back wall was a reception desk, a counter-high reception desk. In other words too high for him to see over. Muttering his annoyance, he grabbed the edge and flipped his body onto the black marble top. A desk clerk dressed in a blue suit with a red flower stuck to his lapel stared back openmouthed.

"Not too friendly a setup you have here." Fafnir tapped his toe. A bit of dirt fell off his boot onto the marble. From here he was taller than the man. Fafnir stared down his nose at him. The dwarf's hand drifted to his belt where his ax normally hung, but the loop was empty. His father and brother insisted that they try to blend when any of them were out in the main human population.

Fafnir despised blending. He picked up his foot and sat his heel down on the clump of dirt, crushing it to dust.

"I'm sorry we... You... We don't—" The man's gaze danced around the room, as if he was afraid to look directly at the dwarf.

A common human ailment, in Fafnir's experience. They weren't comfortable with anyone who didn't look just like themselves.

He ignored the man's stuttering and stepped closer. "I know what you don't. Don't like my kind here, is that it?"

"No, of course—" The man glanced around again, but this time with an obvious intent of finding assistance from some quarter.

Fafnir pressed his advantage, using the man's discomfort to get the information he needed. "There's a couple staying here. I don't know their names, but I need to talk to one of them—the woman." He described the pair, then leaned so his nose almost brushed the clerk's. "You find her for me."

It wasn't a request. The desk clerk, smart man that he was, seemed to realize that. He, however, was having a hard time realizing that it wasn't an order he could choose to decline. "I can't reveal information about our gues—"

Fafnir leaned closer. "Your full-size guests?" His size made many humans uncomfortable. And as much as he'd have preferred to just jam his fist into the man's throat, he couldn't. Not without a lot of extra trouble that would only get in the way of his mission. The spy had done her part; his brother had shared that the dragon's female had come to the club looking for the Collector, had claimed she had some deal to make with him. This at least gave Fafnir a place to start, a job to claim.

"No, our guests' size has no bearing on…" The clerk twisted to the side and picked up a phone. "Who should I say is visiting?"

Fafnir leaned back on his heels, ignoring the clerk's question.

The clerk repeated his question. With a scowl, Fafnir replied, "She'll know."

He waited, hands on his hips while the clerk dialed the number and stammered into the phone. After a few seconds, relief washed over the man's face. He nodded and set down the phone. "She'll meet you in the bar." He pointed to the right.

Fafnir grunted and leaped to the floor.

This plan was going to work. He knew what the witch wanted; he just had to convince her he was willing and able to give it to her.

Chapter 19

The hotel bar was decorated in marigold-yellow and white. It was impossibly cheery and made Amma just a tad nauseous. As did the dwarf sitting perched inside one of the oversize egg-shaped chairs. Sitting back against the cushion, his feet poked out like a child's; somehow that made seeing him even more unsettling.

Fafnir.

Her first instinct had been to ignore the desk clerk's claim that a man had asked to meet with her in the bar. She'd still been stewing over what had happened with Joarr—what her body had done—and was in no mood to deal with what she'd assumed was some human who had seen her in the lobby and mistaken her for someone he had a chance with. But when the clerk had described her visitor as a "little person," she'd told him she'd be right down. She hadn't known which dwarf to expect—but it didn't matter. This mess obviously revolved around the dwarves. She wouldn't pass up the opportunity to see why one had come to call. Besides, the dwarf had arrived only minutes after she'd discovered a vague note from Joarr saying he had been called out. Joarr was a dragon in the human world. Who would call him out? Only someone involved in this tale. And now a dwarf was here asking for her. She couldn't ignore that.

As she entered, Fafnir wiggled forward, closer to the edge so his legs bent and his feet dangled.

An image completely out of keeping with the one set so solidly in her mind of him stabbing the dead dragon, then licking the blood that oozed forth, like a toddler sampling a lollipop. As it was, that image, combined with how he looked perched inside the egg, just made her shiver more.

One hand on each side of the egg, he leaned forward. "You have a chill? How about something warm to drink?" He smiled. His teeth were smooth and white, normal-looking.

Amma shivered again, then shook her head. "I'm fine. Were you looking for me? The clerk said someone was waiting in the bar…" She glanced around as if someone else might be hiding inside the small open space. Then letting her gaze drift back to the dwarf, she added, "But I don't think we've met."

He jerked his head toward an empty egg that sat a foot or so from his. "I understand you were looking for the Collector. Why? Do you have something to trade?"

"Are you the Collector?" She knew he wasn't, but she wanted to hear whatever story he had concocted.

He raised one bushy brow and gestured toward the chair. With a weak smile, she sat.

He resettled himself, staying forward on the cushion, but shifting his legs a bit. "I thought you'd done business with the Collector before."

Sitting inside the egg made Amma uneasy, as if someone might be sneaking up beside her, or that she could be trapped inside the plastic shell. She edged forward, so her peripheral vision wasn't blocked by the sides of the chair.

"I have, but it was years ago."

"You thought he'd changed?" The dwarf's expression was impossible to read.

"I thought perhaps someone new had taken over the title." It was a simple answer, unlikely, of course, but it seemed to satisfy the dwarf.

"No, there is only one Collector as far as I know." He templed his fingers, then patted the pads against each other. "What is it you have for him?"

Amma twisted her lips to the side. She wasn't sure how much to reveal to Fafnir, still didn't know his connection to the Collector. "I'd prefer to talk to him about that," she said.

Fafnir waved one hand. "He's busy, and not available right now, but I am authorized to make deals for him. I am his son, after all."

Amma blinked, but made no comment. If this was true, Fafnir could have the power he claimed, but Fafnir searching her out didn't feel right.

"So, what do you have for the Collector, or perhaps I should find out first what it is you want from him in exchange?"

Amma's eyes narrowed. Asking what she wanted wasn't a standard negotiating tactic. Fafnir's mistake aroused her suspicions anew. The Collector she'd dealt with wouldn't trust someone so obviously unqualified to make a trade for him.

"His standard deal should be fine," she parried.

"Standard?" The dwarf frowned, confirming that he was not representing the Collector at all.

So, why was he here? Amma suspected she knew.

She sighed. "I can see you are much too experienced to be taken in by games. As I said, I did business with the Collector a while back. I traded something to him in exchange for some information. Now, I'd really like that object back. Simple as that."

The dwarf's eyes glittered. He edged farther out of his egg. "And what would you be willing to give in exchange for this item?"

Amma licked her lips and tried to look unsure.

The dwarf took her bait. He jumped back in. "At the club, I heard you were with a dragon. Do you know him well? Would he be willing to help you get this item back?"

The dwarf's eagerness was tangible.

Amma didn't have to fake her uncertainty this time. "I… Dragons are very protective of their treasure."

The dwarf's stubby fingers curled around the sides of the shell. "What if the trade wasn't for treasure? What if it was for something the dragon would never miss, could easily replace?"

"There isn't much a dragon wouldn't miss."

Fafnir smiled. "Handled correctly there is." He reached into his pocket and pulled out a vial. Holding it between finger and thumb, he moved it back and forth. A green liquid sloshed from side to side.

Amma stilled. "What is it?"

"Nothing dangerous, just a sedative. It makes the other part of the task a lot simpler." With his other hand, he reached into the inside of his coat and pulled out a flask. It was glass, wrapped in bands of metal—just like the flask the dwarf outside the portal had dropped and that she'd seen Fafnir fill with the dead dragon's blood.

He handed it to her.

She flipped the flask over in her hands as if studying it. "What could the dragon have that I'd need this?" A sick feeling swept over her. She could barely stand to touch the thing; she knew what it was for, what Fafnir was about to ask her for.

"Dragons are rare," he stated.

She inhaled and nodded.

"In some cultures beings even believe their magic can be used by others."

"Really? I've never heard that."

He shook his head as if the entire idea was distasteful. "There's quite a market for dragon parts."

Amma stared at the flask, wondering if it had been filled before.

"But we, of course—" he laughed "—don't take part in that trade. We only deal in things that leave no one damaged."

"Oh, good." Had Fafnir been saving the dead dragon's body for some reason aside from a source of blood? Did he see that as leaving no one damaged?

She closed her eyes for a brief second, forced herself to remain calm, and injected interest into her voice. "So, this—" she held out the flask "—is for what?"

He smiled. "Blood. I know it sounds odd but these… beings…pay quite well for dragon blood. They use it in elixirs and medical treatments. Some think it may be the cure to some of the worst diseases in the nine worlds."

He made it all sound so very noble.

"And that?" She pointed at the vial of green liquid he still held.

"This?" He shook it as if he'd forgotten he was holding it. "Depending on the dragon and your relationship with him, this may not even be necessary. It's just… well…some dragons we've found are squeamish about the process."

"Squeamish?" she repeated.

His voice dropped. "This—" he held the vial out toward her "—keeps the dragon from even knowing the blood has been taken. Just slip it in his drink. It knocks them out for only a minute or two, but long enough to fill the flask. And they heal so quickly, if they notice the nick, they'll just believe they cut themselves shaving."

Somehow, Amma had a hard time believing that, but she took the vial.

The glimmer she'd noticed in Fafnir's eyes earlier turned to a blaze. Obviously pleased, he relaxed a bit deeper into the egg. "So, now tell me about the object you gave the Collector."

Still staring at the vial, Amma almost missed his request. She set the vial and the flask between her thigh and the wall of the egg. When she looked up the dwarf was watching her, eager and expectant. "It's..." She hesitated. He'd made no mention of the chalice, but this entire journey had started because someone had delivered a note to the dragons claiming they had it and were willing to give it up. So, someone knew it was important; did Fafnir?

"It's nothing really. I'm surprised your father even took it from me." She laughed. "He probably took pity on me. I was a little desperate at the time."

Fafnir waved her comments aside. "Then getting it back shouldn't be an issue."

Amma hoped not. She smiled, tried to appear meek and grateful for his upcoming assistance. "It's a cup. Nothing special, metal with a few jewels."

Fafnir stiffened; his hand, which had been tapping the edge of the egg, stilled. "A cup. The Collector has a number of cups that sound like that. Could you be more specific?"

Amma knew then he realized exactly what cup she was talking about. What she didn't know was if he was willing and able to give it to her.

"It's about this big." She held her hands eight inches apart. "And there are dragons on its sides." She went on to describe the cup in more detail. Finally, Fafnir nodded.

"I think I know the cup you're referring to. Why, may I ask, is it important to get it back?"

"I..." She wasn't about to tell him her real reason. "I'm afraid I didn't come by it honestly the first time. Over the years, the guilt... It was so unlike me to steal, but I was desperate."

He curled his lips into his mouth and hopped down

from his egg. Before she could move, he was in front of her, patting her knee. "You want to undo a wrong. That's very understandable and noble. I'm sure the Collector will want to help you make things right. He, after all, doesn't deal in stolen goods—not if he realizes it." He gave her a judgmental look. "Normally, I don't know that one flask of blood would be enough… but I'm sure I can talk him into it."

"You think?" She widened her eyes, softened her voice.

He leaned closer; she could smell the mustiness of old caves clinging to his hair and clothes. Felt the strange sizzle of magic she'd sensed when she and Joarr had stood near the dwarf in the bar. She'd thought then it was coming from Fafnir, but when she'd tried to draw magic off him, there had been none. This time, however, she was sure the magic was coming from him. She concentrated to keep from reacting.

"Do you think you can get the blood?" He licked his lips.

Amma squirmed before remembering her act. She nodded, but dropped her gaze to keep from having to look at the dwarf any longer. She hoped he took it for shyness and regret for her past thievery. "You're sure it won't hurt him? He won't feel anything?"

He patted her hand this time. His palms were rough and dry. "He won't feel a thing." He pulled a card from his pocket and dropped it on her lap. "When the flask is full, contact me here, and we'll set up a meeting."

She closed her hand over the card and nodded. She didn't look up as he scurried away. She didn't look up when couples and families started filling the bar for brunch, which the hotel apparently served there instead of at the regular restaurant. She was too lost in her thoughts, too wrapped up in deciding what she was going to do. A flask of Joarr's blood for the chalice. It didn't seem like too heavy a price.

Fafnir was right; forandre healed quickly. How long would it take Joarr's body to re-create a pint of lost blood? Minutes?

To gain the chalice and to get away from Joarr, which after her fire-breathing episode had become important. Witches didn't breathe fire, dragons did. She had to believe the child she carried was involved. If it happened again, if Joarr saw it, how long would it take him to guess the truth?

So an exchange of a pint or less of Joarr's blood for the chalice had to be a good deal. Certainly it was for her. If she produced the chalice, Joarr would have to fulfill his end of the bargain, too. She would have sole claim to their son and she could leave before her condition became obvious.

Her son. He was all she wanted... Her mind drifted to waking up in Joarr's arms, warm and safe. She hugged her body, tried to refocus on her baby and to forget his father.

She picked up Fafnir's card and stared at it...black letters on a white card. The words blurred. She brushed the back of her hand over her eyes and wiped away the moisture that had gathered there.

Sole claim to their son. Being honest with herself she knew it wasn't all she wanted, but it was the most she could hope to have.

Chapter 20

Joarr returned to the hotel, annoyed. He'd expected a trap, been prepared for it and looked forward to it.

And he'd got nothing. The bar he'd gone to was filled with dwarves and other beings of the nine worlds—cage fights between dwarves and trolls, dark elves and giants. The crowd had been huge and fired up, but no one had approached Joarr, at least not with an offer to sell him the chalice. Two promoters had recognized him as a dragon and tried to convince him to enter the ring; he'd tossed both aside. One, the last one, he'd had to freeze in place and with more than words.

They had, though, finally got the message and left him alone.

And for the rest of the day and evening he'd stayed that way. He'd sat through twelve hours of matches, drinking warm ale until the thought of it made him nauseous. He stunk of smoke and sweat. And he was fairly certain more than one type of body fluid had been sprayed on him by more than one pugilist.

At dawn, he'd faced the fact that he'd been stood up.

Tired and eager to see Amma, he pounded the elevator button and waited.

A couple with a child walked up behind him.

"He was a little person, honey. There's nothing strange about it. All people are made differently." The woman looked at Joarr, her lips curving into a smile that said, "Kids."

"Why was he dressed funny?" the boy asked.

She placed a hand on the child's head and pulled him against her. "He wasn't." Her cheeks flushed.

Joarr stared at the boy, realization and horror hitting him like a double hit to the gut. "A dwarf? A dwarf was here in the hotel?"

"Sir, really, that isn't—" The woman stuttered.

His day clicked into place. Hours waiting with no contact.

He hadn't been stood up. He had been diverted. Led astray so Amma would be left alone and unprotected.

Joarr didn't wait to hear what else the woman had to say. He was already heading for the stairs.

Amma.

In his mind he was yelling her name. If he'd been in dragon form, she might have heard him, but in this body she couldn't. He jerked open the stairwell door and took the steps three at a time.

The door to the room flew open and smashed against the wall. Amma jumped; a ball of power sizzled in her cupped hand.

Joarr stood in the doorway, his hair and eyes wild. When he saw her, he strode forward and jerked her against him.

She closed her eyes and leaned there. Her nose pressed against his chest, she inhaled his scent and felt the hard thump of his heart against her cheek. She trembled.

His fingers dug into her hair; he tilted her face up. "A dwarf. Was one here?"

She hesitated. She hadn't expected him to guess that, hadn't prepared herself with an answer. The vial Fafnir had given her was in her pocket. She hadn't decided yet what to do, hadn't decided if she trusted that the liquid wouldn't hurt the dragon. Joarr himself had said dragons couldn't be poisoned. Then again, dragons weren't supposed to die except at the hands of a hero, but the body she and Joarr had discovered had been all too real.

She blew out a breath; it smelled of smoke. She clamped her lips closed and turned out of Joarr's embrace.

"If there was, I didn't see him." She looked up, put concern into her eyes. "Why do you ask? And where have you been? Your note… It was vague. I was worried."

He thrust his fingers through his hair. "I was tricked. Someone left a note at the front desk—again claiming to have the chalice."

Her fingers in her pocket touching the vial, Amma froze.

"But I waited for hours and no one approached me— at least not about the chalice."

"Oh." She rounded her lips to blow out a breath, but

stopped herself. She pulled her lips into her mouth instead. "At least you weren't attacked again. Were you?" Her thumb, which had been circling the metal lid of the vial, paused.

Joarr shook his head. "And you weren't, either."

Amma couldn't tell for sure whether it was a question or a statement. Joarr was watching her now, analyzing her reaction.

She laughed. "No, nothing more exciting than a car chase and a few explosions here." She waved her hand toward the TV. She had flipped the device on a few minutes earlier.

She turned her back on the TV and walked to a tray she'd ordered from room service hours earlier. "Are you hungry? I ordered this then realized I wasn't."

Joarr glanced at the tray, but shook his head. "No."

"A drink maybe?" She held up a highball glass and a bottle of whiskey. "I'll join you."

He moved closer. "How could I resist?" He reached for her, but she pushed him away.

If she acted angry, got angry, it would be easier to carry out her plan. "We should talk. I thought we were working together. Then you disappear. And I had no idea where."

She filled two glasses with whiskey. Then carried them to where the ice bucket sat on the other side of the TV. With her back to Joarr, she plunked ice into hers and emptied the vial into his.

When she turned back, he was stretched out on the bed, a frown on his face. "If the note wasn't a trap—for either of us—and wasn't a real offer to deal, why was it left?"

She sat beside him and slipped the drink into his hand.

"Maybe something went wrong. Maybe whoever left the note meant to meet you and couldn't. Maybe they'll contact you again. Who knows, this time tomorrow this could all be over."

He held the glass to his lips and stared at her over the rim of his glass. "Yes, over. The chalice back with the dragons, me back with the dragons and you... Where will you be, Amma?"

She forced herself to smile. "With the treasure you've promised me, of course. Where else?"

"Ah, yes, the treasure," he said and took a sip. "I'd forgotten."

Amma watched as the liquid moved from the glass past his lips, as his throat moved and finally as he pulled the glass away from his mouth.

"What are you going to choose, Amma? Have you decided? Was there something you had in mind?"

She pretended to take a drink from her glass, held it up a second longer than normal. When she lowered it, she held his gaze. "Nothing you will miss, nothing you even know you have."

He shook his head. "I've told you. I know every bit of my treasure, no matter its human worth. Why can't you believe that?" He ran his fingers up the back of her neck and into her hair. "I value everything, and no matter what you choose, I will miss it desperately." Then he kissed her.

She could taste the whiskey she had only pretended to drink on his lips—could taste the liquid she'd poured into his glass, too. Or perhaps that was just in her mind, her guilt sullying the smoky flavor of the whiskey. Just like what she'd done sullied any relationship she and the dragon might have had.

Amma stirred her putrid pink drink, being careful not to spill any onto her skin or clothing. She had left Joarr at the hotel, passed out. He'd been breathing and his color had been good. There had been no signs that the liquid Fafnir had given her had done him any harm.

He had looked one-hundred-percent healthy, except for the tiny gash she'd made in his arm.

She closed her eyes and jabbed at an ice cube. It shot out of her glass and skittered across the floor. The bartender glanced in her direction, but quickly turned away.

She was sitting on the couch behind one of the back bars—where Fafnir had taken the human couple a few nights before. When she'd arrived at the door tonight, a dwarf she'd never met had been working. He'd immediately shut everything down and escorted her here— gone, she assumed, to get Fafnir.

She hadn't seen the blood-drinking dwarf yet, and she was getting impatient. She wanted to get the chalice, take it back to Joarr and get away. She reached for the flask, which hung from a ribbon around her neck. It was warm against her skin. She had hung it there immediately after filling it.

It caused a lump in her blouse, but she didn't care. She wouldn't risk placing it anywhere else. When Joarr woke up, he would know she had tricked him. Her only hope was to be there with the chalice. If she had that, it wouldn't matter how she had got it, the dragon would have to honor his deal.

She laid her hand on her stomach. Everything now depended on Fafnir accepting her trade.

Joarr rolled over onto his stomach; his arm reached out for Amma as he did and hit cold, empty sheets. He blinked, his mind slowly waking, and he groped around again. Still nothing. He was alone in the bed.

He rolled onto his back and moved to sit up. Halfway, on his elbow, he stopped and grabbed his head. A pain throbbed inside his skull, like an army of dwarves had taken up their axes and were mining for minerals there. He groaned and glanced to the side.

His empty whiskey glass sat on the bedside table. He squinted at it, trying to remember. How many had he drunk? Only one that he remembered. Amma had brought it to him, been sitting beside him sipping from her own glass… He glanced around again, saw a second glass still completely full sitting on the dresser.

He cursed and immediately regretted it—the outburst sent the dwarves and their axes back into play.

He threw his arm over his face, blocking all light, and tried to concentrate. Amma had been here. They'd had a drink—he all of his, she apparently only a sip. He'd kissed her and she'd pulled away, urged him to drink more.

Which now of course told him what had happened— what he didn't want to believe had happened.

He forced himself to sit up. He was still fully clothed. He swung his legs over the side of the bed and tried to stand. He staggered a bit before grabbing hold of a chair and willing the world to stop twirling. His pants were wrinkled, as was his shirt. He paused, his gaze locking on a dot of dark red on the inside sleeve. He unbuttoned his cuff and shoved the sleeve up over his elbow. A wound, almost healed, but not quite, leaped out at him.

Blood. The witch had stolen his blood.

Chapter 21

Fafnir walked toward Amma, glancing back over his shoulder as he did. When he reached her, he ducked behind a stalagmite—out of sight, she noted, from anyone in the main bar.

There was a furrow between his brows and his hands opened and closed. "I told you to call me," he said.

She swirled her straw in her glass and, adding a bit of a break to her voice, replied, "I lost your card. So, I thought I'd come here. Was that wrong?" Actually, she had wanted to meet the dwarf on her own terms—not his.

He muttered something under his breath. "It's fine."

"So, the Collector, is he still willing to make the trade?"

At the Collector's name, Fafnir darted a glance over his shoulder. Looking back at Amma, he said, "The Collector...yes, yes, he's still willing to make the trade, but not here. We need to go to my office." He pointed at the boards that swung overhead.

Not the boards again. But she nodded. "Of course."

"Good. You wait here. I have to take care of something." He scurried away, leaving Amma alone again with her pink drink. She had ordered it more as a prop than to quench her thirst, but looking at it reminded her of Joarr passed out on the bed at the hotel. She walked over to a fountain, designed to look like water dripping from a stalactite into a crevice worn into a receiving rock, and dumped her drink inside. Foam bubbled up and onto the floor.

When she turned around she caught sight of Fafnir across the room talking to another dwarf—this one dressed in a red frock coat and a tricorn hat. The Collector. He was here. Her heart raced.

So, Fafnir hadn't been lying, at least not completely. If the Collector was here, the chalice very likely was, too.

Fafnir, his back to her, seemed to be directing the Collector down the stairs toward the entrance of the club. As the older dwarf disappeared from sight, Fafnir trotted back to her side.

His breath coming in a huff, he grabbed her by the arm and pulled her toward a board. She locked her knees and twisted, freeing her arm. "Wasn't that the Collector?"

"Who? That? The dwarf? No, just a...friend of my brother's." Fafnir grimaced. "He's taken to dressing like my father. I'm afraid he has ulterior motives. I asked him to leave."

He waved down a board.

Amma didn't buy his story for a second. "So, is the Collector up there?" She glanced up, tamping down the surge of anxiety as she stared at the vast open space again.

Fafnir shook his head. "No, the Collector refuses to do business here, but since you did come and you do have…" He leaned close and whispered, "The blood." He raised a brow, asking for confirmation.

She inclined her head in agreement.

He smiled. "I'm going to make an exception and step in for him. Don't worry, you'll get what you came for."

"The chalice?"

"Yes, yes, that's right—a cup." He gestured for her to step onto the board.

She twisted her lips and looked at him through narrowed eyes. "Last time, your brother pulled a sword on me." She looked purposely at the ax slipped through his belt.

He held out his hands. "I'm not my brother."

"True." She kept her gaze steady.

With a mumbled curse, he jerked the ax from his belt and waved over a waitress to take it.

As the woman walked away, the ax lying in the center of a tray filled with shot glasses, Fafnir motioned to the board again.

This time Amma stepped on.

This trip was less eventful. In the beginning, Amma stayed tense, but as the board climbed, she relaxed more and more. Her body seemed to move with the board now rather than stiffen with each sway. And she was able to look down, actually study those below without fear clawing at her.

She spotted Regin ordering waitresses around. And just as their board came even with the top bit of jutted-out floor, the Collector walked up the stairs and back into the main club.

Fafnir seemed to have spotted him, too. He shoved Amma in the side, onto a landing. Then immediately began scurrying toward a closed door. "In here."

The door was constructed of one solid piece of thick wood. It was curved at the top, like something out of a fairy tale, and bands of metal formed a Z on its front. It looked ancient and heavy, but opened with just a slight push of the dwarf's hand.

Inside the office was dark. Fafnir slammed the door shut behind them before reaching for a light. There was the snap of stone against steel, then a lamp flickered to life. While Fafnir fidgeted with the wick, Amma glanced around. The room was still dark, completely so outside the three-foot diameter of the lantern's glow.

She looked up. There was an electric, or what appeared to be an electric, fixture set in the ceiling. She pointed at it. He glanced at it as if surprised to see it there. "Burned out. I prefer fire, anyway—don't you?"

For some reason, Amma felt as if the question was a trap, although she guessed it was more likely her conscience nipping at her again. Still, she didn't answer his question. Instead she replied, "I prefer to see what I am trading for."

"Not a problem, as long as you will do the same." He looked up at her expectantly.

She glanced around the room again. She had no sense that she had walked into a trap, but still, it paid to be cautious. Satisfied no one else was hiding in the room and that there was no weapon within the dwarf's easy reach, she pulled the flask up and out of her shirt by the ribbon she'd attached to its lid.

The dwarf's eyes glimmered. His tongue darted out of his mouth to moisten his lips, and in that tiny span of time, Amma would have sworn she saw a flicker of fire deep in his throat.

She wrapped her hands around the flask. Insane. She was going insane—seeing dragon fire everywhere.

He made a give-me motion with his hands.

She pulled the ribbon over her head, but kept hold of the flask. "Where is the chalice?"

He was leaning forward, reaching for the flask. She let magic flow down her arm, into her hand, spread her fingers and held them up in front of him. "You hadn't asked what I am, dwarf—an oversight you might regret, especially if you plan to cheat me."

He pulled back, his eyes narrowing until they were nothing but dark slits. His hand dropped to his belt.

She smiled. "Where is the chalice?"

He growled. "A witch. If I'd known…"

"What, you have issues with witches?" Suddenly she was enjoying herself. She thought of what she'd seen the dwarf do, knew lording her knowledge over him would threaten him more. "I know what it's for, by the way." She held the flask by its neck and shook it in front of his face, her free hand still held out, still sparking with power. "And I'm guessing your father, the Collector, has no idea what his son is doing. What would he do if he found out?"

Even in the yellowish glow of the lantern, she could see Fafnir pale. He dropped his hands to his sides and gritted his teeth. His hands were shaking; his entire body was shaking. He stared at an oversize mirror that hung a few feet away, in the shadows. He seemed to calm. Sucking a breath in through his teeth, he turned back.

"All that matters to you, witch, is that I have the chalice, and I do. Do you still want it or not?" He motioned toward the door as if she could leave, but Amma saw the shake of his fingers, knew if she moved toward the door he would attack. She didn't want that, didn't want to push him that far; she simply wanted him to know she wasn't a pushover.

She curled her fingers in toward her palm, forming a claw before they closed into a fist, extinguishing the magic. "Show me the chalice."

"The blood first." His eyes gleamed.

She tapped the flask against her chest. "A sniff."

He curled his lip, but nodded.

She unscrewed the lid and held out the flask.

His eyes half-closed, Fafnir inhaled loudly.

Amma tensed. How much could the dwarf tell from a sniff? She kept her gaze on the dwarf, stopped herself from glancing at the bandage hidden under her blouse.

His eyes narrowed for a second and his teeth dug into his lower lip. "Different."

Amma readied her magic—let it pulse to life inside her.

"But—" he licked his lips "—I'll get the chalice." He trotted toward the mirror. After glancing at her reflection in the massive piece of glass, he ran his fingers along the frame. The mirror moved, popped open, revealing a room hidden behind it. He disappeared inside, reappearing with a canvas bag.

Back beside Amma, he pulled a cloth-wrapped cup from inside. He held out both hands, one containing the cup, the other empty…asking for the flask.

She slipped the bottle of blood into his hand and grabbed the cloth-wrapped chalice. He held the flask to his chest, watching her as she unwrapped the cup and ran her fingers over its embossed and jeweled sides. It was exactly as she remembered it.

She blew out a breath; a tiny puff of smoke came with it. She pressed her lips together and glanced at the dwarf. He was frowning, but looked only confused… as if he knew something odd had happened, but wasn't sure what. She opened the cloth that had been wrapped around the cup, flicking it in the air to move any lingering smoke out of their space. Then happy Fafnir had kept the lights dim, she made a production of rewrapping the chalice.

"So, we are both satisfied?" she asked once the chalice was rewrapped.

He smiled. "Very."

She nodded and glanced at the door.

"Here." He held out the bag. "You don't want to drop it, or draw attention to it."

She hesitated, but he was right. She hadn't thought to bring a bag of her own and the chalice was too big to hide under her shirt. With Fafnir holding the bag open, she carefully placed the cup inside. He closed the bag, but as he did, he dropped the flask. With a curse, he dropped to his knees and fumbled around the floor. He seemed to find it under his desk. The bag looped over one wrist, he stood and held the flask to the light, flipped it over and over, analyzing it from all sides.

Amma waited, her fingers pressing into her thighs. "Damaged or not, I delivered it to you. I'm not responsible for what happens to the negotiated item after it's delivered into the other party's hands. The Collector knows that."

Fafnir raised his top lip. "He isn't here."

Amma took a step, but the dwarf stopped her by holding out the bag. "However, it seems fine. It's been a pleasure doing business with you. Perhaps I'll add your name to my list of acquirers. Do you spend much time with dragons?"

The bag's handles securely slipped over her shoulder, Amma cocked a brow. "I'm not looking for employment."

Fafnir shrugged and gestured to the door. "Been a pleasure. Get yourself down."

As she walked to the door, the hairs on the back of her neck stood up. She glanced back over her shoulder. The dwarf hadn't moved. In fact his attention, directed at her, could only be called rapt. She pulled the canvas bag more closely against her body and allowed her magic some freedom, until she was like a gun with a hair trigger. The slightest provocation and she wouldn't have to think, power would simply spill out of her.

Slowly, she turned the knob—expecting with each second that some trap would be sprung, but it wasn't. She walked through the doorway and onto the ledge that overlooked the bar without incidence.

Once there, though, things got dicey.

Chapter 22

Joarr brushed past the dwarf manning the club's door. He was done pretending. Let the dwarf challenge him, let the humans see how a dragon handled anyone getting between them and their treasure.

The dwarf didn't complain, but many of the humans did, yelling after him as he strode into the club and down the narrow basement hall. By the time he reached the stairs, he'd left their complaints behind, and a new noise, louder and more violent, caught his attention. It was coming from the main bar. He flew up the steps, barely bothering to dodge the humans flowing in the opposite direction—toward the exit.

The club was filled with dwarves, at least fifty of them. Some were dressed in the same dark clothing as the dwarves who had attacked Joarr outside the portal; others were dressed more traditionally in what appeared to be rough handwoven shirts and pants. And then there was the pirate. Dressed in red and purple, he stood on a board that hung in the center of the room…halfway between the bottom and top floors. In his hand was a saber, as long as he was tall, and on his head was a tricorn hat decorated with a peacock's feather. He slashed his blade to the side and yelled something Joarr couldn't make out. He seemed to be demanding something from a figure that stood on one of the overhangs above.

Joarr followed his gaze and stiffened.

Amma stood on the top overhang, her gaze dancing around her like a trapped rabbit. She clung to a canvas bag that was slipped over one of her shoulders.

The pirate yelled out an order. Boards dropped from the ceiling and dwarves clambered onto them. The small males clung to the ropes, like monkeys, or like pirates themselves. A few even held knives gripped in their teeth, the rest staying more conventional with the dwarves' preferred weapon, an ax, in their free hand. All of them, though, were rising on their boards at breakneck speeds.

Despite the obviously slanted battle, Amma looked cool. She stood, her hand outstretched, but no magic leaving her palms…waiting.

She was waiting for them to be within range, Joarr realized, before she attacked.

He stood frozen, not sure what to do—whose side to fight on. Amma, who had drugged him and—he placed his palm over the crook of his elbow—stolen from him, again? Or the dwarves?

Not the dwarves. No matter what issues he had with Amma, the dwarves' cause was not his.

He should, he knew, help neither. Leave the two sets

of villains to battle each other, wait for the weakest to fail and then, when the victor was still tired, attack.

But…he looked at Amma. Her hair lifted as if there was a wind up above, but he knew it wasn't wind—it was magic, her magic so strong her body vibrated with it and her hair came alive.

He had shared that magic—she had shared it with him.

And despite what she had done, despite the fact that even if she could explain her latest betrayal they could never be together, he loved her.

With that thought blazing inside him, he shifted.

The Collector was waiting for Amma when she stepped out of Fafnir's office. The Collector and forty or so armed dwarves.

He hadn't changed much since Amma had last seen him one hundred years earlier.

He stood with his feet braced on a board only wide enough for one dwarf. It hung from two thick chains—metal rather than rope and thicker than what held any of the other boards. It made his board more stable, less erratic in its movements. In his right hand he held a saber as long as his body. He waved it in the air in a way that could be taken as threat or greeting.

She raised her hands, made it clear she was ready to fight her way out if necessary. But she didn't fire. Despite the dwarves winging their way on boards toward her and the Collector with his blade, none had actually made an attempt to harm her yet. Besides, they would be easier to hit once they were closer. Aim well and shoot once.

She pretended not to notice any of them for a moment; instead she focused on the Collector. If she was going for accuracy, he was out of range, too, but barely. In fact she suspected the old dwarf knew exactly what he was doing, knew exactly where her magic would lose its precision. What he didn't know, however, was that her magic had changed since being with Joarr, since carrying his baby. Power was inside her now, bubbling like lava.

It was stronger; she was stronger. And the Collector had no way of knowing. She put the thought to the side, concentrated instead on studying her adversary.

Physically he was average-looking for a dwarf. Short by human standards, medium height by dwarf. His chin was clean-shaven and his gray, shoulder-length hair was pulled back into a queue. The only thing that made him stand out was his clothing.

Tonight, like the last time Amma had met with him, he was wearing an odd assortment from what appeared to be a variety of times and places. His purple silk pants came only to his knees and his fringed shirt was made of buckskin. On his feet were modern human sneakers—the kind Amma had seen athletes hawking on TV. His frock coat was bright red and his tricorn hat sported a curling peacock feather. All in all he was painful to look at.

As his board rose, his gaze locked onto Amma. He waved his hand for his board to be stilled. As it did, he thrust his saber into the wood and plopped down like a child sitting on a swing.

"Amma. You've returned. Back for new information? Have you something to trade?" His eyes glittered and even from this distance she could feel his gaze roaming her body. From someone else this might have felt like an invasion, but from the Collector it felt exactly like what it was…an inventory.

His eyes were riveted on her bag. "You aren't taking something from my club, are you? Sneaking something out?"

She kept her grip on the bag loose. "Nothing I don't have rights to," she replied.

"And what, sweet little orphan, could that be?" He moved his hand so it was next to the saber. Then swung his legs back and forth, causing his board to sway.

"Your son and I made a bargain," she replied.

"My son? Not Regin—he has too much sense to be making trades without me. So, you must mean Fafnir." Under his hat, his eyebrows lifted. "Fafnir is a fool, and anyone who does business with him is one, too."

Amma shook her wrist, causing the bracelet Joarr had taken from the frozen Svartalfar to jingle.

The sound seemed to transfix the dwarf. He held out his hand. "You lied—you do have something."

Not understanding what he was referring to, she hesitated, but the dwarf was already swinging his board toward her. Then his saber in one hand, he launched himself. Amma stepped back. As she did, the other dwarves still on their boards began to shout.

From her new position she couldn't see what was going on below her, but she could hear what the dwarves were yelling. "Dragon."

The Collector landed solidly on both feet in front of her. He spun and stared down. Then his saber held out in front of him he stalked toward Amma. "A dragon. In my club. Did you bring him here? Is he the same who was here the other night, while I was away?" He took another step, jabbed his sword forward. "If you think to steal my treasure, think otherwise. It's well protected—too protected for even a dragon to steal."

Suddenly, the cup seemed heavier. Suddenly, there was no doubt that the Collector hadn't authorized Fafnir to give it to her. In fact she suspected the entire thing was a setup. He'd got his blood then turned her out, knowing his father and his army of dwarves would be waiting.

But he hadn't counted on her being as strong as she was.

A roar sounded below them. The temperature in the bar soared. Within seconds the dwarf standing menacingly in front of her was dripping with sweat.

Amma smiled. Most definitely they hadn't counted on Joarr.

Behind the dwarf, the dragon rose into view. There were gashes over his body. Dwarf-forged iron could do that, when no other metal could—slice through dragon scales. But he still was strong. He flapped his wings, holding his position in midair as if he were putting out no more effort than it would take to stroll across a meadow. He roared again; fire shot from his throat.

The Collector pivoted, his blade held up like a shield. Joarr's fire hit it and splattered, like water hitting a wall.

That, Amma realized, was no regular saber, not even just a dwarf-forged saber.

Which, of course, made sense. He was the Collector. She had brought him the chalice. How many other beings had brought him things? What kind of riches and weapons did the dwarf have access to?

With a laugh, he reached for his hat and pulled some kind of disk from its brim. Still holding the saber to block Joarr, he tossed the disc at the dragon.

Joarr, lost in his fire, couldn't see it. He wouldn't realize what resources the dwarf had at his fingertips.

Amma screamed, yelling at Joarr, telling him to drop. At the same time she unleashed her magic. It flowed from her strong and hot—fire just like what had shot from Joarr's throat. Not magic, fire…dragon fire.

Amma could hide it no longer; somehow, she was becoming a dragon.

She saw the flicker in Joarr's eyes, knew he had not only heard her scream, but read her thoughts. He folded his wings into his body and dropped like a stone out of sight.

Amma screamed again and raced to the edge. One story below, the dragon hovered, his head turned up to stare at her. And despite all her work, all her time worrying about keeping her secret, she thought about it, imagined her child grown and looking like Joarr. Saw the baby, then the boy, then the man. Cried at the thought of losing him.

And Joarr heard it all.

She staggered backward under the weight of what she had done.

She had lost. She reached for the bag, ready to turn and admit defeat, but as the weight pulled at her shoulder she realized all wasn't lost yet. Joarr had made the deal. Knowing her secret didn't change that. She held the key to keeping her baby.

She jerked the bag from her body and flung it over the edge, toward the dragon. "Our deal. My part is complete. In exchange, I want this." She placed her hands on her stomach. "I want your son." Her voice cracked.

Chapter 23

Joarr couldn't believe what he'd heard, what he'd learned from listening to Amma's thoughts. A son. His son. She was pregnant. And she thought that explained the fire and the smoke coming from inside her. That was why she'd allowed herself to think of her son now while Joarr was in his dragon form and able to read her thoughts—she thought by attacking the Collector with fire instead of magic, her secret, that she was carrying his child, had been revealed.

But it hadn't. There was still another secret, one she didn't know herself, but Joarr suspected the Collector did.

He flapped his wings, ready to soar back up and tell her. Then she threw the bag and yelled what she wanted.

His heart plummeted. He was thinking of her, of

them, and she…she was only thinking of their deal, of taking his son.

A ploy…her sharing her magic, standing with him as he burned the dead dragon's body…everything they had been through together had all been a ploy to trick him into giving up what she knew would be the most precious treasure he could ever hope to find.

The canvas bag tumbled toward him. He stared at it for a second, not caring if it smashed onto the floor below, not caring about anything. Then his sense returned. He needed the chalice; the dragons needed the chalice, or thought they did, and it was his duty to retrieve it. He shot toward the bag and caught it on his back; the handles looped over one of the ridges that defined his backbone.

Then he stared up at Amma. She was farther away now, but he could still read her thoughts if he chose… but he didn't. The last, what she'd done, how she had tossed the bag…had hurt too much.

Betrayal from the woman he loved. Nothing had ever hurt this badly.

He lowered his wings and glided back to the floor. Once there he started to shift; he had the image of his human form in his mind. But suddenly, he snapped. Rage roared through him, crackled through his soul like fire devouring dry wood.

The chalice wasn't enough. Dragons had died, and he had been betrayed. He wouldn't leave things like this, wouldn't fold in his wings and walk away leaving behind those who had hurt him and the other dragons safe and untouched.

He would destroy everything.

He released his magic—all of it, his own and what he had gained from melding with Amma. He left the modified size he'd taken and let himself grow, let his body fill the club. It felt good to shift to his full form and size. He spread his wings, raised them up over his head, their tips going up past the bottom of the ledge Amma stood on.

He could feel her, pulling in magic. There was no way for him to stop her, not while he was shifting. But he didn't need to. She couldn't pull enough magic to stop the rage racing through him.

The last few humans remaining in the club screamed and ran for the exits. Five dwarves fell as Joarr changed, as his body grew and brushed against the boards on which they stood. Amma didn't move. The Collector did, though; he leaped for her.

The witch held him off with fire…Joarr's fire and hers. Her own—she didn't realize that yet.

The Collector pulled some device from his frock coat's pocket and held it in front of him; air surged out of it, blowing Amma's flames back at her. They flickered over her…of course…leaving her untouched. They couldn't hurt her, just like Joarr's own fire and ice could never hurt him.

He concentrated on what the Collector was thinking. A jumble of curses and names flooded Joarr's mind, angry words, mutterings, the Collector wondering where his sons were, especially Fafnir. He thought Fafnir's name again, then cursed over and over.

Fafnir. Joarr had forgotten him…the blood-drinking dwarf. He had much to answer for.

He yelled Fafnir's name into Amma's and the Collector's minds. "Where is he?"

The Collector cursed again, thought how his son had brought this down on him, was risking his treasure. Joarr could feel the dwarf's anger. The Collector glanced past Amma to a metal-bound wooden door, closed and, Joarr guessed, hiding Fafnir.

The Collector spat, then turned and ran, leaped off the ledge. From nowhere a board dropped and the dwarf landed on it. The board twisted and jumped, but the dwarf held on with one hand, the other still holding his saber.

Joarr ignored him. Let him escape. He didn't want the Collector, not now that he had the chalice. He wanted Fafnir, the dwarf who somehow he knew was responsible for the death of the other dragons. And Amma, he wanted Amma, but he wasn't sure for what...

Then clear and determined, the Collector's voice rang out, "Fire!"

The dwarves had regathered, and now instead of axes and swords, they held machine guns.

Bullets flew toward Joarr from all directions. He roared and straightened his wings, held them up to shield the area where Amma stood. The bullets pinged against Joarr's skin, bounced like hail off a sidewalk. The noise was deafening. He added to it, roaring again.

His hold on his dragon half was slipping. Treasure was near—his treasure—and Fafnir, the dwarf who thought he could take on the dragons and destroy them one by one.

Joarr opened his throat and dug deep in his reserves.

He shot back at them—sheet after sheet of icy water that solidified to its solid form as it struck any surface. The dwarves were coated. Icicles hung from their guns, the boards, the rafters. Four fell forward, the ice too heavy for them to hold themselves up. They tumbled like statues onto the floor below.

Joarr stepped forward, searching for the Collector. He found him still on his board, a new toy, some kind of box, in his hand.

"You lied to her, didn't you?" Joarr projected in his head. "Her father wasn't an elf. Why? Were you afraid she wouldn't give you the chalice if you told the truth?"

The Collector shook his head and mumbled, but Joarr could read his thoughts, knew his guess had been true. But at the moment, clearing up Amma's misperception wasn't a priority—finding Fafnir was.

He searched inside the Collector's mind again, looked for his greatest fear. It wasn't hard to find; perhaps the Collector had some dragon in him, too.

Treasure. The Collector was worried about losing his treasure, and now Joarr knew exactly where it was all hidden.

He let his eyes narrow to slits. "You know I can read your mind. I know everything you don't want me to know now. Such treasure you have. Such lovely piles. Your son has been killing dragons. Did you know that? Do you know how?"

The Collector's gaze went wide. His mind scrambled to cover his thoughts and shift their direction, but it was no good.

Joarr roared, fire licking out from his throat. "The

chalice! You knew he had it, knew what it could do, and you didn't stop him. That makes you a murderer, too."

"Joarr—" Amma stood on the edge of the overhang, her body swaying "—our deal… It's sealed." Just minutes before she had been strong and fighting, but now she was pale and growing paler.

Panic lanced through Joarr. He turned back to the Collector. "What did you do to her?"

Nothing. The Collector's thoughts were clear. He had no idea what was happening to the witch.

"Amma," he spoke into her head. "Whose blood did you give Fafnir?"

Her knees bent beneath her and she crumpled to the ground. "Not yours," she murmured. "I didn't trust him. I thought I could trick him."

"Whose blood?" Joarr screamed.

She reached for her sleeve, shoved it up above the elbow. A cloth stained with red was tied there.

"No! The chalice, he's using it to drain dragons. He drinks their blood from it and leeches their powers."

"But…" She ran the back of her hand over her face, looked confused and lost. "I'm not a dragon, and I have the cup. I gave it to you."

Joarr turned back to the Collector. "The bag on my back, take it. Tell me what is inside." He moved closer to the dwarf.

The Collector licked his lips, but reached for the bag and pulled out a cloth-wrapped package.

"Is it the chalice?" Joarr asked.

Joarr could hear the Collector humming in his mind, trying not to answer. "Tell me, or I will tell every dragon who exists where you store your treasure."

The Collector gritted his teeth. "No. It isn't the chalice...not the one you're looking for, anyway." He held up a dented gray metal cup.

"Tricked," Joarr muttered. "Amma, you were tricked." She sat crumpled on the floor, barely looked up as he said the words.

Behind Amma the iron-bound door opened, and Fafnir, his hands wrapped around a gold-stemmed cup, wobbled out. His eyes were fevered, his skin flushed. He took a gulp from the cup. A red stain ringed his lips. His ran his tongue around his mouth, swiping every bit of the scarlet liquid back into his mouth. Then he took another swig and careened closer.

Joarr wasn't sure the dwarf could see them or even knew they were there. He stared at the cup in the dwarf's hand.

"Thief!" the Collector yelled. His saber shot up and the bag he'd been holding tumbled to the ground below. "I knew you'd been snooping around my treasures, but never thought you'd be stupid enough to steal from me."

Fafnir stared at him with only one eye open. "Only supposed to take a sip a day, but I could tell soon as I tasted what the witch brought me, she was trying to trick me. This wasn't dragon blood. It was something else." He tapped a finger against his nose, stumbling to the right as he did. "Couldn't place it, but figured long as I had it, why not enjoy it? And you know, it's good. I might have some more." He leered at Amma.

She raised a hand, or tried to; it fluttered back down to her lap.

"Positions," the Collector yelled.

Fafnir stared into his cup. "I've drank most of it.

Time for a refill." He pulled a dagger from his belt and stalked toward Amma.

Joarr stood tense, gathering fire. As the dwarf took another step, he opened his mouth and a narrow line of fire blasted from inside him—pure fire enough to leave the dwarf nothing but a pile of ash. It hit Fafnir in the gut. Quick, easy and pain-free, at least for Joarr.

He closed his lips and shifted his body, so he could nudge Amma with his nose.

Fafnir, cup and dagger both still in his hands, stumbled back into view. His shirt and pants were burned. Only the cuffs of his sleeves hanging over his hands and the bottoms of his pants covering his feet still remained. The rest of his stout and blackened body was completely naked.

But it wasn't burned. He wasn't burned.

Joarr's eyes widened. His fire had been strong enough to down any being…except another dragon.

Fafnir seemed surprised, too, and pleased. He dropped his dagger, placed the chalice on the floor and then stood with his hands pressed to his bare stomach. "Didn't burn. You shot an inferno at me and I didn't burn." He lifted his chin and laughed. Victory, scorn, pride—his howls contained them all. He lowered his head and stared at his father. "Who's weak now, Dad? Who you going to trust now? Not Regin. Compared to me he's weak! I'm the powerful son now. I'm the dragon!" He ran forward to the end of the ledge and leaped.

At the same time, the Collector gave some signal and bullets spewed toward the dwarf.

Joarr lifted his wing, shielding Amma.

The bullets dug into the wall and ledge where Fafnir had stood. Joarr glanced down, expecting to see the dwarf lying dead and broken on the floor. Instead what he saw chilled him to the marrow of his bones.

One second Fafnir stood with his feet shoulder-width apart, his arms held overhead. The next, there was a flash and where the dwarf had stood was a dragon… but not any dragon—a wyrm.

The wingless beast used his short arms to maneuver his black body across the floor. His tongue flicked out like a snake's. He glanced at his father and grinned. "You're right. I did steal from you. And I don't regret it. Look at me! Dragon fire can't stop me. Bullets can't stop me. Nothing can stop me." It was strange hearing a voice coming from a dragon's body, and disturbing, but no more disturbing than seeing the dwarf lapping blood from a corpse.

Everything about Fafnir was disturbing.

The Collector pulled yet another gadget from his frock coat—a miniature crossbow. He slid an arrow onto it and fired. Fafnir opened his jaws and swallowed it whole. Then he waddled toward his father, opened his lips and dropped his mouth down over the colorfully dressed Collector. He lifted his head. The Collector's peacock feather stuck out from between his lips. Then with a gulp, it was gone.

The Collector was gone.

Fafnir opened his mouth and laughed. Bits of fiery rock spewed from his throat and skittered across the ground. The dwarves who were left dropped off their boards, stumbling and tripping over each other as they raced from the room. Fafnir watched them go. Slapped a forgotten machine gun out of his path.

"Don't mess with my treasure," he screamed. "I know what is there, down to the last fleck of dust. If so much as a coin is missing, I'll find you. And I'll eat you." His short arms resting on his belly, he laughed again.

"Joarr." Amma teetered next to the edge. In her hands was the chalice Fafnir had left behind. "Here," she said. Then she fell. Blood, her blood, flew from the chalice and sprayed over both her and Joarr. With a curse, he lunged toward her. His teeth clamped onto her shirt. Her body jerked and her arms sprang up as if pulled by strings. The sound of tearing cloth ripped through him. He adjusted his grip, nibbling more of the material into his mouth, and prayed her shirt would hold. Her arms dropped, limp and lifeless, but her fingers white with the strength of her grip, she didn't drop the chalice.

He moved his wings in a rapid but shallow way, keeping his body hovering less than a story off the ground. He twisted or tried to. With Fafnir in the space, too, there was little room to maneuver.

Still, he searched for a place to sit her down. He couldn't leave the building like this—not without exploding out of the roof. And this building was older, much sturdier and had been remodeled by dwarves. There was no telling the strength of the beams. He could probably blast his way out, but not with Amma hanging from his mouth, blocking his fire and ice.

Fafnir stood watching, leering.

There was little of the dwarf left now…nothing if he

had had any good in him. The wyrm before Joarr was nothing but a pit of malevolent greed. He had devoured his own father without a blink of remorse, seemed amused by it actually.

And with Amma in Joarr's jaws, he couldn't fight the beast. He glanced to the side, considering whether to put her back on the outcropping.

His movement seemed to attract Fafnir. His eyes glittered and his gaze locked onto the chalice. With no other warning, he lurched forward. "Mine!"

His tongue flickered out of his mouth, sparks instead of spittle falling from it and dropping to the floor. Joarr twisted his neck, jerking Amma out of the wyrm's reach. His tongue hit Joarr instead, burned a trail down the side of his neck. Joarr froze, hissed through his closed teeth.

Dragons seldom fought each other. It took special fire, special energy to build a fire so hot or ice so solid that it could damage another dragon. But Fafnir was doing it. His tongue had blazed its way down Joarr's neck; he could still feel the burn.

Fire flared to life inside Joarr. He wanted to blast the wyrm, incinerate him like Joarr had incinerated the dead dragon's corpse. But that kind of fire was even harder to attain, impossible with only one dragon—it took cooperation. Amma had acted as that cooperating dragon before, but she was in no condition to help Joarr now.

And she still hung from his jaws, still blocked any fire or ice he could produce from reaching its target.

Fafnir attacked again; his tongue reached for Amma and the cup she held. Joarr swung her to the side and with no other choice set her back on the ledge. She lay as he had laid her, her arm stretched out under her head, her fingers still wrapped around the chalice's stem.

"Amma," he urged in her mind. "Amma. Don't let yourself fade. Don't let the dwarf win. Think of our son." He blew heat over her, willed her to pull it in, to share his fire. She didn't move.

But Fafnir did. "The cup is mine!" he yelled. And he fumbled his body forward. His snakelike lower body made a thumping noise as he used his massive arms to move himself forward.

His tongue reached out, fire flickering from it.

His jaws free, Joarr dug into his reserves, thought of Amma, thought of his child. They were dying. He knew that, and he had to save them. Rike had tried to save his son and failed.

But Joarr wouldn't fail—he couldn't.

Ice filled Joarr's stomach. He prayed the dagger-sharp shards would pierce the wyrm's heart.

A sword to the heart. That was how a hero killed a dragon, and while Joarr had never claimed to be a hero, he was the closest thing here—the only thing here.

He pulled air in through his nostrils and started shooting.

Fafnir fought back, using his tongue to slap the missiles to the side, catching a few and letting them sizzle to steam. He laughed as he moved, seemed to see Joarr's attempts to destroy him as a game—a game he couldn't lose.

But he could. Somehow Joarr had to beat him.

Joarr panted for breath, the constant creating of ice

hard enough to pierce a dragon's scales wearing on him, tiring him until he was fighting to stay upright.

Fafnir laughed and patted his stomach—a jolly evil dwarf in a dragon's body. Joarr shook himself and dug deeper, prepared to launch another volley of missiles, but as he stood there rebuilding his stores, Fafnir's tongue lashed out past him and wrapped around Amma's body. Like a frog catching a bug he jerked her back toward his open mouth.

Chapter 24

Something hot and sticky wrapped around Amma. She was tired, so tired. She couldn't remember ever feeling like this before. Joarr's voice had been in her head a few moments earlier. Her first thought was that he was responsible for whatever had wrapped around her. Then her body jerked; she was pulled off the ledge with such force she knew it wasn't Joarr. Even knowing her secret and that she was working to steal his son from him, his voice hadn't sounded angry. It had sounded as if he cared.

Cared... Her mind got lost considering that. She forgot about figuring out what was happening to her.

"Amma!" It was a scream this time—a demand.

Amma didn't do well with demands; she never had.

"Damn it. Fight!"

Now Joarr was angry. Amma frowned. He should be angry. Anger would make all of this so much easier. She frowned and thought of how the dragons would steal her baby, or try to, when they learned of him. Thought of how they separated other children from their mothers, didn't even return them when their fathers died, like Joarr's had. Just left the child to grow up feeling deserted and alone.

It wouldn't happen to her son. She wouldn't let it...

Suddenly she was more awake; she realized a dragon held her. It was a dragon's heat wrapped around her, but not the warm, comforting heat she'd shared with Joarr. This heat was malevolent; it was the only word she could think of for it. Sticky and cloying. It made her skin crawl and her stomach turn...but it was heat. Which meant it was power.

She gritted her teeth and began sucking it into her body.

Amma hung limply from the wyrm's tongue, and Joarr watched helplessly as Fafnir reeled her in. His body was exhausted, his reserves were depleted. He needed time to rebuild them...not long...minutes would do...but he didn't have minutes, didn't have seconds.

He screamed at Amma, angry now. Where was the witch who had captivated him? She wouldn't hang like a broken doll from the wyrm's tongue—she would fight.

He closed his eyes and concentrated on rebuilding the ice. He could feel it hardening, but knew he had to wait. To shoot the shards too early, as he had done before, would cost him and Amma everything. He had to wait, had to make sure they were hard enough this time to do the job in one well-aimed hit.

There was a noise, a whoosh. Joarr opened his eyes. Amma had moved. She didn't just hang loose like a boneless cat. She was twisting, moving so her hands were pointed at Fafnir. Magic poured out of her palms, struck the wyrm between the eyes. He blinked and let out a guttural shriek but he continued to reel her in.

Seeing her mistake, Amma twisted again, this time aiming her power at the tongue itself.

An idea blossomed in Joarr's mind. He might need his ice to kill Fafnir, but there were other ways to save Amma. He moved forward, did what the wyrm had done to his father. He opened his mouth and snapped his jaws down over Amma's body, snapped his teeth through the wyrm's tongue.

Fafnir screamed. Blood spurted from his tongue. Joarr's mouth was filled with it. He fought not to gag, not to spit out Amma along with the blood and chunk of tongue.

Fafnir flailed from side to side, the end of his severed tongue hanging out of his mouth. He groped at it, feeling the end, then touching it again, as if he expected it to grow back…which it might, but not quickly, not within the time it would take Joarr to kill him.

"Amma?" Joarr spoke to the witch, opened his jaws wide enough for her to get air and light. Fafnir's blood leaked from his mouth, ran down his chin and neck. Again Joarr had to fight the urge to spit.

"Put me on him," Amma said. "I can use his power. I can transfer it to you."

Joarr shook his head, slowly, carefully. The idea was insane. He'd just saved her from the wyrm; he couldn't put her back in danger. She was weak. Despite the magic he'd seen flowing from her palms, he could feel she held none now. He said as much in her mind.

"I can't hold magic like I should, but I can pull it and shoot it back out. I can share it with you."

Like she had when they made love.

He nodded, just enough to let her know he agreed.

Fafnir had his back to them now, was still mumbling and stumbling, but Joarr could see his rage was increasing and with it his fire. Steam poured from his nostrils and up, over his head.

Joarr leaned closer, within inches of the dwarf. Amma rolled to her side and crawled out of his mouth onto the wyrm's back.

With Amma safely out of his mouth, Joarr spat, freeing his mouth of the taste and smell of wyrm.

From Fafnir's back Amma held up the chalice to Joarr. "Take it," she said. "It's yours now."

It was obvious she was feeble, that it was hard for her to even hold up the cup. Joarr dropped his gaze. He didn't want the cup; didn't want to go back to the Ormar…not without Amma and his son.

"Joarr." Her voice was weak, but it grew sharp as she called his name.

He looked up at her. "Save yourself, save my son, and I'll give you anything you ask."

It was all that mattered to him now. He would become a wyrm himself if it meant Amma and his son could live.

Amma was dying. She knew it; knew that meant her baby wouldn't survive, either. It was unfair, beyond unfair. He'd waited so long to be born. One hundred human years.

And now because she'd thought she was being smart, had tried to trick the dwarf by giving him her blood instead of Joarr's, she and her baby were going to die. Somehow the dwarf was doing what the elves had failed to do; he was killing her.

Joarr still thought he could save her, and she wouldn't argue with him. There was no time for that. Time wasted meant less time for her to be alive and to help Joarr kill the horrid dwarf.

Helping to kill him might be her last act, but it would be a good one.

She placed one palm flat on Fafnir's back, her stomach and face against his black scales, and pointed her other palm at Joarr. Then she began to siphon.

Amma's power—or Fafnir's through Amma—hit Joarr hard. She was pulling his magic quickly, letting it flow through her body unheeded. At first he resisted. She needed the power, their son needed the power, but then Fafnir turned his head and shrieked. He realized what was happening. He shot balls of molten rock onto his own back, peppered the area around Amma.

In her current state, one strike would surely kill her.

Joarr had no choice but to take what she offered and end this fight once and for all.

He dropped his guards and accepted her magic.

It flowed into him like an electrical charge. He gasped and locked his jaws to keep from crying out. His eyes closed, too. It took every bit of control he had to manage the power, channel it to where his ice stores were building.

Cold, arctic. The temperature inside him was dropping. He could feel the shards sharpening. In his mind he whittled their tips, tested them for cold and strength.

Amma's magic was amazing, intoxicating. It surged through Joarr until he knew he was more powerful than he had ever been, than any dragon who had ever lived.

This is what the Ormar feared. A dragon with this much power could destroy anything, everything, the world even. And if Amma died, if Joarr never got to meet his son, that is exactly what he would be tempted to do.

But not yet. All wasn't lost yet.

He reached into his core, sorted through the diamond-hard ice crystals and selected the sharpest.

Then he waited for the wyrm to turn.

It didn't take long. Fully aware the witch was on his back, Fafnir shuffled his heavy body around. Amma continued to cling. Fafnir switched his tactic, curling his tail and taking swipes at her. Without his tail to balance on, his weight shifted forward onto his arms. It also blocked any clear path to his heart.

"Slide off," Joarr yelled into Amma's head. "Slide and roll."

Amma looked at him. There was regret and sorrow in her eyes. She thought she was going to die.

She was wrong. Joarr wouldn't let her, but he had to move fast. Once she was off the wyrm's back his flailing could easily crush her.

She broke her connection to Fafnir's power. Without it, she lost her grip and immediately slid down under his belly. There she reconnected and hung by one hand from the dwarf's side. Her other hand still gripped the chalice. Joarr wondered briefly if she even could let go of it.

But her move had been perfect. It caused Fafnir to rise back up onto his tail, leaving his chest fully exposed. Joarr focused on the ribbed stripe of scales that covered his heart—only a few feet from where Amma hung.

Then he fired.

The ice shard burst from Joarr's throat and into the wyrm's chest, crunched as it pierced his scales. Fafnir's body flew backward, slamming into the club's wall behind him. A dwarf-made stalactite crashed to the ground. Barware exploded, and the partial floor above Fafnir's head collapsed, raining rubble and debris over him.

Amma lifted her head to stare at Joarr. Her lips twisted into a weak smile, then she released her hold, or the wyrm's power gave out, Joarr couldn't tell which, and she fell to the floor. As she hit, her hand opened and the chalice rolled across the dirty concrete toward him.

With a curse and without bothering to check to see if the wyrm still lived, Joarr shifted and strode to her side, kicking the chalice out of his path as he did. He scooped the witch up and cradled her against his chest.

She was cold and her head tipped back, her hair cascading over his arm.

Desperate, he poured heat into her, willed her to accept it, to grow stronger…to live.

Her skin warmed to his touch, but she didn't move,

didn't gain any power. He was warming her, but as his heat would warm any inanimate object. She wasn't absorbing it; she was reflecting it.

He closed his eyes and pressed his chin to his chest.

"If you want the witch to live, I can tell you how to save her, but for a price, of course."

Joarr's head shot up. Standing on his son's dead body was the Collector, dripping wet, his peacock feather drooping down to his chest. In his hand was his crossbow and it was pointed at Joarr.

"Nice of you to skewer him like that. I wasn't sure how I was going to get out." The dwarf gestured at his son's chest. The ice shard was melting, but Joarr could see that something had increased the size of the original wound, making it into a tear that practically gutted the wyrm. "It's true, you know—dwarf metal can cut anything." The Collector pointed at a dagger hanging from his belt. "But you providing the starting point was quite useful."

"Tell me how to save her." Joarr took a step forward. Amma's hair swung as he moved, but she made no sound. If she was breathing it was too shallow for Joarr to see or hear.

The Collector wiggled his crossbow. "Dwarf metal on the ends of these arrows, too. Don't be tempting me to use them."

"I can survive your arrows," Joarr replied.

The Collector smiled. "But can she?"

Joarr froze.

"Silly girl. She gave the boy her blood." The Collector shook his head. "Why would she go and do that?"

"Because you lied to her?" Joarr asked. "When she

came to you with the chalice, you told her her father was an elf. He wasn't though, was he? There's only one being as hard to destroy as the elves found Amma to be."

The Collector sighed. "Yes. It's true. Your pretty little witch is half-dragon. It's why she was left to be raised by her mother. Unfortunately like your father, her mother didn't live to do the job. She got left with those two hags of sisters she has."

"And you didn't tell her because of the chalice."

"Couldn't be expecting a dragon to give up the dragons' most valuable artifact, now, could I? Sure, she had no loyalty to your kind, but she had some mixed-up feelings about family. I didn't want to risk it. Besides, what was the harm? Wasn't like the dragons were going to accept her into the bosom of their family. Dragons have no bosom of their families."

It was true. Amma would have been turned away, just like the elves had turned her away. But while the elves had no idea how to destroy her when she rebelled, the dragons would have. She wouldn't have been trapped in Gunngar, but she wouldn't have survived, either.

"So, what do you want?" Joarr asked.

The Collector smiled. "Treasure, dragon treasure. All of it. You get me and my dwarves inside the stronghold. No one has to be hurt. No one will be hurt if you do it right."

Joarr's temper flared. "You want me to betray the dragons?"

The dwarf shook his head; he seemed amused by Joarr's question. "You forget who I am. I'm the Collector. It isn't just things I gather. I gather information, too. You never know when some little tidbit will be useful. For example, I know you are the Chalice Keeper, the Chalice Keeper who lost the chalice." He made a tsking sound. "How did the Ormar handle that when they found out?"

At Joarr's raised brow, the Collector chuckled. "You aren't listening, are you? I know everything. I knew my disappointment of a son had stolen the chalice. I knew what he was doing with it, and I knew he sent a note to the Ormar. So, how'd they take it?"

Joarr bit the inside of his cheek and pulled Amma a little closer to his chest.

The Collector's eyes glittered with mockery. "Did they understand? Offer to help you retrieve it? Or did they threaten you, make it completely clear what would happen to you if it wasn't returned?" He tilted his head. "You aren't the first dragon I've dealt with, you know. I understand your kind—I am your kind."

Joarr lifted his brows and the Collector shook his head. "No, no dragon in me. But I understand the need to own, to hoard, to keep others from getting what is yours. We, dragon, are kindred souls."

Joarr doubted if the Collector had ever been more wrong about anything, but he played along because he needed the information the dwarf offered, needed to know how to save Amma.

"You know what happens to dragons who lose everything?" Joarr asked. He looked past the brightly clothed dwarf to his son's wyrm body.

The dwarf waited for Joarr to look back at him. "I've heard the tales." He held his gaze steady. "But I have no control over what will happen after I get my treasure, what the dragons allow to happen. I'm not evil. I don't choose to hurt anyone. I just want my treasure."

Joarr nodded. "I can understand that. I guess it is time to talk." He nodded to the side, asking the Collector for permission to set Amma down. At the dwarf's short nod, he carried Amma a few feet away. He took a moment to arrange her hair around her face, to run his fingers down her face. When he knew he couldn't stall any longer, he turned back to face the Collector, positioning himself so in his larger size he would block any shot the Collector had at hitting Amma with one of his arrows.

"Unfortunately, I don't think we have much to talk about." And as the words were still leaving Joarr's throat, he shifted. He loved Amma, knew he couldn't live without her, but he also knew he couldn't trust the Collector, and no matter how they had treated him, he couldn't condemn even a single dragon to life as a wyrm. He would save Amma; he would just have to figure out how on his own.

The Collector fired his first arrow. It lodged in Joarr's chest, less than a foot from his heart. But Joarr wasn't afraid. He'd seen inside the Collector when reading his thoughts. He knew the dwarf was far from a hero. Without the power of the chalice working for him, neither Fafnir nor the Collector could have downed the tiniest of dragons, much less one of the largest.

The chalice. Joarr glanced to where it had rolled across the floor.

The chalice was the cause of all of this. It wasn't the lucky talisman the dragons thought it to be. No, the reason the cup was important was that the chalice itself could be used to destroy the dragons. It was their Achilles' heel, not their salvation.

Fafnir had drained each dragon's power by drinking their blood from the cup. But what if the cup didn't exist? What if its magic was destroyed?

The Collector reloaded the crossbow and fired again. Then suddenly, as if he had flipped a switch, the arrows began to speed from the bow as quickly as the other dwarves' guns had fired bullets, rapidly, with no pause and no end in sight of his supply. Joarr flung up his wing, shielding Amma and his torso. The arrows pierced the scales on his wing. A few even made their way completely through so their metal tips were visible to Joarr, poking out of the underside of his wing. The metal burned and blood streamed down his scales, like tears. But, as he had told the Collector, they did little lasting damage, and none that a few nights' sleep wouldn't heal.

He glanced at Amma. She hadn't moved; she seemed completely unconscious now. Seeing her lying there, helpless, shifted his focus. He had already decided he wasn't going to take the Collector up on his offer to trade the dragons for Amma, and now he didn't care about the Collector at all, not about his arrows or his unhealthy ideas of stealing from the dragons. Without Joarr's help, the dragons could easily handle one dwarf, even if he was the Collector.

No, the real threat to Amma and the dragons was the object Joarr had been ordered to protect—the chalice. Joarr had to destroy the chalice, and with Amma unconscious, he was going to have to do it alone.

He prayed that what Amma had done for him, the magic she had siphoned off Fafnir, would be enough… that his fire would be enough.

He opened his mouth and thought of her, thought of their child waiting for his chance at life inside her. Thought of the dragons, not as the uncaring, heartless lizards he often called them, but as little boys like he had once been. Little boys who would be much better off once the dragons gave up their outdated beliefs— forgot chalices and bans on male and female dragons bonding, forgot about controlling—and just lived.

And he let fire, hotter than any he had ever created, rip from his throat.

The Collector yelled and a new volley of arrows pierced Joarr's wing, side and neck. He couldn't block the dwarf and concentrate on destroying the chalice, too. So, he let the arrows bite into his scales unheeded, let the pain feed his determination and fury.

The blaze roaring from his throat hit the chalice. The cup moved, rolled away from the heat as if alive and re-treating. Joarr shuffled closer and dug deeper into his core. This time pure blue flame erupted from his throat.

It hit the cup, and the jewels on the thing winked at him, as if he and it were part of some huge cataclysmic joke. His body ached and not just from the arrows. Cre-ating this much fire this hot was taking its toll. Then he glanced at Amma. She moved. Not much but some. Her eyes fluttered and she started to cough.

Suddenly Joarr's pain was gone; his aches and fa-tigue were gone. He closed his eyes and concentrated on nothing but his fire and destroying the cursed arti-fact he'd spent his life thinking he had to protect.

Chapter 25

Amma opened her eyes. Light burned into them, caused her to lift her hand to shield them. And heat… there was so much heat. She tried to lift her head, but it was heavy, unnaturally so, as if someone had tied bricks to the back of it. She let her head fall back to the ground with a thump, didn't even mind the throb as it connected with the concrete. It just felt good to be lying still. She wanted to close her eyes again, to drift off and never wake up, but she knew somehow that was a bad idea…something she couldn't allow herself to do. She had to fight… Someone had said that recently to her, yelled at her and made her angry.

She opened and closed her fingers, forced blood through them, and magic. Where was her magic? It didn't matter; magic hung in the air, tingled around her. Dragon magic, from shifting. She drew it in like spring air into her lungs, refreshing, rejuvenating.

Instantly, she felt more alive, and just as instantly she remembered where she was and what had happened. With rough, jerky resolve, she shoved her body to a sit. And saw why she was hot.

Joarr in his dragon form, his gaze narrowed to the point she doubted he could see anything at all, stood only a few feet away blasting fire hotter than any she'd ever seen or felt at the chalice.

The chalice. She scrambled, trying to stand. He was trying to destroy the chalice, but the dragons needed the chalice, Joarr needed the chalice. Her son needed the chalice. Her brain was foggy, but she remembered her plan—to give the chalice to Joarr, then steal it back.

Confused, she glanced around, but Joarr blocked her view completely. All she could see was the chalice, Joarr and the intent determination with which he was trying to destroy it.

Something exploded. Amma staggered. Smoke billowed from behind Joarr.

They weren't alone; someone else was behind Joarr, fighting him, trying to stop him from destroying the chalice. She should join them, save the chalice, steal it.

There was another explosion; Joarr flinched, but kept up his attack.

She walked forward on her knees, raised her hands to pull in more power. It filled her, warmed her, and suddenly she knew what she had to do.

Trembling with the effort, she turned her hands toward the chalice.

If Joarr thought the chalice needed to be destroyed, she'd damn well help him.

* * *

Something hit Joarr in the back. Something much bigger than an arrow. A small cannonball, Joarr guessed. He'd been hit by them before, but not for years.

The Collector must have grown impatient. Too bad for him, dragons were the most patient beings in the nine worlds. And too bad for Joarr that his battle with the chalice had gone on so long, long enough he could feel the end of his reserves wasn't far away.

Then what? A dragon without fire or ice, faced with the most highly armed dwarf of all time. How long could Joarr last against him?

He guessed he would find out, because nothing was going to pull him away from his mission to destroy the chalice.

As the thought hardened, he saw something from the corner of his eye. At first he thought it was the dwarf or one of his minions, that they had figured a way around him, to his front where he would be more vulnerable. But then he felt the familiar, soothing warmth of Amma and her magic.

It streamed from her hands in two blue bands and joined with his fire as it struck the chalice. Light flared, red, purple, blue. The heat intensified to the point Joarr leaned backward to escape it.

Fire so pure, so intense and so hot, Joarr had never experienced anything like it before.

It struck the chalice. The cup jumped, or seemed to. Then with no other warning, there was a gurgling pop and the cup exploded into gold-tinted mist. Only the jewels remained, still beautiful as ever, red, green and blue, and still winking.

* * *

Amma stared at her hand; it glistened. A golden sheen decorated everything, even Joarr, who was still in his dragon form. He glanced at her and then the dragon was gone, replaced by the man. He moved toward her, his stride quick, strong and determined. She took a step back, remembering what she had done, that he knew she had tried to hide their baby's existence, but he was beside her before she could do more than think about escaping.

"You're all right." He gathered her into his arms and pulled her close to his chest. Warmth radiated from him, and damn her weak soul, she lapped it up, snuggled up against his chest and inhaled his intoxicatingly spicy scent.

She put her hand against his chest and pushed. "Don't. I…" She looked away. What was there to say? "You destroyed the cup."

He placed his hand over her fingers. "The cup wasn't what the dragons thought it was. Fafnir used it to drain the dragons' power. The cup had killed them. I destroyed it so it couldn't be used against the dragons again.

"You gave Fafnir your blood," he added.

She glanced at his elbow where she had pierced his skin. She'd planned to do as Fafnir had asked, but then realized the blood had to be tied to the dragons' deaths somehow. So, she'd used her own. "I thought whatever he was doing only affected dragons. But, after I gave it to him…I got so tired and weak. It was Fafnir, wasn't it?" She closed her eyes, screwed them shut to block out the pain. She'd endangered her son. Her eyes still closed, she forced out more words. "I thought whatever he was doing only affected dragons. I didn't think…because…" She paused; she knew Joarr knew about their son now, but still it was hard to say out loud. She'd concentrated so intently on keeping it from him. "I thought he was only getting my blood." Not their son's.

She had been so stupid.

"What happened to you has nothing to do with our son." Joarr's voice was soft, comforting.

Amma looked at him, surprised. Where was his rage? She deserved it for so many things. Then it hit her. There was no reason for him to be angry; by dragon law he had all rights to their baby. Yes, she'd given him the chalice, but there were no witnesses… and seriously, he was a dragon, would be backed by the entire dragon force. How had she thought she could win?

Her mind was racing, but Joarr didn't seem to notice. He repeated what he'd just said, that her weakness had nothing to do with their son.

She blinked. "So, the chalice didn't just work against dragons? It worked against witches or elves, as well?"

"Not exactly." Joarr turned, his gaze shooting to a bedraggled and angry-looking Collector. "Why don't you tell her?"

The Collector laughed. "For what? I don't give away information for free."

Joarr pushed Amma behind him. "This information was already paid for by her." He glanced at Amma. "Time to pay."

The Collector pulled off his hat and ran his feather

through his half-closed hand. "Surely you have a better offer than that."

Joarr took a step toward him. "Oh, I do. I'm sure the Ormar would be very interested in the deal you proposed to me."

The Collector's countenance darkened.

"And I bet they'd be even more interested in where all your treasure is stored."

The Collector's hand tightened around the feather. It snapped in two. In two short, jerky moves of his body, he turned to face Amma. "Your father was not an elf. Your father was a dragon. Still is as far as I know."

Amma went cold inside. Her mouth fell open and her hand pressed against her abdomen. "But you said... I went to Alfheim..."

The Collector waved his hand in front of his face. "And the elves rejected you." His eyes cold, he lifted one brow. "Trust me, it is better than what the dragons would have done to you."

He looked back at Joarr. "Done. Satisfied?"

Amma had lost all feeling in her hands and feet. She could feel her heart, though; it was beating wildly. She could feel blood and magic coursing through her, too. Based on what the Collector had told her, she had gone to Alfheim and declared herself to some random... She looked at the Collector. Her jaw tight, said, "The elves you sent me to, was there...?"

He shook his head. He looked bored; not one speck of remorse was visible. "Nothing to you. They had shorted me on a deal not too long before that."

And those elves had been responsible for Amma losing one hundred years of her life. The rage hardened inside her. She fisted her hands and took a step forward.

This time when the Collector looked at her, he didn't look bored. His eyes rounded and he glanced to the side. A rope hung only a foot away; he dived for it, digging in his pocket as he did. There was a click as he flicked a switch on some gadget he had stored in his never-ending pockets. His short body wrapped around the rope and it jerked upward. Within seconds, he was at the ceiling. Amma fired, anyway. Balls this time, round, hot balls of fire and molten anger.

She had given up so much, and for what?

The balls smashed into the floor below the Collector. He glanced down once, then hopped onto the overhang and scurried out of sight.

An arm wrapped around her waist. She felt and smelled Joarr behind her…heat and spice, warm and soothing. But anger still pulsed inside her. She wanted to find the dwarf and make him pay for what he'd done.

"He's gone now," Joarr murmured.

Her body stiff, Amma didn't reply. She twisted slightly, her eyes scanning for some sign of the dwarf.

"He'll have an escape route, probably dozens of them," Joarr murmured.

She kept her gaze where she'd last seen the dwarf, as if she expected him to pop back out, like a rat from a hole.

"I won't take our son from you."

Amma's shoulders dropped, but she didn't turn, couldn't.

"It wouldn't be fair to him or you." Joarr swallowed; he blew out a breath. "The dragons don't have to know."

She did turn then. "You're honoring our deal?"

He dropped his gaze to the floor briefly. Then looked back up. Acceptance filled his eyes. "If you choose to look at it like that, but he needs you."

"He…" She wasn't sure how to say what her lips burned to say. It was unheard of in the dragon world. "He needs a father, too."

Joarr smiled, self-mocking. "Not that, he doesn't." He nodded to Fafnir's lifeless wyrm body. "That's what awaits me. Keep him from that. Keep him from me."

He pressed a kiss against her lips. It was soft, lingering and sad. Then he turned and strode from the bar.

The Collector completely forgotten, Amma ran after Joarr, but his legs were too long, his stride too filled with purpose. By the time she reached the street, he was nowhere in sight. She looked up; clouds filled the sky…Joarr as a dragon, flying from her, leaving her and their son.

Her hand on her stomach, she closed her eyes. This was what she had hoped and planned for, but the pain at losing Joarr…she hadn't planned on.

Chapter 26

It had been two weeks since Amma ran out of the Collector's club chasing after Joarr. She'd stayed in the human world. She had nowhere else to go, and after losing Joarr, she'd been lost and morose. She tried to think of their son, but that depressed her even more.

Her son, who would never know his father. If she chose, he would never even have to know his father was a dragon. He'd grow up like her...exactly like her, feeling deserted and disconnected. Of course, he would be three-quarters dragon versus her half. He would be much more likely to exhibit dragon powers from the beginning of life.

Half. She was half-dragon. She still hadn't processed that.

She spent another day trying to come to grips with everything, trying to figure out her next step. Female dragons lived somewhere, together, she assumed. But she had no female dragon family, unless her father had other daughters.

More sisters… She didn't need more sisters that didn't see her as their equal.

She needed a family. Her son needed a family.

What was she doing, hiding here in the human world from the life he deserved?

She headed to the nearest portal.

Joarr sat on a rock, staring out over the mountains that surrounded the dragons' realm. He'd done it; he'd pushed the Ormar too far. He'd returned and told them everything except that Amma was pregnant. That information he would hide from them, protect with his life.

But he'd told them that he'd destroyed the chalice. He'd told them why, too, even though he'd known it wouldn't matter, that they wouldn't listen. They claimed it wasn't his place to make the decision, that even if his story was true, the Ormar should have been presented with the chalice and made the decision.

They didn't care that destroying the chalice had been the only way to save Amma.

She was only a female—to them. To Joarr, she was everything.

The Ormar had taken all of his treasure, his house and his cavern. But that had been a tiny sting, compared to losing Amma, walking away from her.

He'd had no choice. He'd known what would happen when the Ormar heard his tale, known he would wind up here destined to be a wyrm. He didn't want Amma to see that, didn't want his son to know his father as that.

And he didn't want the Ormar to know he had a son.

They might have cursed him to this fate, but he wouldn't let them take his child.

The sun fell in the sky. Streaks of red and blue blended into purple.

So, so beautiful. The perfect place to live his life as an uncaring, mindless monster.

He closed his eyes, thought of Amma one last time, imagined her scent and the feel of her magic, and then, he shifted.

Amma stepped through the portal and into the bar in the dragons' realm. The garm behind the bar glanced at her.

She twisted her wrist. She'd used the bracelet she'd got from the dark elf while at this same portal with Joarr to pay her passage. She missed it; it had been her one memento of their time together. Well, not her only one… She touched her stomach.

When she looked up, the garm was still watching her. He pulled a piece of paper out from under the bar and handed it to her.

It was a flyer, a warning really. A part of the dragon realm had been declared off-limits. A dragon had been exiled for breaking Ormar law. The word *wyrm* was written in four-inch-high letters across the bottom.

She crumpled the paper in her hands. "Is he…?" She couldn't say it, couldn't think of Joarr like Fafnir had been.

The garm opened his mouth, but Amma held up her hand, cutting him off.

Joarr was not a wyrm. The dragons could take everything from him and Joarr would still not turn into a wyrm. There was more to him than his possessions, much more. Besides, the dragons couldn't take everything from him. They couldn't take her love.

She strode out the door.

Outside she found a motorcycle. She didn't bother looking for a key or the owner. Using her magic, she jumped the engine and headed to where the flyer said not to go.

The sun was rising and the scenery was stunning, but it hardly registered with Amma. Wind tore at her hair as she clung to the motorcycle with her hands and thighs. She had to use her magic to stay in control of the thing. She'd never driven one before; it was exhilarating and terrifying…adding to the adrenaline already pumping through her.

The road curved sharply to the right. Two ancient marble pillars shot up from the ground on each side of it—markers to warn her she was entering the forbidden area. She zoomed through them, their massive height dwarfing her.

The road turned a few more times. Then she was there—the cave of the forgotten, the cave of the wyrm.

But Joarr was neither and she was here to make sure he remembered that.

She got off the bike. Gravel crunched under her feet as she approached the cave. The area around it was different from the grassy meadows sprinkled with wildflowers she'd driven through. Things here were barren…torched. Even the rocks that formed the cave opening were blackened with soot.

She touched her palm to a boulder; it came back black.

"Joarr," she called, forcing her voice to be normal and controlled, even though she wanted to rush in and pull him out or just run herself. Everything about this place screamed "run."

There was a shuffling noise, then a snort and fire lapped out toward her. She didn't shy away; she stepped into it instead. Its warmth greeted her, wrapped around her like a hug.

That was when she knew she'd been right, knew everything was going to be okay.

Stronger, she called again.

"Leave," Joarr's voice said, in her head. "You can't be here. They'll find out—" He cut his own thoughts off as if he was afraid someone might be listening, which perhaps they were.

Amma looked around, back over her shoulder at the barren landscape. Joarr was the only dragon she'd ever met. Now that she knew she was one, she couldn't help but be curious about the others—but not about her father. She'd given up that hunt. That was her past, behind her. Now she was looking to the future and her new family, with Joarr.

She turned back to the cave and took a step inside. "I'm here and I'm not leaving. You owe me."

"What? I owe you nothing. I gave you what you wanted, the pick of my treasure."

She forced a dry laugh from her lips. "Hardly."

There was movement, the sound of a dragon shuffling through a tight space.

She held her breath, afraid of what she would see. Joarr couldn't be a wyrm...she knew that... Still, she couldn't stop the frisson of fear that shot through her.

The form moved closer; she held back, waiting, her eyes closed. When she could feel the heat of his body, she opened them.

Sunlight caught on silver scales, reflected back at her, blinded her. Tears of relief, not pain, streamed down her cheeks.

She laughed again, this time for real. She stepped forward. "You gave me our child, but it was under false pretenses. You cheated me—you were holding out on me, hiding something even more valuable. Our deal was that I'd have pick of all your treasure."

Joarr leaned forward, his blue eyes glowing in his face. "You mean you don't want our son? You don't claim him?"

Amma lowered her chin and met his gaze. "I mean I want to name something else."

"But..." He growled, fire flickered from his lips. "If you deny him..." More fire, hotter. It lapped out toward her, danced over her skin, made her hair crackle.

Amma stood strong, embraced the heat.

"What? What did I hide from you?" he asked.

She smiled. "Your heart. I want your heart, Joarr. It's mine and I won't give it up." She held out her hand.

Steam rolled from his nostrils; he shook his head. "I told you, I have nothing. Dragons who lose their treasure are destined to this...life alone as a wyrm. Leave and take our son, save him from this…from me." He turned.

Magic shot from Amma's palm, smashed into his back.

He rotated back.

She held both hands up, let the anger she felt for what the dragons had done to her and Joarr show. "Nothing? You have nothing? What am I? What is your son? You told me once dragons don't value things just because they have monetary worth. Was that a lie? Do we have no value at all?"

"No, but…I don't have…"

The crack she'd given her anger to show him how irrational he was being boomed open. "And since when did you believe dragons' legends? You didn't believe in the legend of the chalice—and you were right. Why do you choose to believe in this one? Is it because you don't value me and your son?"

"NO!" Joarr roared. Fire exploded out of his throat and magic out of his body. It hit Amma like a wave; she staggered under the weight of it, fell against the cave's wall.

"Amma?" Joarr, in his human form, scooped her into his arms. "I do value you and our son, more than anything."

She placed a hand on his chest. "Enough to leave with me? Enough to forget what you've lost?"

He shook his head.

Her heart stilled.

He leaned down and brushed his lips over hers. "You were right. I haven't lost a thing—not if I have you and our son."

He kissed her and carried her out of the cave. The sun was still warm. Amma luxuriated in it. That and the surety that she and Joarr were going to have what dragons had never had before…a happy ending.

* * * * *

PARANORMAL

Dark and sensual paranormal romance stories
that stretch the boundaries of conflict and desire, life and death.

n o c t u r n e™

COMING NEXT MONTH
AVAILABLE MAY 29, 2012

#137 GUARDIAN OF THE NIGHT
Vampire Moons
Linda Thomas-Sundstrom

#138 THE ENEMY'S KISS
Zandria Munson

REQUEST YOUR FREE BOOKS!

2 FREE NOVELS FROM THE PARANORMAL ROMANCE COLLECTION PLUS 2 FREE GIFTS!

YES! Please send me 2 FREE novels from the Paranormal Romance Collection and my 2 FREE gifts (gifts are worth about $10). After receiving them, if I don't wish to receive any more books, I can return the shipping statement marked "cancel." If I don't cancel, I will receive 4 brand-new novels every month and be billed just $21.42 in the U.S. or $23.46 in Canada. That's a saving of at least 21% off the cover price of all 4 books. It's quite a bargain! Shipping and handling is just 50¢ per book in the U.S. and 75¢ per book in Canada.* I understand that accepting the 2 free books and gifts places me under no obligation to buy anything. I can always return a shipment and cancel at any time. Even if I never buy another book, the two free books and gifts are mine to keep forever.

237/337 HDN FEL2

Name	(PLEASE PRINT)

Address	Apt. #

City	State/Prov.	Zip/Postal Code

Signature (if under 18, a parent or guardian must sign)

Mail to the **Reader Service:**
IN U.S.A.: P.O. Box 1867, Buffalo, NY 14240-1867
IN CANADA: P.O. Box 609, Fort Erie, Ontario L2A 5X3

Not valid for current subscribers to the Paranormal Romance Collection or Harlequin® Nocturne™ books.

Want to try two free books from another line?
Call 1-800-873-8635 or visit www.ReaderService.com.

* Terms and prices subject to change without notice. Prices do not include applicable taxes. Sales tax applicable in N.Y. Canadian residents will be charged applicable taxes. Offer not valid in Quebec. This offer is limited to one order per household. All orders subject to credit approval. Credit or debit balances in a customer's account(s) may be offset by any other outstanding balance owed by or to the customer. Please allow 4 to 6 weeks for delivery. Offer available while quantities last.

Your Privacy—The Reader Service is committed to protecting your privacy. Our Privacy Policy is available online at www.ReaderService.com or upon request from the Reader Service.

We make a portion of our mailing list available to reputable third parties that offer products we believe may interest you. If you prefer that we not exchange your name with third parties, or if you wish to clarify or modify your communication preferences, please visit us at www.ReaderService.com/consumerschoice or write to us at Reader Service Preference Service, P.O. Box 9062, Buffalo, NY 14269. Include your complete name and address.

PARA11

Harlequin® Romantic Suspense presents the final book in the gripping PERFECT, WYOMING *miniseries from best-loved veteran series author Carla Cassidy*

Witness as mercenary Micah Grayson and cult escapee Olivia Conner join forces to save a little boy and to take down a monster, while desire explodes between them....

Read on for an excerpt from
MERCENARY'S PERFECT MISSION

Available June 2012 from Harlequin® Romantic Suspense.

"I won't tell," she exclaimed fervently. "Please don't hurt me. I swear I won't tell anyone what I saw. Just let me have my other son and we'll go far away from here. I'll never speak your name again." Her voice cracked as she focused on his gun and he realized she believed he was Samuel.

Certainly it was dark enough that it would be easy for anyone to mistake him for his brother. When the brothers were together it was easy to see the subtle differences between them. Micah's face was slightly thinner, his features more chiseled than those of his brother.

At the moment Micah knew Samuel kept his hair cut neat and tidy, while Micah's long hair was tied back. He reached up and pulled the rawhide strip, allowing his hair to fall from its binding.

The woman gasped once again. "You aren't him...but you look like him. Who are you?" Her voice still held fear as she dropped the stick and protectively clutched the baby closer to her chest.

"Who are you?" he countered. He wasn't about to be taken in by a pale-haired angel with big green eyes in this evil place where angels probably couldn't exist.

"I'm Olivia Conner, and this is my son Sam." Tears filled her eyes. "I have another son, but he's still in town. I couldn't get to him before I ran away. I've heard rumors that there was a safe house somewhere, but I've been in the woods for two days and I can't find it."

Micah was unmoved by her tears and by her story. He knew how devious his brother could be, and Micah would do everything possible to protect the location of the safe house. There was only one way to know for sure if she was one of Samuel's "devotees."

Will Olivia be able to get her son back from the clutches of evil? Or will Micah's maniacal twin put an end to them all? Find out in the shocking conclusion to the PERFECT, WYOMING *miniseries.*

MERCENARY'S PERFECT MISSION
Available June 2012, only from
Harlequin® Romantic Suspense, wherever books are sold.